UNDER THE SHELL

David Wilkinson

Published by Inspired Quill: June 2018

First Edition

Contact the author through their website:
anjelican.wordpress.com

Chief Editor: Sara-Jayne Slack
Cover Design: Venetia Jackson
Typeset in Minion Pro

Paperback ISBN: 978-1-908600-73-8
eBook ISBN: 978-1-908600-74-5
Print Edition

Printed in the United Kingdom
1 2 3 4 5 6 7 8 9 10

Inspired Quill Publishing, UK
Business Reg. No. 7592847
www.inspired-quill.com

Praise for *David Wilkinson*

The intricacy of its world building, the dark themes of political conspiracy and state repression, the heartfelt conflicts of its characters are all sure to bring readers back. It was a well-crafted and enjoyable debut from Wilkinson. If you like your science-fiction intelligent and intense, this is one saga to follow.

—Siobhan Logan,
author of *Firebridge To Skyshore*

It's not a simple matter of good heroes verses the evil empire, but people just trying to live their lives and the people in power having to choose between the lesser of two evils. It feels as difficult as real life.

—Jessica Meats,
author of *Between Yesterdays*

"We Bleed the Same" has reinvigorated my love of the genre. Clear, imaginatively written and with a passion and joy de vivre of the genre that clearly shines through, David Wilkinson deserves plaudits for his concise, intelligent writing that keeps you gripped right up until the last page.

—Matthew Munson,
author of *Fall From Grace*

For Jenny and James.

May you never live in a world like this.

Within the Free City of Engalise there are no laws. Only the Rights of every Free Individual:

1. *To live*

2. *To not be inflicted with pain or injury*

3. *To have one's body inviolate*

4. *To think and speak freely*

5. *To move unimpeded by another person*

6. *To own, retain and protect property*

7. *To vote in choosing the City Corporation every 3000 days, which shall licence individuals to maintain and protect these rights*

8. *To voluntarily give up any or all of these rights*

9. *To re-establish any right that has been given up*

10. *To be free of threats made against any of these rights*

Failure to respect these rights will result in forfeiture of some or all of the rights in the guilty individual.

Chapter 1

TWO RATS TUGGED at the index finger of a white hand protruding from the rubble. *Opportunities*, mused Jaq Pilakin as she tried to stamp on a tail, *dead bodies are full of them*. She managed to land her boot on one and the high-pitched squeaks caused the desired outflow of other rats that had invaded the rubble pile in search of flesh. They swarmed through the cordon holding back gawpers, where street kids landed metal rods on them, scooping up the twitching bodies and deftly tossing them over shoulders into sacks tied to their backs with string.

Opportunities.

Pilakin turned from the street boys, who had got what they came for, and looked at others still waiting for their share. Scrappers gathering up anything they could reach through the cordon – twisted shards of metal and some charred rope; the van from Daskovich Biorendering with two intimidating men inside; the LRT Forensics people, touting for business; several reporters looking for something juicy; and some Engalise City Corporation 5th Right Engineers, who just wanted to tidy up and re-open the street. And there were those like herself. The independent Freedom Protection Agents, slabs in hand, looking for a case.

"Hey, Jaq! Glad you got the message."

Sam Lyttle picked his way over the rubble towards her with a big grin on his artificially tanned face. The same adolescent-like quiff of brown hair still hung limply over his forehead, interfering with his left eye. His boss had been threatening to take it off with a pair of scissors ever since he'd arrived at work five years ago. Pilakin was pleased he had managed to hang on to it in the three hundred odd days since she had been finally forced out of the Engalise City Corporation Freedom Protection Agency.

"Thanks, Sam. You're a nova."

Despite being a detective, Sam still sported an ECC-FPA bomber jacket and carried his gun in a visible holster at the hip. He gestured at the white hand at their feet, so far the only sign that a freshly dead body lay beneath the rubble.

"Oh save it. I mean, I don't know why you'd want it – the guy just got unlucky. As soon as we got here we knew it was nothing we were interested in…"

"So disinterested that you haven't even shifted enough rubble to see his face."

Sam lifted his hands in a mock defensive gesture. "Hey, we pricked his finger. DNA's not in our database so he's not going to be anyone we're interested in. Why break our backs digging him out if there's no money in it? Especially as there's plenty queuing up who will." He smirked at her and continued. "Okay then, Miss Holier-than-thou. You going to get your hands dirty?"

She looked at the filthy pile of rocks for a moment before turning and stalking over to the cordon where a group of five boys waited with metal bars for any more rats that might be about to make a break for it. She smiled as she saw one near the back lift a wallet from the pocket of the man next to him.

"Hey, lads. A credit each if you dig the body out for me and another if you find something with his ID on it."

As they ran past her she grabbed the hand of the last and yanked away the stolen wallet. Handing it back to the surprised victim she let the boy go as the man swore. Pausing only to present him with a view of his middle finger, the boy scampered off after the others, who had already started to energetically heave off the rubble.

The wallet-man's stream of invective grew more colourful and Pilakin suspected he may be about to jump the cordon. If that happened, others might too, and there would be chaos. Voice raised, she pulled her arm back so that the lapel of her jacket rode up to reveal the concealed FPA badge and then rested her hand on her gun.

"Of course, you're free to say anything you like, sir.

But please watch the threats or I may have to detain you for a Tenth Right violation."

He switched targets and began hectoring her instead about the Sixth but, after seeing the look on her face, he threw up his hands in frustration and walked away. Pilakin smiled at a woman who was grinning at the exchange. She wore the uniform shirt of the electronics store right opposite. Pilakin gestured at the scene.

"You see it?"

"Sure. We heard the usual bang up top and the falling rubble. It sounded close but the wailers didn't go off so no-one scattered 'til the last minute."

"Really? No sirens?" Pilakin tapped on her slab's screen.

"Nope. Shit City maintenance as usual. Just a few seconds to get under awnings but you know how it is out here on the rim. Everyone's a cockroach when the rubble's coming down. *He* didn't seem to have the sense of it though – looked like an inny, too. He still had a couple of seconds and everyone shouted at him to get under. He seemed to twig and made to run but his legs collapsed under him. Then the stuff landed. Nasty. I realised as soon as it happened we were going to get half an hour off while you guys did your thing so I went for coffee."

"No one tried to dig him out? Not interested in the reward of a thankful inner-dweller?"

The woman wrinkled her nose and shook her head.

"Didn't stand a chance. He's blatantly dead and the

biorendering guys around here like to guard their business, if you get me…"

Pilakin nodded, handing a business card and a credit note to the woman.

"You think of anything else, you call me, okay?"

"Sure but how long 'til I can get back to the shop? Boss in't gonna pay when no punters can get in."

"Shouldn't be long now."

"But this is a breach of my freedom to move."

"Well, if you can find the Imperial soldier who fired the shell, you can sue him…"

"Hey, lady!"

One of the boys she had hired to shift the rubble was standing near the top of the pile, waving at her with a triumphant look on his face and the dead man's wallet in his other hand. She sighed as she walked gingerly back up the mound. The brief interview had suggested this was just another tragic accident of war, all too common in a city under siege. Paying these boys now was just going to be another waste of her dwindling resources. When she reached the top she took the wallet and distributed the necessary credit notes.

Finally looking down at the body, she noticed the face had a pallor out of keeping with the more expensive gold edging on his shirt collar. She used her slab to take pictures as several the other agents muscled in to do the same. She pushed them away.

"Fuck off. You want pictures, you pay."

They grumbled but stood back, waiting for her to lose interest. She logged the image but refrained from paying to run it against any databases until she'd looked over the wallet. Inside were pictures of a family, some credit cards, money and a business card. She stared at the name and her heart pumped with growing excitement.

Jeremiah Flow.

Bloody hell.

This changed everything.

Chapter 2

JEREMIAH FLOW.

It was certainly an easy name to remember and Pilakin had thought so the previous week when she'd found it on the Kristani Syndicate's revised hit list. The Kristanis wanted him dead and now he was. Surely more than coincidence, however much it appeared to be an accident.

"My case!"

She held up her badge to muttering and expletives from the other agents clustered around the scene. As soon as the name appeared in the wallet, she had dropped it in her haste to grab her slab and log a stake with Central Records. Of course this didn't mean others would not seek out the dead man's relatives and try to get a contract. But it did mean that, for a small fee, Central would lock all the information they held on him for 48 hours. Hopefully, no one else knew his identity yet.

She could see the ECC Agents were on the verge of dismantling the cordon and so frantically waved at the forensics team to come over. Smiling, two of them picked their way over the rubble with a stretcher. Pilakin watched them approach, not leaving the side of the body for fear of someone stealing it.

"Hi guys. I want a full post mortem."

The taller of the two unhooked a computer from his belt.

"No problem. Do you have an account with us, Agent…?"

"Pilakin. No, I don't."

"Then I'm afraid we're going to have to ask for full payment up front."

Dammit, thought Pilakin, *this is going to be pricey.*

The man's computer buzzed and a flimsy piece of paper spewed out of the front. The ludicrously small typeset left her in no doubt it was a contract.

"You'll need to sign."

She stared at the tiny writing for a moment and then up at the man. His ID card showed him to be a doctor and her gut said he was honest.

"I can't read all this. What's going to piss me off?"

He laughed shortly and his eyes twinkled.

"2600 gets you the service. Any additional costs incurred will be charged before the report is released to you."

"So I get nothing until I pay some extra amount

currently unknown?"

The man shrugged. Glowering whilst sighing pointedly, Pilakin signed.

The hoisting of the body on to the stretcher was clearly the moment the ECC Agents had been waiting for to lift the cordon. As they rolled up the tape, Corporation engineers moved forward on a dump-truck with grapple to clear the rubble, and the pent up crowds swirled around them. Inside the tape it had been easy to forget that this blocked street would have been causing people jams for streets around but, despite the jostling, she managed to keep her eyes on the body being carried away and breathed a sigh as it was loaded into the forensics vehicle.

"Fucking bitch!"

Pilakin jumped as the insult came right next to her ear. The Daskovich Biorendering van had pulled up and a very large driver with cauliflower ears and an overhanging brow lent out of the window. He was a prize specimen of the body-snatchers who roamed the City, harvesting the bodily chemicals of the dead. He had a look of rage on his face and he was close enough that his spittle hit her cheek. But she had a dozen years of experience, a gun in her pocket, hundreds of witnesses and several other agents still in the area. The latter, despite the competitive nature of their work, would not allow a fellow agent to get a beating. She smiled coldly at the ape-man.

"I do hope you're not going to threaten me, sir."

"Nope. I respect the rights of others – even body-snatching whores. Bet you shag it later. You're so ugly, no one living would have you."

Pilakin blew the man a mocking kiss as he revved the van's engine and drove it into the crowd, using the loud horn like a force field to carve his way through. She exhaled with relief as she took her hand off the butt of her gun and found it was shaking.

Shit.

She needed a drink.

THIRTY METRES DOWN the street she found a gut-rot bar and, having downed a measure of the filthy, oily stuff, ordered another so as to have reason for remaining on the bar stool. As the fumes cleared her head she connected her earpiece to the call service and dialled a number. The harassed looking man on her slab's screen looked familiar.

"ECC Maintenance Despatch;" he said, "what do you want?"

"Iovanni Chung, please."

A moment later the boyish features of a younger man appeared. He smiled at her and, despite herself, she couldn't help but smile back. He leaned forward and spoke quietly, as if he didn't want others hearing.

"Hello, Jaq! What's up? Finally realised you can't live without me?"

"Not quite that desperate yet, little man. Will you help me for old time's sake though?"

He leaned back and resumed speaking in a normal

tone of voice.

"Sure. Go for it."

"I've just been at a rubble site. Location.... oh hell, wait a minute..."

She fumbled to split the screen in two and find the coordinates but Iovanni beat her to it.

"+0725, −6798, +0002? Yeah, we've got people out there now."

"Okay, thank you, but I want to know where the impact was. You got another job on the same z-line?"

"Hang on... yes. Same x and y. The z is +0247 – private apartment in the Southwind Building. Number 4263."

"Thanks, Vannie."

"Hey, joking apart, maybe we should go for a drink on Sa..."

She disconnected the call, picked up the tiny glass of gut-rot and made the mistake of examining the contents. Flaky bits of something swirled around as she moved it. The oily consistency and bubbly film meant the alcohol was cut with something other than all-too-expensive water to keep the price down. Her sensibilities revolted but she downed it anyway.

PILAKIN LEFT THE bar and headed to the Southwind Building, where the explosion had hit. She stopped off on the way there to look at the siren that had failed to sound the alarm. Bored kids often smashed up Corporation property and she fully expected to find the yellow and black striped metal cabinet in pieces. However, as she inched out along a ledge ten metres or so above the street below, she could see the metre-cube appeared fine. That was odd. Closer inspection showed the doors were still locked shut and the siren appeared to be in one piece. She reported it to the commission as broken anyway, with some justification given the witness statements, and annotated the report with a request for service update.

Down below, the clear-up gang had almost finished scooping up the rubble. Surging crowds of people swirled past it like ants around a fallen leaf.

She stopped and caught hold of herself. Where had that simile come from? Leaves she had seen on, what were they called? Trees… in Gursky Park. But ants? What were they? She shook her head as the alcohol made a fresh effort to hijack her balance. Turning to face the wall, she inched along it slowly back to the safety of the public stairwell and reluctantly resumed her climb up another 235 metres.

Chapter 3

"WELL, LOOK WHO it is…" came a sneering voice as she arrived at street level outside the Southwind apartment complex. Her lack of breath, having climbed a further two hundred or so metres up a public stair, prevented an immediate response but using the Corporation elevator would have been half a credit. It was the same ape-man from Daskovich Biorendering, leaning against the van next to his partner who was filling in paperwork. He took Pilakin's silence as an invitation to answer with his own observation.

"It's the ugly corpse-shagger. You want this one too?"

He jabbed his thumb at the van and grinned. He seemed in better mood now he had a body in there. That was good. He might be more amenable to giving her what she wanted, although this would also mean swallowing the insults. She smiled rakishly.

"That depends. I don't just want any old muck, you

know? Where did it come from?"

"Out of a flat up on the outside of this building. Got hit by an Imp shell. He's pretty cacked up, but whatever floats your boat I suppose…"

"Seriously though, I'm a Freedom Protection Agent and I want that body…"

"Whoa! You can't just have him. We already got a contract with the widow. She said we could take him and chuck him in the vat. In fact she said a lot more, and none of it nice. Also, the lift is knackered. We had to carry him down seven flights, you know. They don't pay us enough for this shit."

"Well, I'd like to buy the corpse off you then, and give you something for your trouble too."

Ape-man looked at his partner, who just shrugged. Clearly a man of few words.

"Okay. I'll call my supervisor."

They should give it to her. Buying and selling bodies was their core business. Even renting them – so that people could have their post mortems, funerals or… whatever… before taking them back to separate out the valuable commodities contained in the corpse. A decades-long siege of a city of millions meant that water, methane, calcium, hydrogenated fats and a hundred other body-borne chemicals had a profitable price. Even hair and teeth could be sold to those in need. In the City of Engalise, the value of a human body could be measured.

"Boss says there shouldn't be a problem," said ape-man, his eyes twinkling with the prospect of his 'tip'. "He just wants to know your name and Agent ID."

"Pilakin, 814159."

He relayed it to his boss and a few seconds later his face turned back to the thunder she had seen earlier. He snapped the connection with a sharp jab of his thumb and then punched the side of the van for good measure.

"Shitting fuck!"

"Problem?" inquired Pilakin.

"Who have you been pissing off? Boss says you've been flagged. We're not even allowed to talk to you."

"So, I'm not getting the body?"

He turned away from her and told his partner to get in the van. Without another word, they pulled out into the crowds. Pilakin stood, flummoxed for a moment, watching the van barge its way down the lane that was supposedly for vehicular traffic. Of course the shortages meant there were very few private cars, especially out here in the poverty stricken rim. She tilted her head back to look up at the large edifice of the Southwind Building; a monument to that very poverty. She sighed and walked through the entrance, where the doors had either been stolen or sold.

APE-MAN HAD LIED about having to carry the body down the stairs. She emerged from the dimly lit and foul smelling but free building-services lift on to the fourth floor landing. Despite being daubed with graffiti, the directory opposite was still legible and she turned in the direction of flat 4263. The doors to the apartments were sturdy plasteel. The designers, no doubt, would claim this was for blast mitigation should the Imps manage to hit the building. Pilakin was sure the residents prized them for their security. Regular Imperial artillery shells kept the outer ring of the City undesirable and thus poor. Yet, counter intuitively, the apartment buildings on the very outside were sought after thanks to their necessarily sturdy construction. Families who lived in them could shut out the anarchy, which was far more likely to kill them than a stray Imp shell. The occupants of flat 4263 were just unlucky.

Outside it she found two Corporation security guards, there to protect the engineers who would be working inside the apartment. She showed them her FPA badge and, after a moment's close scrutiny, they waved her through. Within she was surprised to find another Agent; Gregor Manstein.

"Hello, Pilakin.'"

"What are you doing here?"

He shrugged.

"You know how it is."

She certainly did. Independents without a reputation, like them, needed to investigate anything they could find and hope it turned into something profitable. All the juicy stuff was snaffled by the big agencies.

He led her across the hall and through another heavy

but pockmarked door into the main room. Temporary lights had been set up and cast an eerie glow across the scene. A hole about a metre across had been blown into the room. Pilakin marvelled at the exposed interior of the wall – plasteel encased concrete, almost a metre thick, with two layers of mesh inside.

"Must have been a hell of a blast," she observed. Manstein nodded.

A City Engineer, who was looking out of the hole, turned upon hearing her voice. He nodded a greeting before sticking his head out and shouting, presumably to a colleague outside.

"There's another one here now."

Pilakin looked around the rest of the room. Dust, rubble and shards of metal mesh covered almost every surface. But it was clear that the room had been no palace before the shrapnel got to work. There was only one comfortable chair, which faced the hole. An old fashioned projector system showed the impact wall doubled as the television. There were also two dirty mattresses on the floor, with stained duvets and small bundles of children's clothing for pillows. A low coffee table that had been heavily splintered by the explosion now rested against the far wall, completing the room's furniture.

"Only one person in the room when the shell hit." Manstein consulted his slab, "Youal Fesh. He was sitting in the armchair."

The chair was riddled with pieces of shrapnel and

mesh. It appeared to be soaked through with blood and, by the smell of it, urine too. Death had probably been fairly quick. Manstein continued reading his notes in a tired voice.

"Crystal meth and cannabol user. He spent his days in here before making his partner's life unpleasant in the bedroom at night. The kids slept there." He pointed at the mattresses.

"Are they okay? The kids, I mean."

"Their mother had them in the bedroom doing some maths lessons before she went to work. This building may look like shit but it's built well enough that the blast was kept in here. They've got some ringing in their ears but that's about it."

"And she just sold the body?"

"Yeah. I think the Fesh family's life is going to improve now the patriarch's gone. Multiple Second and Third Rights violations have been filed but he always managed to get her to invoke the Eighth."

"You taking the case?"

"I was about to pack up. Even if we ever got a prosecution out of it, the defence would show the victims' lives have materially improved. Payout'd be miniscule. The poor bitch'd probably end up having to pay the Imps."

"Mind if I take it then?"

His eyes narrowed with suspicion. "Really? What are you working?"

"Oh, it could be something or nothing about a guy the rubble from this lot fell on. Might be able to fold this one in too."

Manstein licked his teeth for a moment as he appeared to weigh up what kind of chances she would have in making a case. In the end he must have decided not much.

"Okay. You can have it as a favour."

Not as insubstantial as it sounded – favours were real currency amongst cash-strapped agents. Manstein put all his crime scene photographs and case notes into a single folder and they bumped slabs to transfer them. Then, with a brief "See you around," he was gone.

Pilakin walked over to the hole and stood next to the engineer who was looking out.

"Hi…"

He looked and smiled at her.

"Oh, hello. Do you want something?"

She now saw they had clamped a platform, outside the hole, on to the side of the building and the engineer's colleague was outside but tethered to some of the protruding steel mesh with a rope. Beyond that, about five metres away, was the 'sink field' – a black, charged plasma held in place by a strong magnetic field. It was there to absorb the energy from weapons fired by the besiegers outside. It encompassed the whole city inside its shell.

"Mmm," she replied, "I was wondering why this happened."

"Well, the Imps shot at us. Kind of happens in a

siege."

"I mean, this is a reinforced building. Why did this shot blow a hole in the side where others don't?"

"The netting's down. Look. Hey, Melissa! Show the lady the rip, will you?"

The engineer outside walked to the edge of the platform and bent down. When she stood again, she was holding up a piece of netting, still hanging at one end from supports inside the field. Pilakin smiled as she looked at the non-ferrous gear the woman was carrying. She knew that standing that close to the magnetic field's main intensity could be dangerous, but the netting was unfamiliar to her.

"What does that stuff do?"

"The sink field keeps out the energy from blasts, nukes, beam weapons, whatever. Physical objects can still pass through it, though. Shells and missiles. That netting is made of carbon nano-tubes with an extremely high tensile strength. It sits just a few millimetres inside the sink. So, when the physical weapons come in they hit it and detonate. Then the energy released by the blast is all sucked in by the plasma. Trouble is the system doesn't negate the momentum of the actual carriage device."

He might have been intentionally using technical terms to flummox her but she had started her career in forensic science – so sod him, patronising arse.

"The shell or missile casing carries straight on and gets shredded."

He looked a little crestfallen but nodded.

"You got it. Most small rubble falls are this kind of shrapnel, small rubble mix."

"So, what happened here?"

"All those casings keep battering the net and eventually we get weak points. They go unnoticed until the spot gets hit again and the projectile just powers straight through them. Then you get a major rubble fall like this one."

"How many big falls are there?"

"City wide? Nowhere near as many as there used to be. Two or three a day."

"But if the Imps have zeroed in on this position, aren't we in danger of them hitting it again?"

"Before we came up here, we got confirmation from the City Defence Agency that they've put up a disruption screen in front of the site. We've got that for," he looked at his watch, "another twenty minutes."

Pilakin felt uneasy. She glanced back at the bloody chair.

"Then shouldn't you be fixing it?"

"The spiders are backed up on another job. Ah, here they come now."

The engineer pointed to where some black multi-legged robots were scuttling up the netting from below. Most went to anchor points and stopped while one, larger than the rest, clacked over to the damaged section. Melissa manipulated some controls on her slab's screen. A large protrusion appeared from the robot's back that turned out to be a high-powered laser, crackling as it cut away the remaining strands holding the damaged section in place. Pilakin was surprised to see how much it was removing.

"Can't you just repair or weld the damaged strands?"

Melissa was now hauling in the excised sections.

"No. It's difficult to repair carbon nano-tubes and even if we did, there would still be weak points. The whole section will be re-threaded."

The last of the netting was in and now the spiders that had been waiting at the anchor points scuttled and jumped, trailing new 'threads' behind them.

"The wires are fast manufactured inside the robots."

It was fascinating to watch as they dipped and weaved. Pilakin had only ever seen real spiders on nature documentaries (ah – that was where she had seen the ants, too!) and it was easy to forget these things were artificial. In less than five minutes the whole section had been restrung. As soon as they were done, the spiders departed rapidly, presumably in search of the next job. The engineers packed up their gear.

"Aren't you going to repair this wall?"

"Landlord's problem."

The broken netting was being stuffed into a bag.

"What will you do with that?"

"The fracture points will be analysed to see why they broke."

"Why? You think it might have been sabotaged?"

The engineer looked at her with a strange expression.

"That's pretty unlikely."

"Then why…?"

His sneer changed to condescension.

"Hey, we're always trying to make the netting better. If there are fewer breakages, then the City doesn't have to employ as many engineers or lease as many spiders."

Pilakin offered her card.

"Will you tell me what you find?"

The engineer took it, shaking his head.

"You're a strange bunch, you agents."

"We have to deal with people who do strange things. Will you let me know?"

"Okay."

She was not confident of ever getting that particular call.

Chapter 4

PILAKIN STOOD BACK against the wall as a crocodile of primary school children filed past in pairs, singing as they went. Happy faces and well-fed bodies so different from the kids of the rim. All were tanned and had braided hair. They swung their held hands in time to the music. Pilakin chuckled as she remembered the song from her own school days.

Th' Emperor wants our freedom
But he is out of luck
Already teacher's had a go
And we don't give a...

The teachers just smiled and ushered them on their way. It was always a relief to come back to the inner city. Though not in one of the most affluent neighbourhoods, the corridor in this apartment building was bright and clean. There was even carpeting on the floor. Finding a graffiti tag on the door came as a surprise.

LIGHT HOG

Pilakin looked up and down the corridor, just catching a glimpse of someone further up stepping back into an apartment. She double checked the address before ringing the doorbell. After the second time a voice crackled out of the comms panel.

"Who are you? What do you want?"

"I'm Freedom Protection Agent Pilakin. I'm here about your husband."

She held up her badge to the camera and, after a long pause, the door clicked open. Having stepped inside, it closed again behind her and only at this point did the occupant emerge into the hall to face her.

"Mrs Flow?" Pilakin asked.

"That stupid name..."

The woman looked careworn and pale – the pallor of her skin just like her husband's. Although not old, lines on her face creased as she grimaced and seemed to indicate days of unrelieved stress. She stood wringing her hands while eyeing Pilakin before bobbing her head.

"I suppose you'd better come in then... and call me Sarah."

Pilakin had expected to see more furniture but the kitchen-living room was only sparsely appointed. She twitched with annoyance as she saw a blind had been drawn over the window.

Light Hog!

She fought down the urge to march over and remove

it and instead took a seat on the sofa. Sarah dropped into the only other chair before speaking in a quiet voice.

"I suppose he's dead, then."

Pilakin raised her eyebrows.

"You don't seem surprised."

Sarah's head dropped forward on to her chest and quiet sobs wracked her body for a minute or two before she took a deep breath and looked back at Pilakin with reddened eyes.

"He was murdered?"

"I don't know."

"What do you mean, you don't know?"

Anger flared in her face and then subsided as quickly. She seemed to be sitting on her emotions in a way suggesting long necessity.

"How did he die? Do you know that?"

"He was buried by falling rubble from an artillery strike. I really am very sorr…"

"Artillery strike? Well, that would mean… What was he doing on the rim?"

"That was unusual?"

"Of course it was! What would a filthy rimmer need of a plumber?"

Sarah's affected inny accent was irksome. It was meant to denote education and social standing but in Pilakin's experience it usually masked insecurity.

"He was a plumber, then? Hence the name, I suppose."

"He *owns* his plumbing business. Yes, he changed his name to that ridiculous… *Need a plumber? Go with the Flow.* He says it's free advertising. That people remember him easily when they're making recommendations to their friends."

"Is that how he picked up business?"

"Well, you know how the rich can be. Cliquey and insular. But water prices being what they are, not many people can afford to have it piped into their apartments. Plumbing is a seriously luxurious commodity, you know?"

Again that supercilious tone. As Pilakin looked around the flat and back at Sarah's untanned face, she knew this woman's life was crumbling. She decided to allow her a little bravado. As she watched, Sarah's shoulders fell once more and despair returned to her features.

"With all the Water Activists about, advertising is a risky… Listen Agent…er…Pilakin was it? Why are you here? You said it was an Imp shell? Where's his body?'

"I've ordered a post mortem on it."

"Why?"

"Have you heard of the Kristani Syndicate?"

"Well, of course I have. Jer was on their damnable death list. Why do you think I asked whether he was murdered? Why do you think I have that…thing…?"

She did not look at the object to which she referred, instead waving her arm in the general direction. The shame in her voice told Pilakin she meant the window blind. Dropping her arm with a shudder, she continued.

"Jer thought we might get bounty hunters with rifles picking us off through the window."

During Mrs Flow's discomfiture, Pilakin had used the distraction to quietly take out her slab and jot things down.

"Sarah, I know it looks like Jeremiah had an accident but I take death lists very seriously. Would you mind answering a few questions about that for me?"

Sarah seemed to stare right through Pilakin for a good seven seconds before she blinked and nodded.

"Do you know why he was on the list?"

"Oh…well that was simple enough. Jer decided to expand his business. He's been doing well enough with City contracts but if you can get private jobs, they pay more. He got a few and made so much off them that he dropped the City stuff. Then the Tank Four riots happened. You remember?"

Pilakin nodded. About thirty weeks ago the city's fourth reservoir tank had been breached by Water Activists. It had caused massive flooding followed by an almost instant 20% spike in the price of water. There had been riots and water-looting, which served to push the price even higher. Weeks of disorder had only ended after the City Corporation distributed millions of free litres around the rim.

"Business dried up after that, did it?" Pilakin winced as she realised her unintended pun.

"Yes. It couldn't have happened at a worse moment. He'd just borrowed heavily to buy a new van and tools. He couldn't afford the repayments so the loan company sold his debt to the Kristanis. They kept threatening to put him on the list so we made…economies."

She blushed and hung her head. Pilakin looked around the room. This would explain the lack of furniture; presumably all sold off. The pallid complexions of both Sarah and Jeremiah's dead body would be another saving – time under ultra-violet bulbs was expensive.

"In the end there was nothing else to give them. He couldn't sell his tools because they were our only source of income, so on the list he went. You think they did for him, then?"

Pilakin shook her head.

"We can't assume that. Debts die with the individual. It would defeat the purpose of the list if more than a few people on it were actually killed. It's just supposed to be a threat…but you mentioned that the tools are still intact. Is the business still operating? Who's taken possession?"

"Jer's nephew was his business partner – Zeb Lander. I don't know anything about plumbing so he'll take all the gear and carry on. He's supposed to give me half the profits. I hope he makes some. There's rent due and Paul's school is only paid for another five weeks. Oh, what am I going to…?"

She was on the verge of breaking down again so Pilakin quickly asked another question.

"Paul is your son? How old is he?"

"He's fourteen."

"Any other children?"

"No, just him. Who can afford more? Only the dirty rimmers have more than they can pay for..."

Pilakin looked at her notes and thought for a moment. The nephew would certainly be a suspect, as would Sarah herself. Then there were the Kristanis, bounty hunters, Water Activists... but if it really *was* a murder, rather than a case of wrong place, wrong time as the Imp shell hit, how could it have been done? Surely several people would've had to be involved.

"Listen, Sarah. I want to investigate your husband's death."

"I won't stop you."

"I mean, I'd like you to sign an exclusive contract with me."

"Why should I do that? Wouldn't I be better with an agency?"

"They won't take it. The ECC-FPA has already refused – I was with them earlier. It doesn't look like murder to them."

"Then aren't there famous independents I could use? I've never heard of you Agent Pilakin."

"They'll take a big cut and they're not as good as I am."

"Then why aren't you...?"

"With a big agency? I was at the ECC-FPA. But with

the contract election coming up they needed to make savings. They could replace me with someone cheaper. Please, Mrs Flow I assure you, I am your best chance of getting justice and compensation for your husband's death."

Sarah looked at her with commingled hope and suspicion in her eyes.

"How much will it cost me? I can't put anything up front."

"That's fine. Twenty percent of the compensation."

"The agencies charge fifteen."

"The agencies won't take it. Look, I'll wait while you call them if you like."

Resolve replaced the suspicion on Sarah's face.

"I'm not going to get my hopes up, you know. Do you really think a rubble fall can be murder?"

"Call it a hunch. I'm going to be investing my own time and money into this."

"Okay, where do I sign?"

Pilakin proffered her slab and stylus where she had cued up the contract. As Sarah signed it, she asked "You said that the death wipes the debt. Does that mean I'm out of danger now?"

"In my experience, yes. It should."

Sarah handed the slab back and then jabbed a finger at the window blind.

"So, I can get rid of that damned thing?"

"Yes."

"Oh, thank God."

She got up and scurried over to the window. Seizing the blind drapery with both hands, she ripped it away. The floor to ceiling window made the apartment feel less claustrophobic and Pilakin got up, moving across beside Sarah to look at the view. It was a narrow canyon of a street but the buildings blazed with illumination. In a city with no municipal lighting under a black dome, there would be perpetual darkness outside but for the ingrained social convention to not blind your windows. From outside, the Flow apartment's darkness would have been as plain as a missing front tooth. No wonder they had come in for abuse. She turned to look at the relief that would be on Sarah's face and frowned. A red light was dancing on her chest. She stared in puzzlement for a good two seconds before the light began to move.

"Get down!"

She leapt on Sarah and they both crashed to the floor as the window exploded into a shower of tiny diamonds.

Chapter 5

SARAH SCREAMED AS Pilakin, gun in hand, pulled her back from the window. With no memory of drawing the weapon, she asked herself what the hell she thought she was going to do with it. The maelstrom of bullets ceased and Sarah shrieked at her. "I thought you said I'd be safe now!"

Sarah tried to crawl across the room but a further shower of gunfire drove her back again. Pilakin breathed deeply and tried to calm herself. It made no sense. She realised she had pulled them both on to the wrong side of the window, the side away from the door.

"Stupid, stupid..." she snarled at herself through gritted teeth. "Come on you dumbag, think!"

She looked up and finally thought of a use for her pistol. Taking aim with trembling hands, she managed to hit the LED array with her third shot. The living room was plunged into darkness. Sarah made to move but Pilakin shouted "WAIT!"

After two seconds a further fusillade of shots dealt with the last remnants of the carpet, the sniper presumably assuming they would have moved into the dark space. After the bullets stopped, Pilakin slowly became aware of their combined heavy breathing. She counted in her head to twenty before speaking.

"Right, Sarah, listen. We're getting out of here. You've exactly two minutes to pack for you and… Paul. Essentials."

"Two minutes…but…"

She was clearly dazed. Pilakin raised her voice to get through to her.

"The gunman is probably on his way here, right now! He might even have a friend waiting outside. I'm going to check while you pack. Understand? This has to happen NOW."

Sarah nodded and they both scrambled to their feet and stumbled across the darkened space. Pilakin groped for the door handle. As she opened it, light from the hallway flooded the room. She turned to see Sarah's frightened face behind her.

"Two minutes, right? Keep it to essentials; we may have to move fast. Do you have a gun?"

"In the desk."

"Make sure you bring it."

Pilakin strode up the hall and hit the button for the spy-hole display. A grainy image of the corridor outside appeared and she was delighted to discover that there were secondary images available from the communal cameras, looking up and down the corridor. It seemed to be clear and the other apartment doors were closed. She jumped as Sarah loomed up behind her.

"Are you packed?" she asked in surprise.

"You said essentials." She showed her a small pack with her left hand and in her right was a simple automatic pistol. She held it in a confident manner. Pilakin reassessed her view of the woman. She had dropped the inny accent and it seemed that after her initial shock she was finding stores of practicality and determination. Growing up in this City tended to give people a core of erith. Pilakin nodded.

"Right. It looks clear out there but someone could be waiting behind a door or round a corner. We'll take the main way out because the bad guys will be taking the service routes. We see anyone, point your gun at them but don't make a verbal threat or you'll be committing a Tenth Right violation. Ready?"

Sarah took a couple of breaths and nodded.

"Yes."

Pilakin yanked open the door, grabbed a jacket from the rack and held it out. Nothing happened so she inched out. Still nothing. She beckoned Sarah to follow and made a run for it. She did the same jacket routine again at the intersection. Two more turns took them to the main elevator lobby. The only people they encountered on the way were a man and a young girl of four or five, who shied away under the muzzles of their guns, him enveloping the girl in the shield of his body. In the lobby was a large group of people and Pilakin indicated to Sarah to put her gun away. She made sure they were hidden at the back of a large group in the lift. Fortunately, the building was above a large tube intersection and Pilakin breathed a sigh of relief as the doors opened and they plunged into the chaotic crowds.

"Right Sarah, let's go and get Paul."

She nodded and they advanced into the human mass.

PILAKIN HAD TO step in on the argument. The weapons detectors on the school gate had sniffed them out as soon as they arrived. A forensic scrutiny of her agent badge had allowed Pilakin to keep hers but the guards were insisting Sarah checked hers in. Inserting oneself into someone else's argument was fraught with dangers of getting sued but some of Sarah's colourful suggestions to the guard were beginning to sound like threats and they really had to get a move on.

"Listen," she said to the guard in a conciliatory tone, "Mrs Flow has been shot at and her son has received death threats. All we want to do is go in there and get him out. Do you have children of your own?"

"Sure I do. And they're in class right now, so no way I am letting some terrified mother with a gun in there. Bad enough I have to let you in."

Damn thought Pilakin, and glanced at Sarah, but she in turn was looking at the guard and the expression on her face made Pilakin worry what she was going to say next, so she jumped in instead.

"The man who shot at her had an automatic rifle. One of those ones that sprays hundreds of bullets a minute. If he gets here, do you think he's going to kill her son with a single shot or do you think he's going to hose the classroom?"

The guard licked his lips.

"Okay. But I'm going with you."

He unholstered his own pistol and the threat was implied but he obviously felt the need to make it plainer.

"You so much as twitch and I'll plug you. If we're not out of here in five minutes, I'm hitting the panic button."

AS THEY CRASHED through the door into a classroom, several students squealed and leapt under their desks. All were watching the guard's pistol in alarm as Sarah ran up to a dark, handsome boy. He jerked and looked up at her. It took a moment for the confusion on his face to give way to recognition.

"Mum!"

"Come on, Paul. We need to go."

AFTER LEAVING THE school, Pilakin led them to the Cold Fusion Cafe. The obsession of City establishments with themes made the blue strip lighting and bubbling tubes of water a ridiculous extravagance for a lunchtime eatery, but this was a place where Freedom Protection Agents congregated to eat and exchange gossip. Half the people in the room were armed and notional allies.

Waiting for someone to answer her latest call, she watched Sarah and Paul. Sarah had refused to say anything about the situation until they had arrived, when Pilakin told her she could relax. Then the look on her face reminded Pilakin of her aunt's expression when she came to tell her about her own father. Gladly, she retreated to the far side of the room to start ringing round the safe-house companies and watched them from a distance. Paul seemed to take the news of his father's death with a certain level of fortitude, although he tried to yank his hand away from his mother's grasp. Pilakin wondered if he would have run from the room if it were not for the white-knuckled intensity with which Sarah held on to him.

"Hello…?"

Pilakin blinked back the tears for her father and returned to the present.

"Oh, hi, yes, hello. This is Agent Pilakin, 814159. Do you have any twin rooms available?"

"Nothing for weeks, sorry."

"Listen, I have a kid in danger who…"

The line hissed. There was no one there and the stool opposite tumbled over as a result of her wrath. Safe rooms were getting harder and harder to come by and it was not even as if she could get a hotel room as a stop-gap. What need for hotels in a city under siege? She looked at Paul again. He really was a good-looking lad. Already over 1.6 metres tall, she assumed he'd still not finished growing. Solidly built, with none of the gangly awkwardness common in his age, his dark features were somewhat softened by his mother's nose and eyes. Large brown eyes he had too; perilous for girls to get lost in. So like… He looked up at her. There was a sheen of tears and she blushed as he caught her looking. She had to make sure he was safe.

Shit. Who was she kidding? She did not have the money to get in anywhere that was still available, and the agencies were keeping their rooms back. Oh well. Desperate times called for desperate measures. She opened a different folder in her slab – the one filled with contacts from her time at the ECCA. She scrolled down to find the one she was looking for and dialled the number. It was answered almost immediately.

"Starlight Sophisticates."

"Hi, is the boss in? This is Agent Pilakin."

"Putting you through."

Sarah and Paul had stood up and were picking their way through the tables towards her.

"Hi Jaq, whassup?"

"Hello, Clem. Listen; huge favour. I need to rent one of your rooms for a week."

"Shit, Jaq, I can't take one of the girls out of the line for that long!"

"Not a girl, just a room. One of your doubles."

"You really think you can afford that?"

"C'mon, mates' rates. One week. The last time I'll ask, I promise. Then we're all square."

Pilakin heard him sigh.

"One week. Not an hour over, d'ya hear?"

"That's great Clem. We'll be right over."

She cut the connection and drummed her fingers on the side of her slab. One week. No point in trying for longer. If she didn't crack this case by then she would be out of money and out of the Agency business for good. As for the Flows? They'd be on their own. Nevertheless she flashed them a reassuring smile as they reached her table.

Chapter 6

"T HIS IS A… *brothel!*" hissed Sarah.

They were sitting in the lobby area – all plush seats and pot-plants. Light classical music played against the background noise of a fake fountain on the far side of the room. Paul's eyes darted surreptitiously as he watched the staff walking around in various outfits.

"Well, no one is going to look for you here, are they?" Pilakin replied at normal volume.

"Aren't there safe-houses for this sort of thing?"

"They're all full."

"But a brothel?"

She kept dropping her voice when she said brothel as if it was a secret that had to be kept from everyone else in the room.

"I don't want my son living in a… Hey, why can't we just go and stay at your place?"

Damn, thought Pilakin. She should have been

prepared for that one. The truth would not do, she had to think of something plausible. Quickly.

"I…er…run my business from it. Everyone knows where to find me. Certainly anyone who could find out that I'm representing you. Ah, here's Clem."

They both rose to greet him. An immaculate suit as always, black jacket, black shirt, black tie but each made with plasilk of a different weft so they caught the light with opposing sheens. He shook Pilakin's hand and pulled her close to kiss both cheeks.

"Ah Jaq, you're as beautiful as always. When are you going to quit the Agency and come and work for me? There's always a room for you here, you know that."

As Clem released her they both turned to Sarah. She looked scandalised. It was amazing how quickly the facade of her snobbery came back once the immediate danger had passed.

"This is Sarah," Pilakin put in quickly.

"Enchanted. And who's this strapping lad?"

Paul smiled with more warmth than his mother managed and shook Clem's hand. "Paul, sir. How many women do you have here?"

Sarah intervened. "For God's sake Paul. I don't want you paying any attention to what's going on here. Mr…er…"

"Just Clem will do."

"Clem, please show us to our room."

As he led them off, Sarah caught Pilakin's arm. Letting

Clem and Paul go on ahead, she carried on with her previous theme in a low voice.

"Look at the way Paul's reacting. You can't expect us to live here."

"Listen, Sarah, it's only for a week. No one will think of looking for you here and even if they do, there's heavily armed security all over the joint. This is a high class place. No kids or junkies or fetishes. It's a place where rich guys bored of their marriages come. It's very discreet and very exclusive."

Pilakin thought Sarah was being very prudish for a native of the City and there was something in the way she turned her head away, lips pursed. Did she have a past that was making her so uncomfortable? The City of Engalise was a huge pressure cooker and everyone was damaged by the strain in some way. Having deposited Sarah and Paul in a room more luxurious than anything Pilakin had ever lived in herself, she left to get back to her own ways of coping.

IT WAS INEVITABLE her feet would lead her to this point. Inevitable as soon as she started drinking that first one with Clem before she left Starlight Sophisticates. She told herself she loved drinking with Clem because it was free and real – this time the finest LaMarquois Shupillier. They polished off the bottle together and he pretended not to notice that she'd had most of it, the same way she pretended not to enjoy him caressing her face.

Then to the CDA Retreat. A gut-rot bar. Cheap. Horrible. But a good way to get properly set for the night, to pick up speed. Propositions by a bunch of soldiers good for the ego.

Towards the inner city. Two bars in quick succession. Beer in both to keep up momentum. Beer – it doesn't sound heavy but when water is as expensive as alcohol, percentages are high.

On to the Calva Club. She only got in because she spent six weeks shacked up with the doorman last year. Lovely lad but he'd put on too much muscle. Inside was a large terrace running round an open space chock full of apple…trees! Of course, trees. Under huge lightbulbs. The orchard insured for 40 million in adjusted credits, she'd heard. The water bill must be ludicrous. Far too expensive but she had to… The frissant of smelling the rich, sweet aroma of distilled real apples before sipping a shot where the alcohol didn't make her gag…

Then it got hazy. More bars probably. And now here. The end of the line. Always the end of the line. Pandora's Pods. As she weaved through the crowds, the top of her brain felt like it was floating while the rest of her body clunked and swayed. She was totally aware of every single thing around her. It was other people's fault that they kept colliding.

The door staff stood in front of her, with back-to-back P's on the arm bands over their black jackets. The queue of hopefuls and wannabes snaked away to the side. Luckily for her, repeat customers got priority. The man with the slab appeared, the short one with the bald head called Fran or Flan or…

"Good evening, Doctor Pilakin."

She smiled. She loved that they used her honorific. When she was here to be at her worst, they treated her as if at her best. And why not? She had worked damned hard for that "doctor"…

"Would you step into the office for a moment, please?"

Oh. Not good. She followed him in and slumped into a chair by the reception desk. Baldy spoke again with that special kind of courtesy that says *fuck off.*

"You know we're always delighted to receive our returning customers but I'm afraid a note has come down from management regarding the extent of your credit obligations."

It was time to concentrate on getting her words out intact.

"Well, can I just pay cash this evening?"

"Unfortunately we have reached the stage where any money you offer will be set against your spending so far. Only if your account is settled in full…"

"Alright, alright. I get it. How much…?"

A number appeared on the desk between them. It was a large number and for a moment she was tempted to pay it off with last of her reserves for just one more night of… She shook her head; not quite enough booze yet consumed to dispense with the last remnants of Dr Pilakin, Freedom Protection Agent. She felt rage building within her.

"Listen Flan…"

"Francis."

"Sure, okay. I'm one of your best customers. I have a deal coming together that will pay this off in full and set myself up a tab."

"Dr Pilakin, we do have plenty of people wishing to sign up as members."

She was going to have to use a name again. Humiliating, but she was jonesing.

"What if someone else paid for me tonight?"

"I'm sorry but we…"

"Hear his bloody name first, Flanboy. Lars Löring-Kristani. Kristani. That name ring any bells? If I give him a call and let him know that a courtesy is not being extended to me…?"

The condescending smile on baldy's face seemed to be fixed in place but his eyes had widened. Pilakin could sniff her chance now and followed it up by grabbing her slab and getting his number on the screen. Easy to do when it was first in the speed-dial.

Baldy copied it down.

"Please wait here, Dr Pilakin. Help yourself to some water."

He left the room and she poured herself a generous measure from the crystal decanter, followed by another. It took him long enough that she had more than half emptied it by the time he came back. He looked with what seemed to be approval at the amount she had taken. He pressed a button on his desk as he addressed her.

"Mr Löring has offered to cover this evening's bill for you."

A host appeared in the room, carrying a security box.

"Eric will take your belongings and conduct you into the club."

Pilakin stood and held out her hand.

"Thank you. I'm…"

"Please don't mention it, Dr Pilakin. We know many of our members are under a lot of strain."

She made to follow Eric when Baldy interrupted once more.

"Oh, one other thing. Mr Löring has insisted that you go to see him at 1500 tomorrow. It will be our pleasure to remind you of your appointment in the morning."

Pilakin nodded and turned to follow Eric out.

Engalise, she thought, *everything comes at a price.*

"WE'LL NEED YOUR gun too."

Eric placed her slab, badge and other accoutrements into the security box, on top of the clothes she had already removed. A large, fluffy dressing gown felt wonderful against her bare skin. She took the gun out of its pocket and placed it, along with two spare ammunition clips, into the box and Eric snapped it shut. They both placed their thumbs on the security scanner and the lock clicked.

"Now, Dr Pilakin, what can we do for you this evening?"

Chapter 7

PASSING THROUGH THE ionising smell of the dampening curtain, the sensory change came in waves. First was the tingling skin on the tip of her nose that advanced backwards across her whole body as she moved forward. Then the smell changed. From the sterilised but stale city air, to a mix of scented chemicals, sterile alcohol, juicy cannabis, tart cocaine and sweetened loob. Next the eyes – from the light outside, through fuzziness, to the dark, dry-ice smoke filled interior. Some aspects of the view became less distinct but the main display lasers cut through with greater clarity. Finally the noise. Music and chatter, a bass beat thumping through her chest.

The central area of the large circular room was full of tables and sofas and staging. The highest value seats were in sunken wells right in the middle of the action. Tonight's show, Pilakin noted disinterestedly, seemed to be a cross between a bukkake party and guy-girl combination pulling a train. None of that sordid public activity for her though, as Eric guided her to one of the upper level booths that ringed the arena.

Behind the curtain, the central feature was a circular bed, three metres across, covered in black silk sheets and scattered with cushions and pillows. Around the walls were a wash area, TV wall, self-service bar, equipment rack and a door through to a small bathroom. The ceiling was one giant mirror. Eric moved around the edge, activating the electronics and unlocking the rack.

"The catalogue is next to the bed, Dr Pilakin."

She picked it up from a small table and started scrolling through.

"Subwoofer in the bed?"

"Yes. The music feeds are next to the bar over here. The vibro channels are numbers sixty-five to ninety-three."

Nothing was leaping out at her from the catalogue.

"Eric, help me out here. You got anything fresh?"

Eric looked at her with narrowed eyes for a moment.

"Ah yes, ma'am. Now I remember your preference. I think you'll like number 43. He's nineteen and stringy."

She looked at the right page. What a beautiful face.

"Excellent."

"Any enhancements? Mr Löring has given you an open tab."

She had never splashed out on the enhancements

before and spent a moment in contemplation.

"A CDA uniform. Preferably a couple of sizes too big for him."

"Interesting choice. Would you like to see the drugs menu?"

"Just bring me the full platter."

"Certainly Ma'am."

As Eric withdrew, closing the dampening curtains behind him, she walked to the bar and dispensed two flutes of shupillier. *If I ever got rich*, she mused, *this place would be my ruin.* She picked up the media remote and went to lie on the bed. First a search through the channels until she found a suitably dark show to set the mood. One of those close up ones where the image was zoomed in, grainy and the curves of fabric and flesh filled the TV wall. Sound down, of course, because she now selected a music vibro channel. The sound filled the air around her while the bass beat and subsonic vibrations got to work on the bed. It varied in effect from purring pussy to screaming sybian, never staying long enough in one place for her body to settle. Later on she would select something more conducive to…

"Hello…?"

She turned her head to see that lovely face peering out from under an outsized helmet, just inside the curtains. His uniform was baggy and he had a rifle slung over his shoulder. Nice touch, although she noted it was safely deactivated. In his arms he held a large tray covered with the drugs and the technical devices needed to use them. He looked nervous and unsure of himself.

"Are you new, sweetie?" Pilakin asked.

He swallowed and nodded.

"It's my first day."

"Well I have you for the whole night, so you put that tray down on the table, pick up those two drinks and come and join me."

She patted the bed next to her.

WHAT WAS REAL and what was dream? It didn't matter. Crystal meth for stamina and hopefully to tweak. Buzz for the touch. A line or two of cocaine off Number 43's flat belly. Meth and marble pills for him. The vibrations of the bed… pleasure… pain… heroin… darkness…

"Happy Birthday. Happy Birthday…"

They're all singing and she feels her face glowing with embarrassment. The whole tower has turned out and they're dancing round her in two circles going opposite ways. Finally they stop and her uncle steps into the ring, holding up his hands for quiet.

"Nearly six years ago, young Jaq came to live among us. She's part of our family now and we all love her. I made a promise to protect her and bring her up decently. I certainly succeeded in the first count and the way she has rejected all the boys who have dared approach her certainly suggests I have done well in the second."

There's laughter around the room and she wants to

crawl away to a hole.

"I know she has long desired to come outside with us and it has been very frustrating for her to be unable to fight. In this I was only fulfilling my promise. But today she is a woman and I suspect that if I keep her out of it much longer she would just walk off to another tower."

"No, uncle. I would never—"

"Hush, zaychonok. It's okay. Anyway, you're going to start today."

A ball of excitement and apprehension engulfs the teenage embarrassment of being centre of attention.

"I thought long and hard of the best way of keeping you safe while letting you fight. And so we have bought you this birthday present. The whole tower chipped in. Itzie!"

The beautiful, tall, gangling boy, comical in his outsized uniform, steps forward with a long box covered in shiny paper in his arms. He blushes as she smiles at him. If only he would ask her out, he would find out he was the reason she'd rejected everyone else.

He lays the box at her feet and steps back. She squats down in front of it and starts to tear at the paper as everyone sings again. Her excitement grows as she uncovers a Simplaeran Royal Arsenal logo on the box. Her hands shake as she opens it to find a grade 1 sniper rifle and targeting kit inside.

"There, Jaq. You can do your fighting without getting your feet dirty."

"Thank you. Thank you so much everyone."

She stands to pose for pictures with the rifle and an enormous smile on her face.

Slowly surfacing, Pilakin's consciousness crept back into a mind that was not yet ready to forgive her the pain. She groped for a remote that would switch off the bed's pulsing subwoofer before realising that her ears were reporting silence and the thumping was in her head. She groaned and rolled over as half remembered images flashed through her mind. Reaching between her legs made her shout at herself.

"Idiot, Jaq. Protection, you stupid bitch. How many times…?"

Her verbal tirade of self abuse was eventually interrupted by the curtain being pulled back, revealing Pandora's resident doctor and a trolley.

"Ah, good morning, Doctor Pilakin. What are we up for today?"

"Hey, Chung-Li. All the usual, please."

"*All* the usual?"

He looked down at the lower part of her body.

"Ah, yes. I thought we'd discussed that last time."

"Fuck off."

Chung-Li started loading drug pastes into the 3D printer to construct her 'morning after' pill. "I assume you'll be after contraceptive as well as biocleaning?"

"Yeah, someone else is paying today, so give me everything you've got. I need a tox flush and painkillers. Lots of painkillers."

Chung-Li walked over to the discarded drugs tray and started taking notes of her usage.

"Love a duck, Jaq. It beats me how you're still in the shape you are, sometimes."

Eric arrived with her security box and they clicked it open. Normally she didn't get this until she'd paid, but she guessed things were different on the Kristani account. He politely reminded her of her appointment with Lars but refused to leave until she had added it to her slab. As she went through her calendar, news reports and emails, she could feel Dr Chung-Li coating her insides with an antimicrobial gel. The 3D printer on the trolley buzzed as it assembled the different drugs, antibiotics, synthetic antibodies, hormones and tissue purging chemicals into a single capsule. While he worked she swiped through her slab and found a call waiting. She initiated the ring-back, without camera due to her position, and it was answered quickly.

"Good morning. LRT Forensics, post-mortem lab 3."

"Oh, hello. This is Agent Pilakin, I have a call back?"

"Yes, Agent. Just a mo'."

She heard the man who'd answered it calling someone in the background just as Chung-Li handed her the newly created pill and a bottle of water. She juggled them to take it just as someone came back on the line.

"Agent Pilakin?"

She quickly swallowed but the pill didn't go down first time. She drowned it in water and got it.

"Hello…?" the man asked again.

"Hi, yes. I'm here."

"Ah good. This is Doctor Vrijbuiter. We've completed your post mortem. Seems your hunch might have paid off. We've found something rather unusual. When can you come down?"

"Well, can't you tell me what it is now?"

"Nice try, Agent. There's some more fees to pay. I'll be happy to brief you when you get here."

Pilakin gritted her teeth.

"Fine."

Chung-Li winked at her and left, pushing his trolley. She looked at her watch.

"I'll be with you in forty minutes."

She broke the connection without waiting for the final platitudes. Picking up a large towel and token that Eric had left her, she headed for the shower room.

Chapter 8

As she stepped out of the club doors, she found part of the queuing area had been cordoned off with Agent tape. Relatively few gawpers meant the bodies must have been there a while and club bouncers had shepherded their early birds away to the other side of the entrance. There were several Freedom Protection Agents in attendance, all in Federation uniform, meaning the victims would be Federation too. Looking at the squad cars, Pilakin rolled her eyes. The Federation's in-house agency was well-equipped and heavily staffed but the quality of their detectives was abysmal.

She recognised one of them as a case in point. Max Locatore. The man was a cretin. He'd been chucked out of the City Agency after six months for recording the department's first ever zero case-closure rate. No wonder he'd ended up with the Free Federation of Anti-Imperial Organisations. Essentially it was a very well funded and equipped terrorist group and, as a result, did not pay its 'volunteers'. In Engalise, giving one's time for free did not sit well with the talented. However, the Federation did pay for its members' living costs and looked after their families, so the talentless and the desperate filled the office functions of their vast headquarters, here in the City.

She crept up behind Max and jabbed him in the ribs with her finger. He visibly leapt and dropped his slab.

"What the Hell…?"

He turned and Pilakin could not help but grin at his shocked expression.

"Wow! Pilakin, isn't it?"

"Hi, Max."

"It's good to see you. Are you still with the ECC-FPA?"

She managed not to blanche.

"No, I've gone independent. Too much vatshit in the Corporation."

"Oh, good for you."

"What do you have here, Max?"

Having picked up his slab, he tilted his head to beckon her over to the cordon. Beyond it were three bodies. Two women and a man, all in Federation boiler suits. Max pointed.

"That one's a fighter pilot and the other two are engineers. The fleet's in at the moment, so they were down on shore leave… dammit."

"What?"

"Forget what I just said about the fleet. Can't get used to the whole secrecy thing."

Pilakin adopted a look of mock surprise.

"You mean you're not a true believer in the fight for freedom?"

"Just trying to feed the kids."

Pilakin wondered why he didn't try a different line of work.

"Anyway," he continued, "they got plugged by two guys with silent pulse guns. You know the ones that set up a shock-wave which punches your insides to hell? They were in and out so quickly, the club bouncers never even spotted them."

"You got a motive?"

"Their Federation badges are missing, so I reckon it's simple – couple of Imperial squirrels want their IDs for some spy-stuff."

Poor old Max. He looked so proud when he said that. A glance at the scene should have told him it was crap.

"Nice theory, Max. Have you reported it yet?"

"Just writing it up. Why?"

"Well, it's just that you, and I, and the Imps all know that Fed badges don't work unless you have rank bars too."

She pointed at the metal strips on the corpses' collars. She didn't know how it functioned but the badge without a real set of bars never fooled the Federation.

Max put his hand to his head.

"Oh for goodness' sake…!"

After a moment he visibly pulled himself together and swallowed his pride.

"Don't suppose you want to do a bit of sub-contracting?"

Tempting though it was to get some easy money out of the Federation, the clock was ticking.

"Sorry, Max. I have to be somewhere." She shuddered as she contemplated using the hideously overcrowded tube with her hangover.

He leaned closer and spoke quietly.

"Can't you at least give me a hint? Where should I start?"

Pilakin looked at him meaningfully and he sighed.

"Okay, what will it cost me?"

"A lift in your squad car down to LRT Forensics"

He nodded.

"In that case, Max, I think you should be looking for a couple of desperate itees who are hoping to use the badges to score some food or drugs. You know – flash the badge and put it on the Fed's expense account."

"Shit, Pilakin. I'm never going to solve that. Itinerants? Where would I start? You can't even tell who's homeless anymore."

"Pulse guns are rare, so you must be able to scare up some intel on how an itee might have got hold of one. Anyway, you asked me what I thought and a deal's a deal. So, get me a driver."

HAVING DEALT WITH the formalities in reception, Pilakin was led through to the laboratories. Doctor Vrijbuiter met her at the door and ushered her inside. Strange blue uplighting ran around the walls and picked out the LRT logo in various places. There were three steel examination tables; two had bodies on them under sheets while the third was being hosed down by a lab assistant. Vrijbuiter took her to the furthest and donned a pair of latex gloves from a box on the side bench. Pilakin had a momentary flashback to the previous night but stuffed the thought away in a corner of her mind and concentrated. Vrijbuiter looked at her and asked if she needed some water.

"No, I'm fine thank you."

He called over to the assistant.

"Can you get Agent Pilakin some water and a stool?"

He looked back at her with a smile.

"Believe me, I've seen plenty faint in this place, although this body isn't so gruesome."

He pulled back the sheet to reveal the corpse and brought up a 3D scan of it on the overhead display. Pilakin nodded her thanks to the assistant as he brought the water and stool. She assumed they would not charge her for it, given the amount she had paid for their services. This report had better be worth it too.

"So what killed him, Doc?"

"A pile of rubble fell on him."

"What the hell?" She was off her stool, anger rising but Vrijbuiter was obviously highly amused by her reaction.

"Oh, and he was murdered."

Was he taking the piss? The smile left his face and was replaced with concern.

"Agent Pilakin, I'm worried about you. Please, sit down. Come on. And I'll tell you what I found."

She glowered at him.

"The victim suffered multiple fractures and internal injuries, as one would expect from the situation."

Red circles appeared on the 3D scan, highlighting broken bones and tissue damage. Pilakin looked down at the body.

"There's no real bruising."

"No, that's because the cause of death was these two fractures here. It will have been almost instantaneous, so the heart won't have pumped blood into the injuries to form the bruises."

The image zoomed in on the head and it was immediately obvious that there were two large indentations with bone fragments scattered into the brain. Vrijbuiter stuck his fingers together and made a chopping motion as he spoke.

"Two rather jagged bits hit his head pointy end first."

"Could that be arranged?"

He smirked.

"I very much doubt it."

Patronising arse.

The 3D scan was replaced by a fuzzy picture of the street on which Flow died.

"This is what we got from the retinal analysis. Quite a good picture, as you can see, because the body was so fresh."

Pilakin leaned forward with interest. This was a neat little technique that had been developed by her supervisor at the Institute. The back of the eye's chemical make-up was fixed at the moment of cell death. So, a high resolution scan of the retina could put together an image of the last thing seen. The quality varied wildly but it could be very useful if the last thing the victim saw was his murderer. Not so good in this street scene, though. People running around – avoiding the rubble fall, presumably. She shook her head.

"Nothing leaps out, Doc."

"Well, that'll be in the report with everything else for you to peruse at leisure. Let's move on to the tox screen."

A series of figures and charts appeared and something was immediately obvious.

"He was high."

"Yes, Agent, he was. From what I can see, he had a cocktail of meth, buzz and some of those designer ones that are alcohol activated. That's interesting because he also had in his system that new slow-release alcohol that came onto the market a couple of years ago."

"Ease the pain with DrAlcohol. Keeps you intoxicated for longer."

"Indeed, but who'd want that?"

Actually, Pilakin thought, *that would be pretty good*

right now.

"So what would be the effect of this lot?" she asked.

"Probably distraction, dissociation with events, warm fuzzy feeling—"

"So it could explain his lack of concern when the rubble was coming down?"

"I would think so. Significant?"

"Maybe." She looked down at her own shaking hands. "But how many of your clients were on something when they died?"

He smiled and nodded. "About ninety five percent. It's endemic."

Yes, she thought. *Jeremiah Flow had serious money problems. He may have been trying to mentally check out.*

"This is all very interesting, Doc, but none of it proves murder. You said you had something significant."

His smile grew broader. He obviously got off on building up to the big reveal.

"Let's return to the injuries."

This time he zoomed in on the legs.

"What do you see, Agent Pilakin?"

"The thighs are both broken…"

"Yes. What's more, they're broken at the same height. Clean breaks."

She thought for a moment.

"One large piece of masonry, with a straight edge, falling across both legs?"

"That's what I thought too, but it looked… well…"

He manipulated the display and a red line appeared along each of the breaks. They were curved and, when he extended the line, they matched up so that they both formed part of the same, larger circle.

"Odd isn't it? I thought maybe some kind of piping, so I had a look at those pictures you took at the scene. There was nothing big or regular enough to break them both."

"So, his legs were snapped by something else?"

"Yes."

"Could he have walked to that spot with broken thighs?"

"No. He couldn't even have stood up."

"So, they were broken right there. Somebody didn't want him to move."

"And that, Agent Pilakin, is why you have a murder on your hands."

Chapter 9

OBVIOUSLY SHE NEEDED to go back and talk to Sarah to see about Jeremiah's drug use, thought Pilakin as she downed a shot of DrAlcohol in a bar opposite the LRT labs. Although, if she waited a bit, she could score a free lunch off Clem while they talked. Reviewing her case notes as a barman refilled her glass, she noticed the Flow's plumbing business was based a few stops down the tube from here. Pulling up the number, she gave their office a call because it would be irritating to get down there only to find the nephew missing.

"Hello, Flow Plumbing. What can we do for you today?"

"Hi. I'm Freedom Protection Agent Pilakin. I'd like to speak to… er… Zeb Lander."

"Certainly Freedom Protection Agent Pilakin. I will be happy to make an appointment for Zeb Lander to come and give you a quote. Please could we have your address?"

"What? No. I want to speak to him now. Is he there? In the office?"

"I am sorry for the misunderstanding, Freedom Protection Agent Pilakin. I would be delighted to make an appointment for you to drop by the office and speak to Zeb Lander about your requirements. When would be convenient?"

"Is he there now? Can he come to the phone…?"

"Please wait a moment, Freedom Pro…."

Dammit, thought Pilakin as she realised she was talking to a machine.

"Cancel. Delete line!" she shouted. The guy across the table was looking at her and smiling. Everybody hated robots.

"New line. Command: Consult Zeb Lander appointment schedule from now forward two hours. End line." she guessed, having had some experience with these things at the Institute. The female voice on the phone adopted a more automated timbre.

"Line. Resource Zeb Lander schedule value null for time stated. End line."

"New line. Command: Test location resource Zeb Lander. End line."

"Line. Resource Zeb Lander at location Flow Plumbing Company Office…"

She jabbed the call disconnect button and downed her drink.

PILAKIN PRESSED THE buzzer next to the large metal roll-up door covered in tags on the front of a squat commercial building. The trip down here on the tube had not been so bad; only a couple of verbal altercations. The City's mood seemed calm today.

"You Agent Pilakin?" asked a man's voice from the intercom.

"That's right," she replied. There was a buzz and the door grizzled as it retracted about a metre up before stopping. Sighing, she ducked under and it closed behind her. The garage space inside was almost entirely filled by a van and she had to turn sideways to inch down the side to a staircase in the back corner. Climbing the stairwell, she could hear a woman's voice and, when she opened the door at the top, heard what it was saying.

"…end line…end line…end line…end line…"

An attractive young man was leaning over a white plastic-covered figure, clearly the source of the monotonously repeating phrase.

"Can't you shut that thing up?" she asked. The man glowered at her.

"It's been doing this since you called. If I could shut it up, don't you think I'd have done it by now?"

Pilakin smiled.

"What's its designation?"

"RK4-Jess"

Pilakin strode over to it saying, "RK4-Jess. React primary sensors."

The robot twitched and turned its head to look at her, still repeating its phrase.

"RK4-Jess, malfunction indicated. New line: break loop. New line: re-boot to primary. New line: reload operating system at last restore point. End Line."

The robot shut down and started twitching as it rebooted.

"Wow," said the man. "you a programmer?"

"I spent some time in the Institute. I assume you're Zeb Lander?"

A nod.

"Well, Mr Lander, how did you know who I was?"

"When Jess started acting up I looked at the call log."

She could not help smiling again at this young man. "Of course. Nice of you to wait around for me."

"Well, once it looked like your abrupt call had broken Jess, I wanted to get the details of the person whose fault it was."

"She's not very robust if a hang-up sent her into a tail-spin."

"She usually does fine but then most callers don't access her command line programme."

Pilakin stroked the twitching, shiny white plastic.

"It's an old one, Zeb. Mark VII isn't it? From before the siege?"

He seemed upset.

"Yeah. Basic model. Graphene processor."

"Naturally. How did you come by it?"

"A cousin with a taste for the retro leant her to me when business went down and we had to let the receptionist go. If she's knackered, he's going to have a major sense of humour failure. Which agency do I send the bill to?"

Pilakin winced at the thought.

"Actually I'm independent."

Zeb snapped his fingers and appeared to instantly relax.

"Ah! You're here about Uncle Jer. Auntie Sarah told me about you."

"So, why didn't you recognise my name from her?"

"She didn't tell me it. Just said that she'd got some desperate independent agent."

Interesting, thought Pilakin. She arched her eyebrows.

"Desperate, you say?"

He smiled back at her for the first time.

"Guess you'd have to be to sniff around a rubble fall. Hey, would you like a drink?"

"God, yes. Thank you."

"Come through."

He led her past a crude partition that bisected the office and she found herself in a basic living area. A large double mattress on the floor covered about a quarter of the space, although the sheets on it looked freshly laundered and there was a large thick duvet rolled up at the end. An induction stove was in the far corner and two chairs were pulled up to a small dining table. An old-fashioned TV on the opposite wall above a cupboard completed the room's furnishings. Sparse, but a damned sight more homely a space than many in the city had to call their own.

"Would you like some tea?"

Pilakin was both disappointed and surprised.

"Tea? Real tea? How did you get that?"

Zeb blushed. "A couple of hydro-guys I know are robo-pervs. They pay me with it to have a go on Jess from time to time."

Pilakin shivered. Urgh! She couldn't help blurting out, "How disgusting!"

Having put the kettle on, Zeb turned round to face her.

"Yes, I know, but it takes all sorts and the work diary's empty. I've got to find some way of paying the rent on this place."

"So, business isn't good then?"

"No. Not since Uncle Jer ditched our City contracts."

"You think he made the wrong decision?"

"Well, of course he did but hindsight is a pretty exact science."

"You don't resent him, then?"

The question hung in the air as Zeb spooned tea leaves into two small porous bags. Pilakin decided to move on.

"How did Jer take it after the business went bad?"

"He got irritated by things. Spent a lot of time whinging about Auntie Sarah and how she was on his back about it."

"She was putting him under pressure?"

"Yeah, sure."

"Was he taking anything to… cope with it?"

The bags had made their way into "Go with the Flow" mugs and, as the kettle boiled, Zeb poured the water on top of them, a cloud of steam rising – it looked like a waste.

"You mean drugs?"

He held out the mug and she fumbled in her pocket for a credit note to pay for the water component of the tea. She was disappointed when he took it.

"Well, I suppose it wasn't as bad as Auntie Sarah would have us believe. He was drinking a bit and taking some calmers, but nothing hard."

Pilakin looked at the bag floating in her mug and wondered whether she was supposed to take it out or drink with it still in there. Smiling, Zeb came to her rescue.

"The longer you leave it in, the stronger the flavour gets. If you've never had any before, I'd take it out round about now."

She fished it out using the string and dropped it into a small bowl that Zeb held out for her. They sat down at the table.

"Do you know where your uncle was killed?"

He blew on his tea.

"Yeah, out on the rim somewhere."

"Do you know why he would be out there?"

"Sure."

That was surprisingly simple. Less likely to be the murderer, though.

"Care to enlighten me?"

He looked shifty and embarrassed for a moment before taking a deep breath.

"We were bidding for a job."

"On the rim?"

He nodded.

"Some guy contacted the office but when he said he was from out there, Uncle Jer balked. Then the guy said he'd pay for us to come to a meeting, and for each consultation after that, so we thought 'what the hell'."

Pilakin took out her stylus and activated her slab.

"What was his name?"

"Well, the one he gave us was Artyom Rimsky."

"You think he was lying?"

"Maybe, given what he wanted to do."

Pilakin looked up and raised her eyebrows.

"That was…?"

"He'd come into a bit of money and wanted to invest in a hydroponics set-up."

"Growing?"

"Cannabis, coca leaves, the usual."

"Well, no need for him to be cagey if that's all he was into."

"True. But when we spoke to him, it turned out that was just a front. The specs he handed over were for fruit and vegetables."

Pilakin winced. Real fruit and veg were serious cash crops and firmly in the hands of the syndicates. This may be significant after all.

"And your uncle decided to run with it even after he found out?"

"He came back and we laid it all out. He told me how much of a financial mess we were in and how much we could use what Rimsky was offering – it would have cleared all the debts in one go. We discussed it for hours."

"And decided to go with it?"

"No. We decided to turn him down. Next day we called Rimsky. He sounded disappointed but said he could respect the decision. He wanted to end it in person – make sure Uncle Jer had taken the plans out of his pad, have one more chance to try and change our minds, whatever. We were going to say no but he offered expenses for the trip. That was what Uncle Jer was doing when he was killed."

"Why didn't you go with him?" she asked calmly. He flushed red and his voice rose a little.

"I had to go out to quote on a job. We weren't in a position to risk losing work."

"So, there will be a corroborative witness?"

He sounded angry now.

"No. It was a waste of time – the people at the address said they'd never asked for me. I don't like the way you're—"

"Excuse me…?"

Pilakin jumped at the woman's voice but relaxed a little as the robot walked into the room. Zeb lowered his voice again.

"We're fine Jess. Agent Pilakin was not a threat to me."

Jess advanced a little further.

"That is good, Mr Lander. However, you misconstrue my reasons for interrupting you. I merely wished to thank Agent Pilakin for clearing my system glitch."

At those words, Pilakin felt the adrenaline of pure fear rush through her body. She leapt out of her chair, drawing her gun in one easy movement, and aimed straight at the robot's head.

Chapter 10

"THAT'S NANOMATRONIC BEHAVIOUR!" she grated. Tunnel vision had robbed her of the ability to see anything except the back of her gun and the robot's blank features. It came as a surprise when Zeb's face obscured it.

"She's not nanomatronic," he shouted. "I installed a gratitude software package. The robo-pervs like it."

"What?" Her gun quivered.

"Seriously! They get off on the idea she's grateful for what they do. I mean, come on. Would a nanomatronic be able to stand by and let you point that gun at me? And stop doing that, for God's sake, or I'll report you for a Tenth Right violation."

Pilakin shook her head and her mind cleared. What the fuck was she doing? Where had this terror come from? She felt ashamed. Re-holstering her gun, she spoke in a low voice.

"I have no idea what they're capable of. I've never

knowingly met one."

Zeb had gone white and was breathing hard.

"I think you should leave, Agent Pilakin. I don't think I like you and I certainly don't feel safe having you around."

Pilakin nodded. Prime suspect or not, she knew she had overreacted.

"Look, I'm sorry. Here," she held out her business card. "I hope you'll still help me to find your uncle's killer."

"Of course I will, but don't come back here, okay?"

PILAKIN MANAGED TO snag a seat on the tube back to Starlight Sophisticates on the Upper. The smell of unwashed bodies, inadequately masked with cleaning chemicals, was particularly overpowering today. The recent spike in water prices seemed to have turned into a plateau and, as a result, more and more people were economising by putting even longer intervals between their showers. Although she herself was clean, thanks to Pandora's that morning, she looked down at her clothes and was irritated that she hadn't asked them to do a wash as well. Her sleeve cuffs were looking grubby and a surreptitious sniff confirmed that her shirt was adding to the melange of odours in the carriage. After lunch she should go to her laundry. The last thing she needed was to give Lars something else to nag her about at their meeting in the afternoon.

She alighted at Rottan Rode Station and made her way to the news vendor. Pressing the buttons on top of the pod, she selected the Angel Chronicle, the ECC Daily News, the Federation Gazette and the Free Radio Transcript Download. Bumping her slab on the rubber pad then debited a credit from her account (*Four for the Price of Three!* the vendor's advert proclaimed) and downloaded the day's news feeds. A quick scan of the indexing program showed that none had any interest in the Flow case, the gunning of Sarah's flat or the artillery strike. The only oblique reference was in the ECC Daily's round up of city maintenance, referring to the net repairs. What a stunningly interesting journal it was. But it was surprising that neither the Gazette nor Free Radio had taken it up; they loved stories running down the security situation.

She pondered this as she shouldered her way through the door of Starlight Sophisticates. Clem was in the lobby and came straight over to her, looking at his watch.

"Jaq Pilakin walks into my lobby – it must be lunchtime."

She kissed him on the cheek.

"How are they? Have they come down to eat yet?"

"Oh they're fine, as far as I can tell. They're taking their meals in the room. She's a total prude, Jaq. Where did you find her?"

"Be careful, Clem. I think she's got more about her than you'd think. How about Paul?"

"That lad will put me out of business, the amount he's eating. Also, someone looked at the porn channels at about one a.m. – I bet that was after her majesty went to sleep."

"You didn't charge me for that I hope."

He grinned.

"And *I* hope your attention is focussed on paying the bill for this lot. Jaq… you do have the money, don't you? I heard there was a bit of trouble at Pandora's last night…"

She squeezed his arm.

"Bless you for asking, Clem, but I'm fine. Will you send lunch if I go up there?"

He smiled and nodded.

"Of course. Same old Jaq."

SARAH LOOKED DOWNRIGHT irritated when she opened the door.

"You did check it was me, didn't you?" Pilakin asked.

"Of course. They called up from reception to say you were coming and I checked the screen."

Paul, lying on his bed with headphones on, was playing a game on the room's entertainment console. His bag had been emptied and its contents were lying all over his side of the floor. She could almost see a demarcation line running down between his half and the stark emptiness of Sarah's. Pilakin imagined the kind of arguments they'd been having.

"You know, Sarah, if you're going a little stir crazy in

here, Clem would be happy to lay on a bouncer to take you down to the dining room."

"I'm not having him down there, mixing with those people."

Despite Paul's headphones, Pilakin lowered her voice.

"You know, it might do him good to see the working girls are real people…"

"What are you doing to get us out of here?"

Once again she wondered what had made Sarah so intolerant.

"Shouldn't we go somewhere away from…?"

She nodded at Paul.

"We can talk here. Once he's got those things on, he can't hear a thing. Here let me show you. Paul? Do you want to go down and chat to the girls? See? Not a flicker. So tell me."

Pilakin sat down on the bed and after a moment, Sarah joined her but right on the edge, back tense and rigid. Pilakin pulled out her slab and started flicking through.

"Well, firstly I've got the forensic report back and we've been able to confirm that your husband was murdered…"

A stifled scream stopped her in her tracks. She looked up and was startled to find Sarah biting on her hand, tears welling up in her eyes. Sarah's mask had slipped again. Pilakin felt something akin to compassion and reached out to squeeze her shoulder. Sarah shook it away and closed her eyes for moment. When they opened again, she pulled out a handkerchief and wiped the tears.

"How?" she asked in husky voice.

"I'm sorry, I'm not in a position to tell you that yet. There are still confidentiality agreements between me and the forensics people—"

"Vatshit! I'm not stupid."

Pilakin nodded.

"Okay. I'm still getting to grips with the case and I haven't been able to rule anyone out yet."

"That sounds more like the truth. So I'm a suspect am I?"

"Yes."

"Telling your client she's a suspect…well I suppose that shows you're after the truth. I've been wondering after all that business that got you chucked out of the ECC-FPA."

Pilakin was taken aback.

"That's right, Agent Pilakin. I've been checking up on you. They said you were corrupt."

"I was made redundant."

"Alright. Some influential blogs said you were corrupt."

"There's an election coming up. They needed to cut costs to get the services bill down…"

Sarah waved her hand.

"Okay, whatever. I suppose your case clearance and compensation rates were impressive. Now, since you won't tell me what's going on, I guess you're here to ask me some questions."

Pilakin cleared her throat and looked down at her pad.

"I'm sorry if this is painful, but could you tell me how Jer was in the last few days before he… was killed."

"How do you mean?"

"Was he stressed? Worried? Angry? Distracted?"

"Well, of course. We had real money worries you know. Love him, he was most concerned about what would happen to Paul but he didn't want me going back to…"

Pilakin waited but Sarah didn't continue. From the look on her face, she wasn't going to either.

"Okay. But was his behaviour more erratic? Was he drinking or something?"

"No. Absolutely not. Well, not at home, anyway. If he was doing it, he kept it out of the flat."

"Anything else?"

"No. I'm sure of it."

"It's just the tox screen came back as…"

"Oh, the calmers? I gave him those. I have my own supply. I swear he was the only person in the city not to have his own."

Either the woman was a far better liar than Pilakin gave her credit for or Jeremiah was not using in a big way. A knock at the door heralded the arrival of lunch, so she let it drop. The three of them ate in a frosty silence.

AS SOON AS she was done eating, Pilakin got out of the claustrophobic atmosphere. She took the back way out to avoid Clem's further questions about how payment would be made. Outside, two burly bouncers were giving a beating to an errant punter and the one of them gave her a smile and a wink. She nodded back whilst lighting up a heroette and checked for messages. It was a surprise to see a return call request from ECC maintenance and, as she called, she moved down the alley to get away from the sounds of the altercation. She briefly voiced her frustration as it went to voicemail but the small hit of opiates from the heroette kept her from getting too agitated. Looking at the clock on her slab, she saw she still had time to get to her laundry and clean up before going to see Lars.

"DO YOU WANT a shower token as well?" asked the laundry clerk as he put her clothes into a tagged sack and dropped it onto the conveyor behind him.

"No thanks, I had one this morning."

Pilakin hugged the threadbare laundry dressing gown around her, quite a contrast to the luxury cotton fluff she had been given at Pandora's. Clutching her receipt, she went through into the locker-storage room. She opened number 263 and, having looked around, reached inside her spare pair of shoes to retrieve the worryingly small roll of credit notes. Taking about three hundred, she sighed and locked up her remaining clothes. Could she really sell her last dress? She replaced the three bullets she had used and rattled the remaining four in the ammunition box as if she could find one that might be hidden.

She slammed the door shut and went to sit on one of the benches, trying ECC maintenance again and was satisfied as, this time, it was answered.

"ECC Maintenance, Engineer Melissa Walden speaking."

"Hi, this is Agent Pilakin. You gave me a call?"

"Oh yes, you're the one who was speaking to my colleague at the Southwind building. Sorry if he was a bit of a dick back there."

Pilakin tried to keep the impatience out of her voice.

"Sure, no problem. Did you find something, then?"

"Yes. He left a file. Hang on… here it is. Mmm, that's odd. It shows here that the net was cut."

"Cut?"

"Yep. No striations in the ends so it looks like it was done with a high temperature laser."

"Is that significant?"

"Well, if it had been cut manually, the person or device would have to be on the spot. Laser cutting could be done from anywhere with direct line of sight."

"Ah, I see. Wouldn't that be rather dangerous though?"

"Nah. The sink field was right behind it and absorbing that energy would be like swatting a fly."

"You seen this kind of thing before?"

"Sure."

Pilakin was surprised.

"Really?"

"Spiders get a little twitchy sometimes. Some go off the grid altogether. Don't tell anyone but there's at least a dozen we've never found."

Pilakin smiled with increasing satisfaction. The MO was beginning to make sense.

"Listen, Melissa. If I needed a bit of freelance analysis, could I call you sometime?"

Melissa lowered her voice.

"Sure. I'll send you my private number."

The end of the call coincided with her ticket number appearing on the laundry's completion screen.

Chapter 11

As Pilakin passed through security at the entrance to the Kristani Building, she felt relief at having stopped off for a launder. She smelled fresh for the full body pat-down and was less conspicuously poor in the plush lobby surroundings. Everything from the wasteful use of space to the immaculate business suit worn by even the lowly receptionist showed that the Kristani Syndicate operated as one of the richest organisations in the city. Invited to take a seat, she smiled as she looked over the other inhabitants of the waiting area with bulges showing muscles and guns. It would take an army to get into this place and no one with an army had any interest in doing so. The syndicates could pretty much do as they wished. And what they generally wished was to make money out of ignoring the Free Rights of the Individual.

A large ornate scroll high on one of the walls listed the many companies and concerns under Kristani ownership and a workman was adding recent acquisitions with a fine paintbrush. She idly scanned the names before one jumped out and she felt a cold prickle on her neck.

Daskovich Biorendering.

Biorendering was a pretty unpleasant, shady world and most syndicates had their own subsidiary, if for no other reason than to conveniently get rid of inconvenient bodies. But it was a hell of a coincidence – the Kristanis owning the company that had red-flagged her for no discernible reason. Her thoughts were interrupted.

"Agent Pilakin? Mr Löring-Kristani is ready to see you. Please follow me."

She followed the young secretary through another security check and into the warren of offices and meeting rooms. One of the big chaps from reception fell in behind, not saying a word and certainly not needing to. She wondered how many times she would have to visit before she was trusted.

The secretary knocked on a familiar door and held it open, closing it quietly after her. It took a moment for her eyes to adjust to the dim interior; soft yellow light from triangles on the walls and a downlight on the desk. As usual, Lars didn't get up from his desk to greet her, the rude bastard.

"Hello, Jaq."

"Hiya."

She sat down in the plush, real leather chair opposite. He watched her quietly through glasses that flashed as his head moved. Lars Löring-Kristani. Of course, she'd known him since he was plain old Lars Löring, although high up in the syndicate even then.

"You look like shit, Jaq."

"Well, you look old."

He opened a box of thick steamers and offered her one. They both took a moment to light the chort leaf and inhale the sticky vapours. It had a sweet scent of roses but with a tart puckered feeling in the cheeks that made her mouth water.

"Simplaerosian?" she asked.

"Yeah."

They sat in silence for another minute. He obviously wanted her to start first but fuck him. He had summoned her. Finally he shifted in his seat and rested the steamer against a Tintesian amber ash tray.

"Are you okay, Jaq?"

"Sure."

He ran his fingers over his desk and a list appeared with a series of numbers against it.

"I've had your bill from last night's excursion to Pandora's. Obviously, when I see a section on medical expenses I tend to get a little concerned."

"I'm fine."

"Yes. But it appears that a young man who used to work there needed some attention."

Pilakin felt cold.

"He's not…?"

"Dead? No. Pandora's management feel he's not cut out for their establishment. So, there's also a line for the cost of hiring his replacement."

Pilakin said nothing and looked down at her hands, surprised by their steadiness. Lars broke into her thoughts.

"You do know it's only a matter of time before…?"

"Yes! All right. I get it. You've given me my telling off. Can I go now?"

She was on her feet but Lars put out his hand and spoke sharply.

"No. Sit down."

"You're not my fucking father."

"I said, sit down!"

She stared for a moment as she tried to get her anger in check. Or was it shame? Slowly she resumed her seat. Lars went back to his tone of calm concern.

"I'm worried about you. Look at this drug consumption. Do you even know what you took last night?"

She shook her head and he continued.

"I'm surprised you're even up and about. How come you are?"

"I'm working a case."

He raised an eyebrow and an amused expression finally broke through his blank features. "Really?"

Patronising arse.

"Yes, really. It's a murder. I've got the contract. And the most interesting part is I think *you* lot are involved."

That wiped the smile off his face.

"Us lot?"

"The Kristanis."

Lars picked up a payment keystamp from a rack at the side and tapped it on the electronic bill still lying on his desk. Bunching his fingers made it appear to screw up into a ball and he flicked it off to the 'bin' in the corner. He picked up a stylus and tapped the notepad icon. A fresh electronic sheet opened up.

"What was the victim's name?"

"Jeremiah Flow."

"Are the drugs out of your system yet?"

"He's on your hit list."

"That certainly doesn't mean we killed him. You know how it works – the list is a threat. Only the most incorrigible or those with no hope of paying ever get green-lit."

"Well, was he?"

"Oh, come on. You're seriously asking me to reveal syndicate paperwork to you? The members would take a very dim view. Of the terminal kind, you understand…"

Pilakin took out her slab and flipped through the contents. Finally she found the ECC validation stamp and turned the screen so Lars could see it.

"What's that?"

"It's my old bounty-hunting licence. Still valid. And as a City Corporation approved BH I'd like access to the active elements of your current hit list, please."

Lars sighed and searched through the desk-top's contents.

"Here we go. No. Mr Flow was not green-lit."

"If that's true, why do you want me off the case?"

"Do we?"

"Daskovich Biorenedering is a Kristani outfit, isn't it? Well, they've red-flagged me."

"I lose track of our subsidiaries. Hang on."

He eschewed the desktop in favour of a screen he could use without her seeing. After a moment, he frowned.

"Shit, Jaq. Why didn't you tell me? The flag is syndicate-wide. I'm going to have to answer some serious questions as to why I've even seen you."

"Why have I been flagged?"

"I can't tell you."

She swore again.

"How close to the edge are you, Jaq?"

"I'm fine."

"Did you find somewhere to live?"

"Lars, seriously I'm fine. This case breaks at least half way right and it'll tide me over to after the election. Then the ECC or one of the big agencies will start recruiting again and—"

"That's not going to happen! You do know that don't you? I'll always be grateful for what you did but the ECC is never going to forgive or forget. Do you have any idea how much it cost me just to get them not to revoke your FPA credentials?"

"You don't think it was worth it? You just say the word and I'll get out of your life for good. I'm sorry I'm such a burden to you."

Lars sighed and muttered, "It certainly feels like a father-daughter relationship."

Pilakin's hot retort died on her lips as she saw the bleak expression on his face. Their old, shared sadness calmed her and after a moment's silence, she held out her hand. He reached across the table and squeezed it before looking up at her again, clearing his throat.

"What are you doing this evening?"

Pilakin shrugged.

"Working my case."

"Come on. Blow it off for a couple of hours and come to the opera. I've got box tickets."

"What's playing?"

"The Dragon Hunt."

She loved Chitellios and closed her eyes as she recited:

You leave, my love, and I imagine you engulfed in
*   dragon's breath*
And so my purpose would be gone; I'd follow in
*   untimely death.*

She heard old screaming and was overwhelmed with grief, screwing up her eyes against the escape of tears.

"Well, Jaq, you'll certainly appreciate it more than anyone else I could take. It'll do you good to put on a nice dress for the evening."

"I sold them all."

"Right. Well, I bet you haven't sold your old City Defence Agency uniform. Does those society types good to see a row of medals occasionally. And there's plenty who'd reward a CDA hero, if you need it."

"There was nothing heroic about what I did out there. I'm sorry but this case may be my last shot. You understand I have to take it."

Lars nodded slowly.

"You're so like her… Okay but promise you'll come back to see me if it all falls flat. And listen… be careful okay? You need any bullets or anything, let me know. Now, I have to make a call to explain your presence here or they won't let you out. There'll be someone outside my door to escort you back."

He picked up the phone and, as he did so, used his fingers to slide one of the e-papers across the desk top. He swivelled in his chair and, as he began his call, presented her with his back. She looked down at the shining surface and quickly scanned the text. It was an account derived from the hit list. She could see the symbol for those who had been condemned and saw that Lars had told the truth about Flow not being one of them. However, there was still an entry against his name in the bounty payment column.

Ten thousand credits paid out to Artyom Rimsky.

Chapter 12

PILAKIN'S HAND HAD not left the butt of her gun since arriving in this particular district. Waiting on the street corner for Zeb Lander was not good for the nerves and, although she did her best to project the image of a hard-ass, it felt like the thugs and itees round here could see right through it. Fifteen minutes late, she assumed Zeb was punishing her after their earlier encounter. Although, to be honest, it was a relief he'd agreed to come at all.

SHE HAD CALLED him after leaving the Kristani building.

"Hi, Zeb? It's Jaq Pilakin."

"Oh," a long silence. Then, "what do you want?"

"I need your help. Can you take me to the bar you went to and see if we can find Artyom Rimsky?"

A huffing sigh hissed out of her earpiece.

"So, you've decided to believe me now?"

"Look, Zeb. In this job I can't afford to take anything

at face value."

"So what's changed?"

"Corroboration. Rimsky's name has come up in a separate line of inquiry."

Another silence before he said, "Well...?"

Well what? She thought with rising frustration before saying, "I want to find your uncle's killer for Sarah and Paul's sake as much as mine. It'll get her off your back about business profits too. You gonna help me?"

"You're very mercenary, Agent Pilakin. All I wanted was a 'sorry'. I'll meet you at the corner of Fortune Road and the Inner Rim Circle at seven."

"Will it be busy that early?"

"I think people there do business early before it gets too dangerous."

"Okay, I'll—"

But he was gone.

FINALLY SHE SAW him weaving through the crowds from the direction of the tube. He'd put on a rim-style jacket and, what with his black shirt and trousers, looked quite dashing. He stopped before her and folded his arms.

"Christ, Pilakin. Shades? You're not a syndicatist you know."

"Good to the look the part, somewhere like this. Be nice if no-one knew I was an agent too."

Zeb obviously did not know why syndicate members wore them. The inbuilt sensors could detect concealed weapons. Further, they recorded everything and downloaded it into her slab. There, facial recognition software would link with the public city databases and the web and throw up information about people on to the insides of the lenses. Of course the technology was old and simple but shortages of key components and materials under the siege meant the glasses were rare. Or so went the story. Pilakin suspected the hand of the syndicates. Her shades she had got from an ECC-FPA evidence locker. Shagging the stores clerk had bought his silence when she liberated them upon losing her job. The bastard had still cut off her access to the ECC database though, so her slab could only examine commercially available records.

"Well, Zeb? Where's the place then? Or are you going to keep a girl standing on a street like this all night?"

He smiled and turned on his heel before crossing the road, heading down a small, dingy alley. Pilakin looked up and down the street but saw nothing suspicious. The only thing that pinged on her glasses were a couple of Freedom Protection Agents' locator beacons somewhere in the vicinity. Hoping they were going to stick around – it would be handy to have some back-up if things got tight – she strolled after Zeb.

He waited for her at the next intersection and they turned right into an even narrower passage. To Pilakin's trained eye, it was clearly designed as an access control because at the end they entered a wider courtyard with no windows at ground level but plenty of small ones one floor up. Two bouncers stood outside a plasteel door, above which the name *Cubilicious* had been painted. The burly men looked wary, so Pilakin smiled and slipped her hand into Zeb's. The guy on the right nodded and knocked twice on the door. A moment later it opened and they stepped inside.

Pilakin was relieved at the lack of gun-check. Passing through a black curtain, they entered a darkened room with tables everywhere and little in the way of lighting. The smoke from a dozen drugs gave the air a woolly quality and she was sure that if her system wasn't so used to it, she would have got high very quickly. The thought made her wonder what affect it would have on Zeb, or whether it had had anything to with Flow's tox screen.

As they advanced in search of a table, her glasses began reporting on which people had guns. Fairly simple: everyone. Everywhere she looked, small red pulsing blobs were superimposed under people's armpits, at their waists, at their ankles, although many wore them openly too. She grabbed her slab and disabled the weapons threat alarms. Her glasses then started reporting the large number with bounties on them, or syndicate members or dealers who had uploaded their own faces to the city databases to act as adverts for their wares.

Near the centre of the room a glass box sat atop a raised platform. Inside a man and woman were having sex. Along one side were a series of buttons and, for a couple of credits, drinkers could select the sexual position the couple should adopt. Pilakin felt for the girl; she must be desperate. In a place like this the clientele would probably have sadistic tastes. As they passed in search of a table, Pilakin paid for twenty minutes of missionary. Let her lie down for a while and have the guy do the work. The girl smiled at her through her running mascara and mouthed, "thank you." Interestingly the man also nodded at her with a grateful look on his face. She realised they must actually be a couple and poverty had driven them to this particular pursuit.

She led Zeb over to a dimly lit table against one wall where they could command a decent view of the room. Shortly after sitting, a waitress arrived and Pilakin was amused to see that she openly wore a stun-baton hanging from her belt.

"What can I get you?"

"You got any sealed brands?"

Pilakin did not fancy the thought of drinking anything in this place that could have been adulterated.

"Yeah, some. Off-world?"

"No. Cheap end of the spectrum, please."

"We got OBV."

"Old Bottom Vat – the yeast vodka? How much is it?"

"Twenty eight for a litre bottle."

Pilakin winced.

"Okay. And bring two glasses."

Zeb looked at her as the waitress departed.

"I'm not going halves, you know. This is your gig. I

doubt I'd get half of it anyway."

Pilakin guessed he was going to keep insulting her in retribution for… For what? Pointing a gun at his damned robot? She swallowed it nevertheless, in the interests of the case.

"I tell you what. At 55% ABV I'm planning to take plenty of it home anyway."

"Oh? Where's home then?"

"I've brought you here to do a job, Zeb. I need you to take a good look round and see if there's anyone at all you recognise, be it Rimsky or possibly someone else who you remember seeing here at the same time. I sat you on that side so you can see the door. Do you smoke?"

"No. Why?"

Pilakin pulled out her packet of cigarettes but then reconsidered as stinky breath would not help her solve tonight's bed situation by enticing Zeb. She put them away and retrieved one of the big steamers she had lifted from Lars' office.

"Because I want to put a hazy fog in front of your face so others are less likely to spot you."

She lit up and slowly blew the steam across the table. Zeb blanched a little but then seemed pleasantly surprised by the sweet smell. The vodka appeared and, as Pilakin busied herself with the serious business of pouring out measures, he began to look methodically round the room. She passed him a glass and he raised it in salute before sipping a tiny amount and resuming his observations.

"So, Agent Pilakin. You going to tell me where Rimsky's name popped up?"

She considered for a moment.

"I've heard a… rumour… that he may have been involved in collecting a… bounty on your uncle's death."

Zeb smiled.

"Oh, come on. I bet what you have is a lot more solid than that."

Pilakin tilted her head and shrugged before taking a much larger sip of the vodka. Even with her prodigious tolerance for alcohol she shivered a little as it went down and felt vaguely sick afterwards. She decided to change the subject again.

"Tell me why you really have that robot."

She watched his expression carefully. His face didn't change but his eyes widened and then narrowed.

"What do you mean?"

"Its functions could easily be performed by a computer hooked into your phone line. Why go to the expense and trouble of having a robot? They're not exactly popular and if the luddites found out, they'd smash it up."

It was his turn to shrug.

"I guess I'm sentimental. She's been in the family for a long time."

Despite her needling him for another few minutes he wouldn't be drawn further and they sat in silence for a while. He carried out his survey of the room before glancing at Pilakin and smirking. Her discomfort must have been plain so she grasped at the first topic that came to mind.

"What does Christ mean?"

Zeb smiled again and turned his attention to the door. He seemed to have relaxed somewhat and was drinking more of the vodka. "What are you talking about?"

"When we met outside you said 'Christ, Pilakin. Shades?'"

Zeb laughed shortly.

"Christ Pilakin, nothing much gets past you, does it? Maybe you're not a shit detective after all."

She smiled warmly back him.

"Thank you for such fulsome praise. But this time I really am going to have to insist upon an answer."

"Okay, agent. I'm a Christian. I believe that a man called Jesus Christ is the son of God and died for all our sins."

"Really? Christian? Never heard of it. A man being the son of God? That seems a strange idea... what? What is it?"

Zeb had gone rigid and grabbed her hand before turning his head so he faced the wall.

"It's Rimsky!" he hissed.

"Where?"

"He's just gone behind that pillar. Hang on... he hasn't come out the far side."

"Okay. We'll have to go and find him. Is that a gun under your arm?"

"I work in a service industry; of course it is."

Pilakin slid out of her chair, not forgetting to slip the vodka bottle into her jacket's inside pocket.

"Don't get your gun out but make sure you can grab it in a hurry. Come on."

They both sidled across the room, making for the pillar. On arrival they discovered that behind was a staircase leading up to gloomy second level. Pilakin looked back around the pillar and noticed for the first time a murky mezzanine floor above with several shadowy figures looking down over the rail. Presumably they were getting a better view of the sex-cube below. She retreated behind the pillar again and drew her gun.

"You okay coming up there with me?"

Zeb reached under his arm and drew out a small but efficient looking pistol.

"Sure."

"Keep that down by your side. We don't want to provoke anyone."

She led him slowly up the stairs, letting her eyes get used to the dark. At the top she stopped and peered round the corner, finding a series of dimly lit booths set back from the balcony. Extra private for business or…? She beckoned Zeb to follow and led him to the balcony rail. Walking slowly behind the watchers' backs she signalled for Zeb to look into the booths. As they drew level with the fourth there was a flash and bang. A gurgling shriek came from right next to Pilakin. She dropped to the floor. The screamer toppled over and landed heavily on top of the sex-cube. The woman inside, still on her back, screamed. An instant later all was pandemonium.

Pilakin didn't hear the second shot but winced as it ricocheted off the metal rail next to her head. The third wouldn't miss so she leapt to her feet and dragged Zeb into an empty booth.

"Are you hit?" he gasped.

"No. You?"

He shook his head. Pilakin grabbed the table.

"Help me."

They tipped it over as a barricade and its heft indicated plasteel. Good. Barring seriously heavy ordnance, they'd be protected. Pilakin took stock. The sounds coming up from below suggested a free for all – shouting and screaming, scattered gunshots, the clatter of chairs and tables toppling. She risked a glance around the side, just in time to see a crouching man's head explode in a shower of red gobbets. Multiple flashes at another figure's waist became loud taps on their table barricade. Pilakin squeezed off a couple of shots blindly in vaguely that direction, more to discourage an approach than in hope of scoring a hit.

"Zeb! Keep firing the odd shot. I'll get help."

"How?"

Wincing at the noise of Zeb's gun, she grabbed her slab. She opened the emergency application system and set off an Agent Distress Call. The agents she had seen in the area should drop whatever they were doing and get down here to help. Should.

As several minutes passed things seemed to calm down. The only noises left were shouts and groans. Pilakin risked another look over the table and ducked again as another fusillade of shots battered her barricade.

"Shit!"

Where was that agent? Zeb changed the clip on his gun. How could he afford that? Even so – they weren't geared up for a siege. She had to buy time.

"Who are you? What do you want?" she shouted. No reply.

"Who are you trying to kill? We only came in here to talk to someone."

More shooting rewarded her efforts. Then the establishment's emergency lights bathed the whole scene in harsh white. Dazzled, she screwed up her eyes, hoping the assailant was in the same position. A voice called up from downstairs.

"Agent Pilakin? I got your distress call!"

"I'm up here!"

She covered the top of the stairs with her gun. A stranger appeared, gun in hand.

Pilakin shouted, "Stop there. Break out some ID."

The stranger kept her gun by her side and reached to her belt with the other hand. A badge appeared and Pilakin's shades, having scanned it and compared it to the City database, confirmed the agent's name and number.

She finally allowed herself to feel relief. With the release of tension came the end of the adrenaline and she slumped. Zeb sat next to her and laughed unexpectedly. The agent appeared above her head.

"What the hell have you two been up to? It's carnage out here."

Pilakin dragged herself to her feet and shook the woman's hand.

"Thank you so much. I…"

Her words died as another figure loomed up behind her benefactor.

"Manstein! What are you doing here…?"

Realisation dawned and rage washed through her.

"You bastard!"

Chapter 13

MANSTEIN HOLSTERED HIS gun and held up his other hand in a placatory gesture.

"Hey, take it easy, Pilakin. I was in the area and saw your distress call too."

"Bollocks! That's vatshit. You…"

She was still shouting and the other agent stepped between them, placing a hand on Pilakin's chest.

"Take it easy. What's going on?"

Pilakin didn't take her eyes off Manstein.

"Why the hell are you here? A city this size there is no way we just happen to bump into each other. You're still working the case!"

Manstein shrugged.

The other agent interposed.

"What are you talking about?"

"He gave me a case in return for a favour but he's still working it."

The agent turned to Manstein.

"Is this true?"

"No," he said, quietly.

She gestured to the stairs. "I think you ought to leave."

Pilakin smiled at the outrage on her face. Manstein mumbled some kind of apology and shuffled off.

"Thank you," said Pilakin.

"No worries. What a bastard; that's just not done."

She turned and walked over to look at the man with half a missing head. Pilakin and Zeb climbed over the pock-marked table to join her. She turned the victim's head with her boot.

"Looks like your case has got pretty hot, eh? You want this one too?"

"No. I think we've got our hands full. You can have it."

The agent shook her head.

"Nah. Look at all this shit." She gestured over the balcony. "Shoot out in a place like this? Nobody'll talk. Even if they did, there's no CCTV to figure out the hierarchy of shots and I'd spend the next couple of years arguing with dangerous people in shady courts."

Pilakin looked down into the main room. The sex couple were crouched, hugging each other in the corner of their box. Bullet-proof glass, it seemed, from the criss-cross pattern of cracks. She could see at least half a dozen bodies lying around it and a couple more people who looked on the verge of death. Zeb startled her by talking for the first time since the end of the shooting.

"You reckon anyone's called an ambulance?"

"I doubt they have medical insurance and no one will come out on the off chance that one of them may be rich enough to pay."

She looked at the table where she and Zeb had been sitting. The wall behind it was filled with bullet holes. She shivered – her own medical had also been sacrificed on the pyre of her budgetary problems.

ONCE OUTSIDE, AWAY from the stench of gun smoke and blood, Pilakin lit a heroette with a shaking hand and offered another to Zeb. He shook his head.

"You okay?" she asked.

He looked thoughtful for a moment and then a smile slowly spread across his face. "Yes… and I've no idea why. That was terrifying."

Pilakin grinned back at him. "Feels strangely good, doesn't it?"

"Does that kind of thing happen to you often?"

"Not as much as you might think. Not these days anyway. Back when I was shooting lions…"

"Shooting what?"

"Never mind. I think our survival calls for a celebration. What would you say to going for a decent drink or two?"

"You think I can keep up with you, Agent Pilakin?"

"Call me Jaq."

ZEB REPEATEDLY TRIED to insert a keycard into the lock for his garage door but whenever he got close Pilakin jabbed him in the ribs and they both giggled. Eventually the door grizzled up by itself and, despite her inebriation, Pilakin gripped her gun. Zeb smiled and placed a hand over it, shaking his head. Once the door had retracted enough she could make out in the gloom two glowing red eyes set in his robot's mechanical form.

"Jess!" Pilakin shouted and leapt forward to hug it. It did not flinch or move.

"Jessie, Jessie, Jess," she shouted in mock affection, kissing it on its face before licking its eyes to leave smudgy marks on the glass.

"Oh for God's sake, Jaq…" muttered Zeb as he pulled her away, leading her past the van and up the stairs.

Once in the living room, they sat at the table and Pilakin retrieved the OBV Vodka bottle from the cavernous inside pocket of her jacket. Useful pocket that. She'd kept all kinds of things in it. Zeb reached for his tea mugs and she poured them both hefty measures. Zeb sipped his and winced.

"Why on God's green Athréa did you ever want to become a Freedom Protection Agent anyway?"

"Bookdog and the Worm."

"What?"

"Bookdog and the Worm. Didn't you ever watch it as a kid?"

Zeb shook his head. "Apparently not."

Pilakin giggled and tried to suck fumes out of the vodka bottle. Disappointed she threw it aside where Jess deftly caught it and took it to the sink.

"Useful feature," she slurred before lapsing into silence, contemplating what happened to recycled bottles. Zeb pulled her train of thought back.

"So?"

"So what?"

"Ratdog and the Worm?"

"Bookdog and the worm. It was a cartoon about police dogs."

"About what?"

"You heard of police? Out in the ...er... outside. You know." Pilakin gestured expansively with her arm, trying to convey the universe.

"Yeah, sure. It's what governments use to repress people."

Pilakin leaned forward, conspiratorially. "Well... they have these little aliens or something, called police dogs, who help them."

"Aliens?"

"Well, sure. What else would they be? Anyhoo, two of these police dogs, little four legged bastards they are, decided they got fed up with repressing people and they'd like to actually solve real crimes. So, they escaped and came here to Engalise to work for the City. Cracking all the crimes the human agents couldn't."

Pilakin pulled her emergency hip flask out of her

pocket. Upending it in her mouth, she discovered it was empty. Disgusted, she threw this aside too and found it interesting to note that the fucking robot didn't bother catching this one. Odd. Did it know it wouldn't be damaged? Or that it was firmly her property and thus would have no salvage value? Or maybe Jess just hated her and hoped her stuff would break. Any of the alternatives led to disquieting conclusions.

"Why was one of them called The Worm?"

Pilakin brought him back into focus.

"He was long for some reason. Oh, I don't fucking know. It's all a bastard sick joke anyway."

"How do you mean?"

Pilakin felt her nose twitch and couldn't help a sneer. "Because when you get good at solving crimes, the ECC don't give you a promotion and a TV series. Oh no. They give you a nasty case, with a shit outcome. Then they tell you to forget it when you find the answer. Then you do something about it and they show you the door. Hey listen, Zeb." She reached out and patted him on the chest, belching as she did so. "You're better off without your City contracts. Work for real people. They'll appreciate you more."

Zeb sat and looked at her for a while, so she looked back; drinking in his handsome features. After their experience in the shoot-out he seemed to have thawed. A little shared danger did wonders for a relationship. She felt herself swaying on the chair and decided that she'd better make her move now while there was a chance she would stay awake and not disgrace herself. She nodded in the direction of his mattress.

"Is it comfortable?"

"Don't you have a home to go to Agent Pilakin?"

He was smiling nonetheless.

"I'm not entirely sure it would be in the interests of public safety for me to wander the streets in this condition."

"The public's safety or yours?"

She stood, turned and fell, hopefully with some grace, on to the bed before rolling over to one side and patting the mattress next to her.

"Come on Zeb. Do you get much warm flesh in here? I don't expect you to put me up for free, you know."

PILAKIN WOKE, IN a woozy haze but without the accompanying headache, which meant she was still pissed and couldn't have been asleep more than a couple of hours. Zeb's arm lay affectionately but chastely around her waist and she smiled. He'd been a real gentleman alright. At first his rejection had annoyed her but then he tenderly helped her undress, tucked her in and gave her a large glass of water that he refused to take payment for. He had undressed only down to his underwear and snuggled in beside her in a way that implied he was glad of her presence and, more interestingly, that he was used to sharing his bed with another. She had spent enough nights with single guys to know the awkward misplacement of arms, knees in the back and fidgeting of the habitual lone sleeper. However, Zeb had rolled in behind to spoon, slipping his arm under the pillow, high enough not cause discomfort. He'd not mentioned a woman in his life. Yet, she couldn't imagine he would be this intimate if there was someone serious…

SHE AWOKE AGAIN. This time with a raging thirst and the kind of headache that creeps up from the base of the skull. The bed felt empty. Rolling over, she discovered Zeb gone. While scrabbling around for her slab to find out the time, a red glow on the other side of the room caught her attention. Two red glows. As she sat up to get a better look there was the sound of movement. Something heavy crashed onto her chest and the glowing red eyes of RK4-Jess were right in her face. Close enough that she expected to feel hot breath on her cheek. The absence of it was even more frightening. Her legs were pinned. Her arms had some movement but beating the plastic sides of the robot was painful and useless. As she started to scream a rubbery hand clamped down over mouth.

"Now listen here, you bitch," snarled an inhuman voice. "He was happy until you came. You get out of his fucking life, do you hear? Zeb didn't kill Jer. Zeb couldn't kill anyone. In the morning you will be gone. One way or another. Clear?"

Pilakin could only stare at the blank, emotionless face

in terror.

"I asked if you understood me, fleshbag."

Pilakin nodded as best she could.

"Good."

And then Jess started to tighten its grip, cutting off her breathing altogether. She tried to struggle again but was too firmly held. The throbbing in her head increased. She saw stars and the world went green. Panic gripped her completely. The green went to grey and finally black.

Chapter 14

*W*HY HAD SHE *got an invitation to this party? Second year in the Institute, living on her City Defence Agency payoff. It would be ridiculous to turn it down though – shut-down parties always have free drinks. She's interested to meet this guy too. Professor Damian Reigel, roboticist.*

She can't see him. She picks up two whiskies and heads to the largest knot of people. Hopefully he's in the middle and he likes whisky.

He's not there.

Another tour of the room finds a man, by himself, shabby, obviously drunk, slumped on a sofa.

"Professor Reigel?"

"Who wants to know?"

"I'm Jaq Pilakin."

His eyes focus and his head rises. He holds his hand out for the whisky. She sits down close to him and he speaks.

"It was you then – here's to you."

He takes a large gulp of the whisky.

"What did I do?"

"You made it embarrassing for the bastards."

"Which bastards?"

"The faculty board. The ones who shut me down and paid for this. Make sure you walk off with as many bottles as you can."

"How did I embarrass them?"

He grins broadly.

"You signed up for my course."

"Was I the only one?"

"Quick girl. Shame I won't get to teach you. What are you majoring in?"

"Forensic Physics and Engineering."

Reigel signals to a passing waiter-drone – a cruel joke by the department – and obtains another bottle of whisky from its tray. He kicks over the drone. People turn to the noise but, seeing Reigel, shake their heads and return to conversation.

"Why pursue robotics, forensics-lady?"

"I did fundamental because it gave credits to my ethics module. I did basic and standard because fundamental had grabbed my interest and one day, when this siege is over, I think we'll be using them again."

"And you signed up for nanomatronics because...?"

"A.I. scares me."

Reigel laughs deeply and took another slug of whisky,

filling her glass at the same time.

"That's an honest opinion from a besieged city dweller."

"I find the best way to deal with something that scares me is to find out more."

"Well, now there's nothing to find out about. Robotics in this city is over. They're already clearing my laboratory for recreational drugs research."

"Why did they shut you down? Was it just the student numbers?"

"And the anti-robot riots. And the bottom falling out of the market… that's all vatshit. They didn't like my proposed next path of research."

"What were you planning?"

"How much do you know about nanomatronics, young Pilakin?"

"Not much. Just that you grow a brain using microscopic, artificial cells containing simple computer processors."

"Right. They are much the same as human brain cells but they're bigger so we can't use as many. We make up for that by the fact that each has significantly more… er… computing power than a brain cell. So you get all the complexity of a neural network matrix but with each point capable of its own processing."

Pilakin downs her drink and never takes her attention away from this intense, old man. The glaze is gone from his eyes.

"You strike me as a man with a plan."

"*I don't generally apply for research until I've already started it. Better to make sure something's possible so you don't look like a fool.*"

"*What did you do?*"

"*You know how we make nanomatronics safe? For us, I mean.*"

"*Respect for human life and the instructions of their overlords are hardwired into them.*"

"*But the brains we grow are too complex for programming everything. They have to learn the same way we do, although at a much faster rate. So, the hardwiring has to be done into every cell. But that hardware takes up room that could otherwise be turned to something more productive.*"

Pilakin feels her eyes widen.

"*You removed the inhibitors!*"

"*Every bit in the cells has been given over to free processing.*"

"*How many…?*"

"*Sixty.*"

"*What have the faculty done with them? Are you getting to keep any? Will you train them?*"

Reigel leans forward conspiratorially.

"*Already done. The faculty have no idea. My parting revenge.*"

"*They're in robots?*"

"*Half of them are in plastiforms. I let them loose, sold some, just sent others out to fend for themselves. I don't give much for their survival chances."*

"No. They'll be smashed to pieces. You said half?"

"I had thirty humaniforms in cold storage from before the siege. Just waiting for something worth putting into them.

"Oh my god... there are thirty uninhibited, nanomatronic, A.I., humaniform robots out there?"

"Running around the city for over a hundred days now."

"Can you find them again?"

"I've destroyed all records, including images. The only piece of advice I gave them was to not get caught."

PILAKIN BECAME DIMLY aware of the smell of coffee and frying breakfast-flavoured yeast cakes. For a moment she could not recall why she found this incongruous but revelation accompanied a rush of adrenaline and she leapt up, back against the wall. Zeb stared at her, spatula in hand.

"What the hell, Jaq?"

It took her several gulps of air before she could respond.

"Jess...!"

"What?"

"Jess! Where is it?"

Zeb frowned.

"She's in the office, staffing the phone. What the hell's wrong?"

"It attacked me."

Zeb looked incredulous for a moment and then laughed.

"Stop it, you bastard."

"Oh come on, Jaq. You've had a bad dream or something."

"Well, where the hell did you go last night?"

"I had an emergency call out. You remember I have a job? Water prices the way they are, if someone springs a leak in the night they aren't slow about calling out a plumber. I get to charge a fortune for something like that…"

He tailed off as Pilakin slumped to the floor and let out a sob. Picking up a bottle of water, he poured it into a bowl and brought it over to her.

"Here, splash this on your face."

She took the bowl and he squeezed her shoulder.

"I think you need to detox and take some time off."

"This is a waste," she replied as she looked at the bowl.

"A little treat after last night's job."

She pushed her face into the water, eyes closed, and held it there for a good ten seconds, letting the cool feeling seep into her. After the adrenaline of her waking, her hangover was starting to creep in and she dreaded taking the soothing feeling away from her brow. But then a whisper of panic yanked her head out. Zeb passed a towel.

"Come and have coffee."

She couldn't relax. No matter what Zeb or common

sense said, Jess' attack just seemed far too real. She unclipped her gun from her harness hanging on the chair and sat facing the door to the office. Frequently pausing to glug the coffee, she ate the bacony yeast cakes in near silence. Having said thank you to Zeb, she explained she needed to get on with following up leads and asked him to escort her from the building. He tilted his head and looked at her.

"Jess! Come in here please."

Pilakin moved her chair back and put her hand on her gun. The robot appeared in the doorway. Actually, it had just crossed the threshold, in order to follow Zeb's order precisely. Graphene robots were supposed to do that.

"Good morning, Zeb Lander. Good morning Freedom Protection Agent Pilakin."

Pilakin fought down her desire to shoot the damned thing as Zeb spoke to it.

"Jess. Please tell us the extent of your interaction with Agent Pilakin last night."

"At 0348 Zeb Lander said he must depart for a job and instructed me to keep an eye on Freedom Protection Agent Pilakin until he got back. I stood in the corner of this room and watched her. At 0422 my human-distress alert was triggered by Freedom Protection Agent Pilakin moaning, crying out and moving in an agitated manner. Cross reference on human behaviour indicated this was the phenomenon known as a nightmare. I moved to Freedom Protection Agent Pilakin and tried to wake her to save her further distress. Her eyes opened but she appeared to still be under the influence of the nightmare. I laid my hand upon Freedom Protection Agent Pilakin's face in an attempt to wake her but then her eyes closed, her breathing became regular and I calculated that she had returned to normal sleep. I then returned to the corner and continued monitoring her until your return at 0754."

Pilakin looked hard at the robot, shaking.

"Vatshit. Get the damned thing out of my way."

"Jaq… oh come on."

"I want to leave."

"Tell her to get out of the way yourself. She has to follow orders."

"RK4-Jess, go and walk into that wall."

As she walked through the now empty doorway she heard the robot hitting the indicated wall and Zeb swearing.

ONCE OUTSIDE SHE kept walking at a brisk pace until she had put a couple of blocks between herself and the office. Stopping in a doorway, she used shaking hands to light a heroette and, as she took a drag to calm herself, smiled at the thought of the robot blindly walking into the wall. A frown replaced the smile as she thought about the noise. She had been too keyed up to notice it when she was in there but now, as she replayed the incident in her head, she realised – the impact had sounded hollow.

Why on Athréa would Zeb have a hollow wall in his

flat?

Well, no way of getting into that now – she had work to do. Pulling out her slab she scrolled through the messages.

Whinging from Sarah about their accommodation.

Lars asking if she was okay. Again.

Pandora's offering a payment plan for dealing with her bill.

A service update from the Safety Commission. She opened this one.

> To: *Freedom Protection Agent Pilakin*
> Case number: *SM-R-269-219*
>
> *Thank you for taking the time to report to us* **the failure of siren 269**. *This was due to* **vandalism**. *We are* **delighted** *to inform you that* **the unit has been repaired**. *If you require any further information do not hesitate to* <u>call</u> *us. Please remember this swift response when voting to re-let the ECC contract.*
>
> *Siren Maintenance Team*
> *Safety Commission*
> *Engalise City Corporation*

Vandalism? She'd been up there and seen the box for herself. It was in one piece and still locked. She jabbed the call link and waited an interminable time for someone to pick up. Eventually there was a click.

"Er… hello?"

Pilakin frowned.

"Hi. Is that Siren Maintenance?"

"Er…yes. Yes it is. Who are you?"

"My name's Pilakin. I made a report on siren 269. Your message said I could call you…"

"Wow. Hold please. Hey guys… someone's actually called. I need to get up the report on 269. Can someone do that while I speak to this nutcase? Hello ma'am. Sorry for the delay – just getting the details."

"You know you didn't actually put me on hold then?"

"Oh. Er…"

"Sorry?"

"Yes. Sorry. Very sorry." She could hear the sound of laughter in the background and couldn't help smiling. She loved this city.

Adopting a cold tone through her grin she asked, "What is your name?"

"It's Engineer…er…Smith." More laughter from the poor guy's colleagues.

"Well, Engineer Ersmith, your message was very unenlightening. How about you tell me how a siren could be vandalised without leaving any visible evidence."

"Sure. Oh, that's interesting. The inside had melted a bit."

"I'm going to need more than that."

"Okay. It looks like someone had squirted something corrosive through the keyhole."

You mean like acid?"

"Sure, like acid."

That was interesting. Acids were not easy to get hold of.

"Thank you, Engineer Smith. Now I'd like you to send me a customer satisfaction form."

"Absolutely, ma'am. I'll do that as soon as you get off the phone…er…I mean as soon as we're finished talking."

"That moment has arrived."

Pilakin threw away her cigarette butt and chuckled as she cut the connection and stepped down into the street.

"Hey, lady. Got a light?"

She pulled out her lighter as she turned and saw a smiling man with a cigarette between his fingers. He was well dressed and tanned and if it had been the evening she might have tried to further the conversation.

"Thank you."

He handed back the lighter.

"So, you having a good day, Agent Pilakin?"

"What the…?"

She backed away rapidly and two beefy arms wrapped around her chest. She flexed her knee instinctively and brought her heel up hard into the guy's crotch. His squeal turned to a wheeze and the arms fell away from her. She jumped backwards over his collapsing form, turned and ran while fumbling for her gun. The swearing of another pursuer got closer, so she gave up on the gun and concentrated on headlong flight. She reached the corner and a ground car screeched to a juddering halt in front of her. It was far too late to stop so she leapt in an attempt to get over the bonnet. Her legs went out from under as she rolled across the warm, metallic surface. She fell off the far side and kept rolling, shins hurting like hell. Before she could get up two people leapt on top of her and pulled her arms back, forcing her to bend double. They harried her into the car's open back door, throwing her into the foot well, before climbing in and holding her down. The carpet smelled freshly cleaned. A black hood was yanked down over her face and the car sped off.

Chapter 15

DEPOSITED IN A chair. No, *dumped* in a chair. Two men were standing in the corners. Several questions on her part had elicited no response, so she decided to act tough. *Act as if ye have faith, and faith shall be given unto you.* Where on Home had she heard *that*? Leaning back in the chair, she planted one heel on the desk and crossed the other ankle over. It was surprising that they didn't stop her and she did indeed feel a little rise in her confidence. Then, a new voice.

"Thank you chaps, you can go."

She decided to perpetuate her nonchalant facade by not turning to see the speaker and, despite her belly feeling like it was in freefall, picked her fingernails as an affectation. A familiar looking man came round and sat behind the desk, placing her slab and gun down in front of him.

"I'll give you these back on three conditions, Agent

Pilakin."

"I don't like conditions."

"Well, I hope you'll make an exception this time. One: don't kill me. Two: don't call for help. Three: stay and talk with me for while."

The off-world accent meant Pilakin finally twigged who he was and, thus, where she was.

"Okay, I'll agree to conditions two and three. Take it or leave it."

The man smiled and pushed the gun and slab across the table. She picked up the gun immediately. The full clip meant they'd given her seven bullets on top of what she had come in with.

"Compensation for the manner of your arrival, my dear."

"Patronising arse," she retorted, although the misogynistic speech pattern confirmed her suspicions about her location and led her to holster the gun instead of pointing it at his stupid, fat head. She looked him straight in the eye, the knot in her stomach finally unravelling.

"You're Gustav Frieder. Head of Imperial Intelligence."

Imperial. The Empire. Besiegers of the City and rulers of most of the known galaxy. They were apparently hated out there in the worlds they ruled and so the Free Federation of Anti-Imperial Organisations was created with the sole purpose of bringing it down. For some reason she didn't understand, the Federation were headquartered here in Engalise and the 'Imps', as Empire personnel were disparagingly known, were trying to dislodge them. It all seemed so irrelevant and distant a thing for City dwellers to suffer and die over.

"Head of Intelligence? Nothing so grand. He never leaves the Home World. Yes I'm Frieder, but I'm Head of the Engalise Field Office of 3rd Imperial Navy Intelligence."

Pilakin frowned. "But if you're an Imp spy, why do I recognise you?"

"The Federation are running an advertising campaign to get my face out. You seen that one where the surface scum of the sewerage tank coagulates into my features?"

Now Pilakin laughed. "Oh yes, of course. *Talking to an Imperial agent will just add to the shit.*' Well, now I know who's behind my kidnap, it's actually worth suing your goon squad for…"

"You won't do that," he interrupted.

"Why?"

"Because I'm going to give you information instead. That's our currency around here."

"What do you know that I might think is valuable?"

"The exact location of the murderer you're looking for."

It took a moment for this to sink in but the amusement on Frieder's face at her silence and apparent discomfiture spurred her detective's suspicion back into action. She picked up her slab.

"What's the name?"

"I don't know."

"But you just said…"

"I said I can give you his location and I can."

"You said 'his'. How do you know it's a he if you don't know who it is? Or is it just your natural Imperial sexism?"

"Because I know what he is and, given his location and function, it has to be a man."

She balked at asking the obvious question. Frieder was sitting there smugly with an "I-know-something-you-don't" expression and she was damned if she was going to give him the satisfaction of asking him outright. On the other hand, she was a detective. This was a lead. And it was her job to ask questions. Dammit.

"What do you want to tell me?"

"You've seen the Meadow, I think?"

Pilakin shifted in her seat. "I spent some time living on the shell when I was young." Probably not a good idea to reveal any more. Frieder gazed at her evenly for a moment before asking his next question.

"What do you know about it?"

"The City of Engalise sits in the middle of the Eglitzé Crater. When the rest of the world became a colony of the Simplaerosian Kingdom, Engalise was given special status as an independent and free city, encompassing the whole crater. Things were fine until the Federation who fights you came and set up shop here. You Imps decided to get rid of them, but the Simplaerosians who own the rest of the planet said no. You lot set up a siege operation inside the crater in the hope that the Simplaerosians would leave you to it. But they didn't. So now your troops are in a big, radioactive and poisoned wasteland right round the City. With the City Defence Agency, The Federation and the Simplaerosians all fighting you. Hell's Meadow. And it's of your own making."

She stopped, realising she had gotten angry and said more than she intended. Frieder's face didn't flicker.

"You're remarkably well informed, Agent Pilakin. But I guess your information is a little out of date now. Did you know the Federation have destroyed almost every Imperial artillery battery within range of the City?"

"Well, they clearly haven't got all of them."

"No they haven't. And don't you think it's strange that the remaining dozen or so are spread out in a ring and can hit every bit of the rim?"

"Vatshit."

Frieder shrugged. "It's true."

"Okay, let's say it is. What then?"

"Well, it's strange that the Feds can't finish off these last guns, but it starts to make more sense when you find out that they've disrupted our communications lines to the emplacements."

"How do you know?"

"We decided to cancel our policy of requesting firing solutions on the City three years ago and yet they keep on firing."

"Well, maybe they're getting their orders from outside."

"They're not. We've been listening to the orders being given. We can decode them because they're issued with Imperial ciphers. They have to be because whoever's ordering them is pretending to be us. Furthermore, the signals have been triangulated and are emanating from within the City."

"Syndicates drumming up construction work?"

"That's what we thought too."

"Why don't you warn the gunners that you've been compromised?"

"Because our signals are now subject to jamming. Only one organisation has the capacity to do that and it's the same one letting the batteries exist in the first place."

"The Federation?"

He smiled at the incredulity in her voice. "Why not?"

"They're on our side. They're fighting against you; trying to lift the siege."

Frieder leaned back in his chair. "Sure they're fighting the Empire, but only here. There's no wider insurrection."

"You've gone round the bend."

"No. All that propaganda they spout is rubbish. There is no fighting beyond Athréa. The galaxy is at peace. The Federation *used* to be what it says it is but now it only exists here in the City."

"That's bollocks, Frieder. They have colonies and bases and prisons everywhere. They just headquarter here because it is beyond the Galaxy and has the Simplaerosians helping to defend it."

"It seems to me that you're a little too ready to swallow Federation propaganda."

"Well, if what you're saying is true, what are they still bothering for?"

"Let me ask you something, Agent Pilakin. What motivates the syndicates?"

"Money and power."

"Then why do the syndicates never bid for the City Corporation contract?"

"Because they'd get womped in the election. No matter what they offer, people aren't going to vote for an outfit that ignores our free rights."

"And the Federation never bids for the contract either. They're rich, organised, competent, they have a vast media machine; don't you think this means they have a dirty little secret that makes them unelectable?"

"What is it?"

"They run themselves as a representational democracy."

Pilakin shuddered in disgust.

"Government!"

"Yes. The denizens of this city will vote in letting a business contract to a company to run services that have to be run and licence people to run them. But no one in this city will vote for any kind of government that will then have power over them. And yet the Feds have got used to having power and money. And now the larger fight is over, the only way they can continue to wield it is by prolonging the siege; trampling on people's rights every day. Agent Pilakin, the Federation is nothing more than the biggest syndicate in the City."

Pilakin sat in silence for a minute. This guy pedalled misinformation for a living. So why was it speaking to her gut?

"What's all this to do with my case?"

Frieder pulled a piece of paper out of his drawer and slid it across the table. It had a CDA Meadow grid reference on it. She recognised it as such from her time on the shell. Frieder tapped it.

"This is the location of the battery that fired the shot and killed your client's husband."

Pilakin smiled and shook her head.

"Nothing doing, Frieder. It wasn't the shot that killed him. I already know someone else stopped him from moving. Any normal person would have run, so the murder wasn't committed by the Imp shell."

"I'm not talking about Flow. I'm talking about Youal Fesh."

Pilakin started and felt guilty. She'd forgotten about that violent drug-head in the apartment. Of course – he was killed by the shell directly. But…

"But the Imp soldier won't have anything worth suing him for and Fesh's wife will have trouble proving to a court that she's any the worse off for having him gone.

Where's the percentage in my risking a trip into the meadow to pick him up?"

"Things haven't been so good for you since you went independent, have they? The clients aren't exactly buzzing round. You need a reputation. Imagine the media storm around the Agent who actually managed to bring an Imp Soldier to justice."

The seething resentment in the rim's population due to its impotence in the face of Imperial shelling would explode. She'd be a star. Frieder cut in on her thoughts.

"And of course it could be a fairly significant lead in your other case."

He was right. If everything he said was true, it would take her search for a suspect into the heart of the Federation. That could be very lucrative indeed. Money and fame! The first she wanted and the second she needed. She turned a suspicious glance onto Frieder.

"Typical intelligence operative; selling out your own man. But why? What's in it for you?"

"Such a City attitude... My job is to hurt the Federation's cause any way I can. One soldier who would probably welcome the chance to get out of the Meadow versus a massive public relations disaster for the Federation that could see all popular support for it evaporate."

"Why bother? If this is such a localised war, why doesn't the might of the Empire finish it?"

"We're men of peace and the Emperor is merciful.

We've been trying to negotiate with the Feds for years but they just won't come to the table. If we can kill off public support for them through scandal – show how *they've* been the ones killing City dwellers – then they'll be forced to make peace just to save their own skins. Agent Pilakin, I'm offering you the path to solving your case and the opportunity to do your part in ending this siege."

Was he a liar?

She picked up the piece of paper with the grid reference on it.

Chapter 16

ADVANCING UP AN access tunnel, the smell increased until it pulled Pilakin's mind back to her youth. It was over fifteen years since she'd last visited the shell but the melange of sulphur, soot and petroleum, all mixed with the swamp-gas sickliness of a hundred thousand rotting bodies, dissolved the passage of time. Given her previous service, the City Defence Agency – the CDA – had not balked at lending her some fatigues and kit. She smiled at the feel of a rifle slung over her shoulder once more, the butt brushing against her backside as she walked, like a persistent pervert handling her on the tube.

Reaching the top of the tunnel, she looked up, breathing hard despite the rancid air. She couldn't help it; over a decade in the city had robbed her brain of its ability to comfortably process the concept of a sky. Granted it was a low one – black clouds artificially seeded with metals and carbon structures, known as the blanket. It was there to prevent observation or scanning from orbit, but it was still a higher vault than anything in the city – even the ceiling over the Anjelican Temple itself. She knew above the blanket was a blue sky, filled with suns, white clouds, moons and stars but she had never seen such a thing and even the idea of looking out to infinity made her nauseous.

She walked across to the parapet and looked out on the Meadow from a firing slit. Hell's Meadow, the Imps called it. It was startling how little had changed. Until this very moment she found it had been impossible to recall the view but now it was so utterly familiar. The earth dark brown and black, the muddy shell holes filled with metals and dust falling from the blanket in rain squalls here and there. Rain was common because the particulate acted as permanent cloud seeding. In the distance Simplaerosian fighter-bombers flitted back and forth showering the unfortunates below with a range of deadly technology. Here and there were grey bunkers. It was impossible to tell from a distance which belonged to who, although the CDA and Feds maintained meticulous maps of the apparent chaos.

Close to the shell-wall, stretching across the whole view afforded by the firing slit, lay the Imperial front line. Mostly a chewed up trench, the ring of shell craters indicated the occasional strong point. She could just make out the tops of Imp helmets bobbing around in the trench and she pictured herself in an embrasure just like this celebrating her birthday by rotting number one. She started and drew back as another forgotten memory forced its way home. For the first hundred or so she had not fixated on the lions, she just went for those helmets.

Turning her back on the meadow to push the memories away, she instead gazed up at the dynamic yet unchanging murk of the sink field. From this angle, it appeared to rise like a vertical cliff. Only distance would give the perspective needed to see the dome that enveloped the City in its protective shell. The only home she had ever known.

Despite leaving the access tunnel at the closest exit to her objective, she still had to walk five hundred metres or so. The nasal assault from the Meadow came in waves on the occasional breeze and the crackle of electrical discharge from the sink field heralded the tart smell of ozone. She fancied she could feel a prickling sensation and, upon waving her hand above her brow, she encountered strands of hair escaping the front of her helmet; standing to attention thanks to the static. If she came across someone she could give them a truly monumental shock with her finger, as if she'd been skidding on nylon carpets for hours. Most shell guards drove small metal nails though the heels of their boots just to stay earthed.

She walked past Defence Tower 17 but kept going on her way to 18. No-one in 17 knew her; there would be no way they'd take her out into the Meadow. At least, not without a lot more money than she could offer. Finally she stood at a reinforced door and battered its metal surface with her rifle butt. After a second time the tiny viewing grill snapped back.

"Who are you? What do you want?" came a rasping voice that was probably female. She held up her badge.

"I want to see your tower captain."

"Fuck off."

"He knows me."

"The Hell he does…" More uncertain this time.

"Tell him it's Jaq Pilakin."

Silence. Then "Pilakin…? Really…?" She heard a sigh.

"Okay, wait here."

The hatch snapped up and, as if activated by the motion, a dozen explosions not far from the wall rent the silence in quick succession. She felt each one in her chest and couldn't help ducking, despite the parapet being higher than her head. She'd have to fight that instinct or these people would never take her seriously.

The sound of withdrawn bolts presaged the door opening and she stepped back to let it swing wide. A large man with a bushy moustache stood with suspicion in his eyes as he mentally aged her face from the last time he had seen her. Then his eyes twinkled and a broad grin burst across his mouth.

"It *is* Jaq!"

He threw his arms wide and she fell into a bear-hug that lifted her off her feet, swung her around and into the tower. The door clanged shut behind them.

"Oh, my sweet girl," he bellowed as he dropped her back to her feet. "It's so good to see you out of a vidcall. I'd forgotten you have a third dimension. Why don't you ever come out to see us, eh? No don't answer. It'd be 'Why don't *you* come into the city?' Oh hang it girl. Let's not argue…"

She seized upon his intake of breath to leap into the conversation.

"Vanya…?"

"Isn't here. Out patrolling. Well, *she* calls it patrolling. Everyone else calls it bartering for supplies. I call it shopping. Come on – come in and meet everyone, although there's hardly anyone left from your day I bet. Not many stay on the shell as long as we do…"

He continued talking as he took her down the spiral stair into the tower's main guardroom. Camp beds for those on watch were clustered together in one corner while in another, comfortable chairs were drawn up around a heater and television. The five people sitting there turned to look with suspicion as Pilakin came in. Well, four were suspicious. The fifth, the oldest of the group, seemed curious and more friendly. Pilakin thought she recognised her.

Kit lay strewn around the room. More kit than just the five and Tomasz would need, so Pilakin surmised that the others were probably out on Vanya's 'shopping trip' or were off-duty and snugly ensconced in the more homely living quarters deeper inside the tower. Tomasz cleared his throat.

"Hey everyone, shut up. This is Jaq. She's a Freedom Protection Agent…"

He was interrupted by a very young woman. She had red hair – the kind you didn't see much in the City – gathered into a severe bun, and glowering, blue eyes. The freckles on her face ran down onto the shoulders, visible thanks to a sports vest. She spoke with a distinctly off-world accent.

"Is this about that whiny bitch at the Flyers' Club? Made a complaint has he? Well maybe he shouldn't have…"

"Stow it, Crustetin," growled Tomasz in an exasperated way that suggested he said it several times a day.

She kicked a crate but another look from him silenced her.

"What are you here for, Jaq?" he asked.

"I need to go into the Meadow."

A moment of silence greeted her statement followed by a cacophony of mixed reactions. Tomasz muttering under his breath. Crustetin laughing in a mirthless way. Two others asking if she was serious and a lad whose voice cut across everyone else.

"What possible reason would make us want to risk our lives taking an agent into the Meadow?"

The older woman finally spoke, with a croaky voice that nonetheless commanded silence.

"Because she's the Lion Hunter, kid."

The boy's jaw visibly slackened. Someone whispered, "Wow…"

Crustetin broke the silence.

"Who the fuck is the Lion Hunter?"

It was 'the lad's' turn to answer.

"Top scorer in the entire siege history. She lived in this tower. Six hundred and something kills in one year…"

"Six hundred and thirty nine," broke in Tomasz. "Two thirds of them from the Meadow itself."

Pilakin looked at her boots.

639 kills. 639 victories. 639 reasons she drank. 639 reasons she drugged and shagged her way around the City and sought oblivion every night.

639 reasons…

639 reasons she was a hero.

She had to remember that. She had to say it to herself day after day to hide from the thought that threatened to overwhelm her in the sober times.

639 times a murderer.

Chapter 17

"I T'S VOLUNTEERS ONLY," said Tomasz, "but come on guys. What else are you going to be doing? Nice trip out into the Meadow. Just what the doctor wants to sell you, eh?"

There were grumbles but most were accompanied by nods. Crustetin was a notable exception but Tomasz threw a combat jacket at her anyway.

"You're a volunteer by definition, Jé-Anne. Intel sent you out here to gain experience."

Crustetin swore but put it on. Her attitude and accent were explained as Pilakin saw a Federation Intelligence badge and collar bar denoting the rank of trainee officer on the coat.

Pilakin briefed them on the case and the reason they needed to go to the battery. They were picking up and loading their guns when another thought struck her.

"Hey, people. This is an investigation, not a mission,

so we're not going out there to kill anyone."

"What?" shouted several.

"Fuck that shit," said Crustetin.

Tomasz looked at her. "Oh, come on, Jaq. I know how you feel about the First Right but we're out of the City now."

"No, Tomasz, we're not. We get used to thinking of the City as everything inside the shell and sink field but the charter of colonisation extended the limits all the way to the edge of the Eglitze Crater. Anyway, the First Right is universal. It's just that the Corporation can only licence agents to enforce it within the City."

The lad sounded puzzled as he asked, "We kill people all the time. How are we not committing rights violations?"

Pilakin smiled at him. "You are. And you've just admitted it to a Freedom Protection Agent. I hereby detain you pending prosecution by interested parties."

He looked panicked and started to retreat towards the stairs, raising his gun. Everyone laughed and he blushed.

"I'd lower your gun if I were you," said Tomasz, "before she slaps the Tenth on you too. Don't worry about it kid. Everyone turns a blind eye to what happens out here. I mean who really gives a toss about what we do to the Imps? They came here and attacked us."

"Oh, so that's why we can get away with it." The lad looked relieved.

Pilakin shook her head. "No, it's still a violation

because there's no collective responsibility for anything. The only way you can legally kill someone is if they are attacking you personally. As Tomasz says, the rest we turn a blind eye to. This time, though, because this is an actual investigation I need us to comply with the rights in full. Only kill someone if they're trying to kill you."

"So what are we supposed to deploy instead," growled Crustetin, "colourful language?"

Tomasz was dragging a dusty crate across the floor.

"Non-lethal, people. Load these into your secondary barrels."

"What are they?"

"Zapper rounds."

There was plenty of muttering as they all loaded the electrical stun shells into the large, underslung rifle barrels. After a brief kit inspection Tomasz led them all down to a door in the front of the tower and out into a deep slit trench. They climbed a small incline which gave into a sap, zigzagging out into no-man's land. They paused at the sap-head as Tomasz reminded them of the rules of engagement and arranged the order of march.

"Jaq, you're in the granny-spot."

There was laughter at that. The front half of the column would be first into trouble, the middle would get hit in an ambush and the back picked off by snipers. Three quarters of the way back was the safest and that was where Tomasz was putting her. Not that they needed to have worried. For fifteen minutes they advanced through the mud and shell holes, seeing nothing of either friend or foe. Occasional Fed communications crackled through the headset inside Pilakin's helmet. As they neared their target a Simplaerosian aircraft directed a message at them.

"AOP129 to CDA column at 1462-K39. Be advised, I can see an Imperial infiltration unit seventy-five metres West North West of you and moving towards your position. Get your heads down and I'll take it out."

Normally they would be delighted to watch the fighter-bomber do its stuff but Pilakin shot Tomasz a look. He scowled back at her before responding with a resigned tone.

"Negative, AOP129. We're going to have a crack at them ourselves. How many Imps please?"

"Oh, okay. Looks like four or five. Have fun."

"Will do."

Tomasz waved up at the circling machine before arranging the ambush. They took up position behind some spent bomb casings and part of a fuselage. Pilakin had the olfactory honour of leaning on a pile of corpses, having been given the task of shooting whoever was second from the right. Looking through rifle's scope instantly took her back. Her fear disappeared. Her breathing slowed. The stench, the noise, the case... all left her. With a jolt she took her finger off the lethal trigger and put it onto the secondary. She pulled the stock of the rifle more firmly into her shoulder. The first of the Imps' helmets appeared. Then two, three, four... Helmets were no good. Tomasz was cool though. He would wait to give the order. She squeezed the slack off the trigger. Old experience told her it was a hair's breadth away from firing. Tomasz' command would tip the balance. She wouldn't have to think, so all concentration could be devoted to aiming. It looked like there were only four. She selected the one second from the right. He was dark skinned. His eyes black holes in white holes.

There was the lion. She placed her cross hairs right on it.

HE SCREAMED AND collapsed, clutching his chest and twitching violently. She could've sworn she had had nothing to do with it. She didn't remember firing but as they ran up to look at their ambush victims ambush she could see two zapper rounds fizzing in his chest. One of them was slap bang in the lion's head. It must have been hers. Crustetin knelt down and touched one of the men's faces as he writhed, gasping.

"What happens now?"

Tomasz was the one to reply.

"They get zapped for about three minutes. It stops for a couple of seconds in every thirty so they get to breathe a bit."

Crustetin stood and kicked the poor unfortunate. "This one's pissed himself look."

"Alright, Jé-Anne. I think he's having a shit enough day without you piling in." He winked at Pilakin. "Beats being dead though, eh? Do these four count on your balance sheet?"

She shuddered and felt sick.

"No, Tomasz. I don't think so. Come on, let's get out of here."

THEY APPROACHED THE bunker obliquely. The muzzle of a field gun protruded from what appeared to be a muddy mound. A net of mud-encrusted camouflage hung in rags over it. Tomasz signalled they stoop down to pause as he came back down the line giving deployment instructions. Two of the group ran up to the door and squeezed explosive putty around the hinges and lock. Tomasz briefed the people around Pilakin.

"I'll go and drop a puke bomb into the embrasure. When you hear it go pop, count to five, blow the door and chuck in a couple of flash-bangs. Only shoot anyone who raises a gun to you."

Tomasz looked at Crustetin meaningfully until she lowered her eyes.

"Okay, boss."

"Right. Respirators on. Here goes."

Tomasz dropped his kit and rifle by the door and scaled the muddy incline up to the embrasure. Pilakin fumbled with her gasmask, trying to remember the right way of achieving the tightest seal. When Tomasz got close, he lobbed the puke bomb into the bunker next to the artillery barrel. They heard a pop and a moment later a cloud of sickly-looking yellow gas blossomed around the gun and Tomasz came slithering back down, holding his nose. Someone handed him a respirator and he donned it easily as the door blew off its hinges. Crustetin was first in and the other members of the squad muscled Pilakin aside. There followed a lot of shouting and swearing, demands to drop weapons – all muffled by respirators. Nothing was being shouted back at them and when she finally got in she saw why.

The bunker consisted of one cubic room, dominated by the large field gun mounted in the middle. Bunks were along the back wall and ammunition cases, which had been set up as a table and chairs, were in disarray. Dog-eared playing cards lay mid game and a pile of rat bones were obviously being used as gambling chips. Half a dozen Imps were doubled up on the floor, retching hard. Pilakin had seen puke bombs deployed before and expected a carpet of vomit but there was nothing more than the odd bit of sputum. Given the noise the Imps were making, dry heaving was causing them no small amount of pain. Having made sure their guns were well away from them, Tomasz snapped the lid off the anti-canister; the red smoke that billowed out was designed to react with the puke gas and turn it inert. As the air cleared, the Imps stopped heaving and lay still, groaning and breathing hard. Pilakin followed the others in removing her respirator. Crustetin kicked the Imp with sergeant stripes.

"Sit up, you twat."

She lifted her boot again but the sergeant raised his arms and nodded. He struggled but managed to get up, his back against one of the ammunition crates.

"What do you want?"

Crustetin stepped back and looked at Pilakin. "He's all yours," she sneered.

Pilakin advanced and sat down, taking out her slab. "What's your name, sergeant?"

"What the…?"

"Please, sergeant…" she glanced meaningfully at Crustetin and back at him.

"Oswin."

"Thank you. I'm Freedom Protection Agent Pilakin."

"You're what?"

"I guess you would think of me as a police officer."

"You're kidding."

"Not at all. I'm investigating a First Right violation – a murder – back in the city and your unit has come to my attention."

Oswin shook his head, a look of bemusement on his face. One of the other Imps asked "Can we have some water?"

Tomasz answered him. "Sure. Get it, but no heroics."

"No. You don't understand. We want your water."

"You don't have any?"

"Only what we can collect from rain and we drink it straight off."

"That stuff is filthy and full of heavy metals."

"Gotta drink something."

"Don't you get any in your ration packs?"

The sergeant barked a derisory laugh. "Not had anything for forty or fifty days. We ration ourselves to one meal every seventy-two hours now."

Pilakin looked at his emaciated face and wondered what his body would look like beneath the heavy Imperial combat clothes. She handed her water bottle to him and saw the others doing the same.

"Where's your officer?"

"He ran away weeks ago. Said he was going to get more supplies. Fucking bastard."

Pilakin realised this was probably going to be easier than she had imagined.

"Listen. I know this is going to seem weird to you but I need to know about a shot you fired two days ago."

"Weird? No. Why would that be weird?"

"The exact time was…"

"You only need to say morning or afternoon. We only fire about once a day."

"Afternoon."

Oswin shifted in his seat uncertainly.

"What if we did?"

"Then I'll arrest one of you."

One of the other men lurched to his feet.

"Hey, sergeant. Fuck that shit…"

Crustetin whacked him in the chest with the butt of her rifle but a raised hand by Tomasz prevented the second blow. The sergeant shouted at the man.

"Can it, Wade."

Before Wade could speak again Oswin turned back to Pilakin.

"Arrest us? As in take us away from here?"

"Of course. Back into the City."

"And what happens to convicted murderers?"

"Usually about thirty years' incarceration with the pay from obligatory work going to compensate the victim's family. Although, given who the victim was in this case, the compensation level will be low so I guess you'd be out in less than ten."

"And we'd be safe, warm and fed?"

"Safe as you can be in a prison but yes to the other two."

The sergeant looked meaningfully at his men. There was hope in his eyes and she could see them all come to the realisation that what was on offer was certainly a hell of a lot better than staying here. Each nodded and he turned back to Pilakin.

"What do you want to know?"

"You keep an order log?"

He pulled a scrappy notebook out of his breast pocket. She opened it and to her satisfaction found the time and date that matched the explosion under investigation. The target co-ordinates were there and the CDA would be able to translate them for her from Imperial to City numbers. She logged it as evidence and put it in her own pocket.

"The order came in the usual way?"

"Yep – just like all the others."

"Was it the usual person who gave it?"

"How do you mean?"

"Was it the same voice?"

"Oh, we don't hear anything. It comes in on that thing."

He pointed at a worn out decrypter. That was a blow to her linking the Fesh case up with the Flow one, but at least this was now looking like a certain thing.

"So which of you is the trigger man?"

The sergeant's eyes narrowed.

"Why do you want to know that?"

"Rights violations can only be committed by individuals. There's no such thing as conspiracy or joint enterprise…"

As soon as the words were out of her mouth, she regretted it. As the import of what she was saying struck the Imp soldiers they all started shouting and swearing at once. It took several moments for Oswin to get his men back under control before he could speak to her again.

"So, you're only going to arrest one of us and leave the rest out here to rot?"

Pilakin could see they weren't going to give up the individual unless she gave them all a way out. She could hope that desperation might lead him to step forward but then they all would.

"Listen, Oswin. You all want out of here, don't you?"

"Yes."

"Tomasz? Do you have a Federation medical distress beacon?"

Tomasz growled but Pilakin gave him a pleading look and he reluctantly reached into a pouch and showed her a white baton.

"Right, Oswin. You activate this and a Fed medical lander will come and pull you out. You'll be going into Federation hands but they'll look after you."

The gobby soldier, Wade, spoke again but remained seated on the floor this time. "Don't tell her, sarge. You know the Federation fuck you up."

"We don't know that," Oswin shot back. "They say they'll send us back home. They say they'll give us hospital treatment. I think it's a risk worth taking to get out of this shit, even if we do end up in a POW colony. How long do you think we're going to keep living in the meadow with no food, no water and the weekly nuke?"

The others shouted their approval and Oswin looked Pilakin straight in the eye. "You have a deal."

Before he could finger anyone as the trigger guy, Wade butted in again. "This is shit! They're never going to let us get out of here. They'll torture us and kill us."

Crustetin grabbed him but he kept on shouting. "Tell them the truth! We don't fire at the city any more. We're not mad."

Pilakin stepped over to Crustetin. "What's this? Let him speak."

Oswin and the other men were telling him to shut up but a threat from Tomasz cowed them. Wade carried on defiantly. "You all want me to shut up because you want out. Except, I'm the trigger man. I'll be the one doing time while you all swan around in a Fed hospital or get right-of-returned. Pilakin, wasn't it? Yeah, we got the order. Yeah, we fired the shot. But we don't shoot at the City any more. You go ahead and ask them…" he gestured at the Tomasz. "We want to live so we don't do anything that would invite the Feds or the CDA to get rid of us. We get the order to hit the City and so we fire one round and plant it at the foot of the wall in no-man's land. Every time."

Pilakin felt anger and looked at Tomasz. "Is this true?"

"I don't know. We can't see this emplacement from our tower. You'd have to ask the guys in number seventeen."

"Well, does an emplacement you can see do it?"

"Yes… don't look at me like that, Jaq. It doesn't mean I know what every barrage round the City is doing. Why would I think that no one is shooting at us anymore? It doesn't make sense."

Pilakin kicked over a stack of crates, which fell to the floor scattering small-arms ammunition. She took a moment to seize control of herself, breathing deeply and focussing on the Imperial coat of arms burned into the splintered wood at her feet. One of the jagged edges had gone right through the eagle.

"We're wasting our time here."

"Great," said Crustetin.

Pilakin looked up. "I'm sorry, Tomasz."

"It's okay. Maybe we should have done more prep-work, eh? Okay people, let's get ready to leave."

"Hang on a fucking minute," roared Oswin. "You're just going to abandon us? We acted in good faith. We were co-operating. And now you're going to leave us in the shit because we actually refrained from shelling the City? We want to defect. Let us defect."

He's got a point, thought Pilakin, and gave Tomasz one of those looks he could never resist.

He swore. "Oh, what the hell. Okay. Sergeant Oswin, come here and I'll show you how to use the beacon."

The relief on the Imp's faces was gratifying and they stopped looking daggers at Wade. While Tomasz was talking, Pilakin tapped the badge on Wade's chest.

"What's this lion badge about?"

"Eh?"

"I've been… seeing it for years. The lion with a sword but with chains on its wrists and ankles. It's a strange symbol. And I've never seen it on officers."

"We call it the lion-patch. It shows we're puniserves."

"Puniserves?"

"Yes. On punishment service. We've been convicted of sedition against the Empire and have been sent out here to rot and die. Most of us are innocent of what they said we did but we certainly all hate the Empire…"

And the bottom fell out of Pilakin's world.

Chapter 18

*I*T ISN'T THE *first time she's been sent on holiday to Uncle Tomasz' tower. Dad often has to go to work for several days and since mum... Well, there's no-one dad trusts to look after her in the City. So, he always says the same thing. "Jaq, do you want to go and see the sky?"*

"Some sky. Always the same black clouds."

"Better than anything you get in the city, my little chimp."

Normally she pouts and sulks at that but today she wants something.

"I can stay here, dad. I'm ten standard. I promise I won't open the door to anyone. Mrs Flizen over the hall can take me to school and back."

He shrugs on his coat with the badge attached to its breast pocket before taking the bars off his shirt collar and reattaching them to the one on his jacket.

"The Flizen girls are not good for you to be around."

"Why? You always say that. Why can't I pick my own friends?"

"We're different to the City people, Jaq."

He sits down in front of her and looks deeply into her eyes.

"You mustn't forget who we are. Yes, your mother sacrificed to get us here and this city has saved us. But you'll leave one day. You'll go back out there. That's why you need to see the sky."

She feels her anger rising just like it always does when he mentions her mother. But today there's something in his eyes that stops her tantrum. He reaches out and strokes her hair… And then she's in Uncle Tomasz' tower. The younger children – her wild Pilyarkin cousins – screaming round the room acting out their favourite scenes from Bookdog and the Worm. And Auntie Vanya is in the doorway. She has a look on her face that Jaq hasn't seen before. She looks scared. Auntie Vanya is never scared, even when the Imps are shelling. She beckons Jaq outside.

And that is where she tells Jaq that her father is dead.

SHOUTING. A STING on her cheek.

"…akin…!"

More stinging. A slap? She struggled against the grasping hands as they lifted her to her feet. She grabbed the hair at her temples and breathed deeply before letting the shriek in her guts out in one long, primal sound.

"Jaq Pilakin," shouted Tomasz. "What in Hell is *wrong*

with you?"

"I killed innocents. It wasn't defence. It was never defence. But at least it was killing those who wanted to kill us. Take our freedom away. But now I know it wasn't even that. I'm a multiple First Right violator. I'm a murderer. I've always been a murderer. I know that. But now I've murdered innocent people. People on our side. I've killed six hundred people who hate the Empire as much as we do…"

Tomasz grabbed her into a bear hug.

"I killed all those boys. All those beautiful, innocent boys. I couldn't bear to look them in the face. The lion badges were over their hearts. I didn't want them to suffer. I never wanted them to suffer. But I couldn't look at their faces. So I shot them in their lion hearts… Oh, Uncle Tomasz. I miss my daddy so much."

He pressed her face into his fleshy chest, holding her firm as she struggled and fought. His bulk absorbed her torrent of verbal self-flagellation and the wracking sobs that came after it. And the wail after that. When she felt the fight go out of her and went limp, he finally relaxed his grip. She held him and cried softly. He stroked her hair.

"I do too, Jaq. I do too."

The others stared. The Imperial prisoners looked scared but Tomasz's face seemed to challenge any of them say anything. One by one they looked away. The shell had different rules. Inside the city people got twitchy if you freaked out. People who lose it in the city often end up shooting people. Out here, instability was the norm.

WHEN SHE GAINED enough composure, they moved out. Tomasz set up a cordon formation with her in the middle for protection and took a different and more direct route back. Before leaving he had told the Imps not to activate the beacon for fifteen minutes so as to give time for Pilakin's group to get back to the shell. The walk back was uneventful. Pilakin could feel the stares, although the only one who whispered was Crustetin. No-one engaged with her.

THEY GOT BACK to the shell bang on the quarter hour at the foot of Tower 17. They gained access and, ignoring offers of coffee, hurried up to the parapet, peering through their rifle scopes at the battery they had left.

"There, at one oh two."

Pilakin scanned round to the heading and saw the large, rectangular white form of a federation medical lander heading towards the battery, floating on what appeared to be a cloud of mud. She could make out the screaming sound of the mighty retro engines keeping it airborne.

"What the hell?"

She didn't know who spoke but they then gave another compass point and Pilakin swung her rifle to see two fighter-bombers. They banked, showing Federation markings. That was rare. 99% of aircraft over the Meadow were Simplaerosian.

"They'll just be escorting the medical lander," said Crustetin.

Pilakin doubted that. One of the few niceties of war actually observed in the Meadow was the sanctity of the medical landers. She saw the planes dip their noses in what was undoubtedly a bombing run. She swept the ground ahead of them but the only objective that appeared to be on their route was the battery. People started to shout.

"No. Surely not."

"They can't be…"

"What the fuck…?"

Pilakin's ear piece joined in the cacophony.

"Medical lander to Federation fighters. Wave off! Wave off! We are on rescue mission."

Straight lines of smoke with burning heads, almost too fast to see, connected the fighters with the battery's bunker. The medical lander veered away with a drunken lurch and the fighters sat on their tails in a vertical climb. A second later the bunker disintegrated on the outside of a bubble of fire. Pilakin's scope automatically dimmed the bright light but she could still see that bubble for minutes afterwards.

INSIDE THE TOWER, Tomasz led her down into the domestic area and, as she entered the kitchen, the delicious smell of sizzling meat hit her with a wall of memories. A large woman was stirring a huge frying pan as two small children ran screaming round with toy landers locked in mortal combat. She looked up.

"Oh my… Jaq!"

"Auntie Vanya!"

Her uniform was as striking as it ever was, stretched across huge breasts. Pilakin ran across the room, buried her face in them and sobbed for a few moments as if she were still a girl. Vanya wrapped her beefy arms around her and made a good attempt at crushing bones. Pilakin felt like she was home for the first time in a very long while. Finally, when she'd stopped shaking and crying, Vanya released her and stepped back. Pilakin was grateful. Vanya always seemed to be able to suck the despair out of her and she never returned her to the world until she was composed once more. She looked at Pilakin and smiled.

"Look at little Jaq. You've turned into some kind of woman. I always said you'd look good once you grew into your bones. Didn't I say that, Tomasz?"

Tomasz grunted. He tended to turn taciturn around Vanya but Pilakin had seen too many held hands and stolen kisses to think that their marriage was anything other than happy.

Vanya picked up the spatula again and gave the meat a vigorous turn over. Pilakin inhaled the renewed aromas carried by the steam.

"That smells like rat," she exclaimed.

"Just the legs. We've managed to get so many I could put the rest in a stock." She indicated the large pot from which bubbling sounds came.

"What's the special occasion?" Pilakin asked. As a child, real meat was for festivals and birthdays. "Did you do it for me?"

"Well, there's the girl who has the high opinion of herself. No, dear Jaq. They're not the rare commodity they used to be; we traded them off the Imperial soldiers in the front line. Things have changed since you were out here. Those poor guys are literally starving. They'll take our yeast bricks and we get fresh meat."

Pilakin shuddered as she remembered the foul tasting bricks. Vanya grinned as she saw it.

"They taste a lot better when you're truly hungry and they'll stave off starvation far better than a few mangy rats. These are plump enough; they've feasted on human flesh. Although I've had to throw away the ones with high radiation."

Pilakin laughed, despite herself. Vanya had always tried to put her off her rat when she was small. It hadn't worked then and it sure as hell wasn't going to work now that she knew rat carcasses went for over twenty Credits a piece in the city. The CDA were feasting like Syndicatists and they probably didn't even know it.

"You say they're starving? How do you know?"

"You can see it. Not just the hungry look in their eyes – everyone on the Meadow has that. No, their cheeks are hollow, their uniforms hang off them, their hands and wrists are so bony."

Pilakin thought about the guys in the bunker. It seemed that it wasn't just a problem of their supplies. It felt like some bigger picture was just beyond her grasp.

Vanya started scraping the meat into a huge serving dish.

"I tell you, Jaq. Things have changed out there. I don't know what, but the Feds are up to something. I reckon we're going to live to see the end of this siege. Imagine that."

Pilakin found she couldn't.

Chapter 19

"Hello?"

"Engineer Melissa Walden?"

"Speaking."

"Hi, it's Agent Pilakin. Can you talk?"

"Yeah, sure. I'm at home."

"Great. You doing anything for the next couple of hours?"

"No, but I'm tired. I've just got off work."

"Would a hundred credits get your shoes back on?"

"I guess it would. What do you want?"

"Southwind Building. Was it really hit by a shell?"

"As opposed to what?"

"Having a bomb planted on the outside."

"Why would—?"

"Can you find out?"

"I don't see why not."

"Do you keep your analysis stuff with you?"

"Of course. If I left it at work someone would walk off with it."

"Okay. How long will it take you to get to the scene?"

WHEN SHE GOT to the apartment, Pilakin discovered the front door was missing. She went in and knocked on the bedroom door. It opened a crack and the barrel of a gun emerged.

"Mrs Fesh?"

"Who are you?"

"My name's Agent Pilakin. I'm—"

"We are not leaving. He's reported me for a Sixth hasn't he? Well, I'm paid up fully so here I stay. You want to do something, get rid of the fucking squatters."

"I'm investigating your husband's death."

A moment of silence.

"You work with Agent Manstein?"

"No ma'am. He sold the case to me."

Mrs Fesh laughed and opened the door wider, although the gun stayed pointing at Pilakin's chest.

"Well then you must be a simpleton. Why don't you go and investigate real crimes that might end up with a payout."

"Actually, it was murder."

She frowned at that.

"Really? How?"

"Well, I have an expert coming to examine the hole again. It's still there, isn't it?"

"Sure it is. That bastard landlord said he wouldn't fix it while I was still living here. He wants me to leave so he can accuse me of breach of contract and let it to someone else for more money. But I've got six months paid up in advance so I'm not leaving. Then he took the fucking door off its hinges so the place would fill up with squatters but I did a deal with them. As long as they stayed in the main room and didn't touch me or the kids I wouldn't get the agents on to them. Already a better life than with that bastard Youal."

"They've stuck to it?"

"Yep. They're mostly junkies but one of them's a big-guy. He cries every time he sees the kids. I guess he's lost some. One night some freaks tried to get in and he beat them up. Killed one right where you're standing and threw the other out of the hole. I guess word's got round. There's been no trouble since. This your expert?"

Pilakin turned to see Melissa standing behind her with a large kit bag over her shoulder.

"Thanks for coming."

Melissa nodded and shook her hand. "Let's get this done. I want to sleep sometime tonight."

Mrs. Fesh stopped them.

"If you go in there cold, the big guy might hurt you. Choker!"

Some muttered swearing came from behind the living room door and they heard some things being knocked over. Finally the door opened and a colossal man with no hair and a face covered in a spider web of burst blood vessels stood swaying in front of them.

"Choker. These people are trying to find out what killed Youal and they need to look at the hole in your room."

"Youal?" he slurred, "Who the fuck is Youal? And why the bollocksing fuck do I give a shit what killed him?"

His voice was rising and he started to advance.

"He was the kids' father."

Choker stopped in his tracks as if winded. "Oh… those kids. You here to help them?" He dipped his head to look Pilakin in the face with glassy, bloodshot eyes. For a moment Pilakin wondered if she was looking at her own future.

"Yes, sir. If we can prove something we might claim enough comp to get them out of this place."

He nodded slowly and Pilakin tried not to shy away as he extended an arm to pat her on the shoulder. "You're alright. Come in… I'll look after you."

Pilakin was used to the scene awaiting them on the other side of the door. The fact that Melissa gasped suggested she wasn't accustomed to the stench of body odour, ammonia, shit and a melange of burning drug smells. There must have been twenty or thirty people in the room and the only light came from the hole in the wall. Fesh's soiled chair had been set up facing the hole and no one lay or sat between the two. This was clearly Choker's throne. Addicts of many kinds were piled around the rest of the room, some with needles in their arms, some bleeding from their noses and at least two that Pilakin could see were dead. Few acknowledged their arrival and the ones who did lost interest almost immediately. A girl of maybe twelve or thirteen had been honoured with one of the horrid mattresses next to Choker's chair, presumably as part of his mission to help children. At least Pilakin hoped so. She was curled in a ball, so the shit from one end and puke from the other had run into each other as they soaked into the bed.

"What's the matter with her?" Melissa gasped as Pilakin knelt down beside the girl.

"She's jonesing. What does she use, Choker?"

He dropped himself back into his chair and looked down with a sad expression. "My lovely Polly likes the heroin."

Pilakin reached into her pocket.

"Polly? Can you hear me? I don't have any smack but these are heroettes. They'll take the edge off, okay?"

Polly raised her head at the word heroette with an eager expression and nodded. Choker handed down a lighter so Pilakin lit one and put it into the girl's mouth. She started to draw deeply.

"Slowly, Polly or you'll burn yourself. There's only fifteen left in there so make them last, okay?"

Choker reached down and grabbed the packet.

"I'll make sure she does."

The look on Pilakin's face must have betrayed her

mistrust.

"Skag isn't my thing. I won't nick 'em. Anyway, she's more use when she's functioning. Now do what you got to do and get out."

A glance at Melissa's face showed she was thinking about leaving, so Pilakin decided it would be best to do as Choker said. They picked their way over to the hole. Melissa removed various instruments from her bag and started taking measurements while Pilakin's attention was divided between interest in what she was doing and watching the room's inhabitants. Polly seemed to be relaxing and Choker was staring into empty space.

"Talk to me, Melissa."

"There's a distinct lack of shrapnel."

"The place has been cleaned up a bit. I know it doesn't look like it."

"I don't mean loose bits. Most of that will be amongst the rubble pile anyway. But there should be small fragments embedded in the concrete."

Pilakin watched as she roved over the surface with a device projecting a tight beam of very bright light, while observing the results with a microscope eyepiece held in her screwed-up socket. When she appeared satisfied another tool emerged from the bag – a rotating, metal scouring brush with a vacuum tube. It buzzed and the small cloud it created was sucked up and collected in multiple vials down the back of the instrument.

"You going to chuck that in the GCMS?"

Melissa nodded as she replied. "You know what it looks like? Get it out of the bag will you?"

Pilakin retrieved the circular box and laid it on the floor. She switched it on and unclipped one of the vials on its surface marked calibration and slotted it into the input housing. After a couple of minutes' whirring the machine heated up enough to evaporate the sample and send its known molecules down the tubes for their masses to be measured. The green light blinked ready.

"Okay, we're set."

Melissa slid her sample vial into the top and opened a programme on her slab to see the results. Pilakin frowned as the graph of a familiar explosive appeared on the screen.

"Will the type really tell you whether it is a shell or not?"

"No, but it will tell me whether it was manufactured inside the city. All the ones produced here have isotope markers in the molecules. It's supposed to be to help a forensics team but really I think it's for advertising. People who set bombs for a living watch how other attacks go. If you're a terrorist, a nice big body count is something to take best-practice from..."

"So, if it's an Imperial shell..."

"Or pretty much any ordnance from the outside..."

"It won't have any markers."

"Correct."

"And...?"

Melissa almost smiled. Professional satisfaction,

Pilakin assumed.

"This one does. The explosive used here was produced by Radical Marketing Solutions. They're based over in South Central somewhere."

"Know anything about them?"

"I think they got bought out by one of the syndicates a couple of years ago."

"Do you remember which one?"

Melissa frowned.

"I'm not sure."

"The Kristanis?"

She shrugged and started putting away her equipment. "Could be."

"So, let me get this straight. The explosion was not delivered by any kind of shell or missile and the explosive used was manufactured inside the City?"

"That's about the size of it."

Pilakin leaned forward and peered out of the hole. Above and below, other than the area around the explosion site, the building's outer wall stretched in an unbroken surface. Almost as if to mock her, a loud rumble like distant thunder reverberated; another impact somewhere on the rim that she could more or less feel through her feet. She pulled her head back inside.

"Do you have any idea how the bomb could have been fixed to the side of the building?"

Melissa paused and shrugged.

"Well the platform you saw us using worked on

vacuum cups. We put it in place with a hovercar lifter."

"That's expensive and would attract attention. Could someone drop down on a rope and attach…?"

She stopped, frowning.

"What is it, Pilakin?"

"I seem to remember…"

Come on, Pilakin, think. In the rubble pile… there was a scorched length of frayed rope… an unusual object. Not rare but certainly unusual. The frayed end…

"What?"

"Are you done here, Melissa?"

"Yes."

"Thank you so much. I'll pay you…"

She nodded to the door. She didn't fancy waving a fist full of credit slips around in front of their present company. She patted Choker on the shoulder, pulling him out of his stupor for a moment.

"Look after Polly, won't you?"

The big man looked up at her with tears in his eyes and nodded.

OUTSIDE, PILAKIN HANDED over the payment.

"Thanks again for coming out. You go home and get some sleep."

"What are you going to do now?"

"There was some rope in the rubble pile. I'm going to head up to the roof and see if there's any evidence it was attached and used to go down the side of the building.

Listen, can I borrow your micro-eye?"

"Why don't I come with you?"

"To be honest, I can't afford to pay you for something I can do myself. Here…" She held out another couple of credits. "Give me your address and I'll bring it back when I'm done okay?"

"Okay."

PILAKIN EXITED THE stairwell and stepped out onto the roof. It only took a glance to see plenty of places where a rope could be secured – pipe work, silent A/C units, the stairwell itself. Blanching a little as she saw the complete lack of handrail at the edge, she nevertheless edged toward it. A metre or so short, she dropped to her hands and knees on the dirty, concrete surface, kidding herself that it was just to make her task easier. A peep over the edge showed she was not directly above the hole; it lay five or six metres to her left. Crawling along, she looked ahead hoping to find the end off a rope still secured but had no such luck. Once above the hole, she felt along the edge of the building and found it had a sharp, rough corner. She lay flat and, using the micro-eye, slowly looked along the edge. After thirty seconds or so she grunted in satisfaction as she came across some fibres on the outer corner of the concrete. Taking out her own small forensics kit from a pouch on the back of her belt, she used the tweezers to collect several samples and drop them into an evidence tube.

Before she could get up to leave, something heavy landed in the small of her back and slammed her down into the roof. The wind left her body and into a moment of silence she could not fill there was a voice.

"Now you're gonna pay, bitch."

Chapter 20

PILAKIN TRIED TO move but a foot was planted on her cheek and pinned her down. She gasped several times before finally managing to wheeze "Who are you?"

"Who am I? My name you mean? You already know me but you don't give a shit about my name do you?"

"What… do you mean?"

"You know me by a title other than my name, bitch. Say it!"

Pilakin struggled to turn her head but couldn't move it enough to see more than the edge of a ragged jacket.

"I'm sorry… I don't know."

"I knew it. I knew you wouldn't even remember who I was if you met me again. I'm number forty-fucking-three."

The hazy fog of two nights ago cleared and it all made sense in an instant.

"From Pandora's."

"That's right you nasty piece of shit. I'm the guy

you..."

He choked, clearly emotional. Distracted. Pilakin's mind raced as she weighed her options. From what she remembered he was a bit of a twink. No body mass or muscles to speak of. He'd probably had no training in violence and if he was armed it was unlikely to be with anything expensive. More likely a knife than a gun. The decision came. Upward movement wasn't possible so she put all her strength into her right arm and leg to roll sideways. It worked. He unbalanced and as he tried to gain his footing her hand slipped quickly and easily into her jacket holster. Now it depended on what he was holding. She brought her gun to bear with both hands while still lying on her back and breathed again when she saw nothing more than a knife in his hand. It was plasteel, serrated and vicious. Her mind shied away from what it could have done to her. She focussed on the fact that she now had the advantage.

"Step back!"

His face was twisted with anger and frustration but there was no fear. That wasn't good. She resorted to the freedoms she was supposed to enforce.

"You've just committed Second and Fifth Rights violations against me. You are currently committing a Tenth with the First. I feel the threat is current and so inform you that I am about to take measures to defend myself against the perceived threat in kind. To summarise; step back or I will shoot you in the head, you shit-eating bastard."

She cocked the pistol with her thumb and resettled her fists around the butt, aiming with steady hands. Her speech seemed to have an effect but not for the reason she anticipated. He moved back two or three steps, the knife still in front of him as if to ward off the bullets. "You're an agent. He didn't tell me you're a fucking agent."

"Drop the knife."

After a moment's more hesitation he complied.

"Now kick it away. Nice and far but not over the side."

After he did so she got up, keeping the gun trained on his body. He was no longer a threat and she hadn't formally detained him but she took the gamble that he wouldn't know enough about the niceties of Rights Enforcement to realise he could make a break for it.

"Who didn't tell you?"

"What?"

"Who didn't tell you I was an agent?"

"No one."

Pilakin sighed. "Turn round and put your hands out behind you."

"Why?"

"I hereby detain you pending prosecution by interested parties."

He turned and with deft experience the single loop plasticuffs from her trouser pocket were zipped on to him in a second.

"Now twinkboy, believe it or not, it's your lucky day.

The interested party is me and I really don't have time to pursue a prosecution." *Not that he'd have anything worth suing for.* "So, you start talking and we can avoid all the unpleasantness."

He shook his head. "Warm cell in a detention facility looks pretty good right now."

Oh, for goodness' sake.

She yanked him roughly by the arms and dragged him to the edge of the building, pushing him forward. He screamed and then his arms went taut as she held him by the cuffs, hanging at an angle. He looked down at the distant street, the crackling sink field only a couple of metres away. Pilakin shook his bound wrists.

"Who?"

"Hanging around Pandora's. Hoping to get back in. This guy asked if I wanted some work. Said he wanted someone watched. Told me to go and wait outside that apartment you were in and follow whoever came out."

"Did he tell you who I was?"

"No… I still don't know. I just recognised you as—"

"Who was he?"

"No name. Just said he worked for a syndicate."

"Which one?"

"I don't know."

"The Kristanis?"

"I swear I don't know. Please – pull me back. I promise you'll never see me again. I swear."

She hauled him back with so much force he stumbled,

turned, and faceplanted into the roof. She put her knee into the back of his neck and used his hair to yank his head backwards. He cried and her anger started to ebb. She needed to finish this before the feeling of righteous vengeance left her entirely.

"What did he look like? Sound like?"

"Normal city accent. Tall. Grey hair. Wore a suit and those big dark glasses the syndicates have."

Hell, that could describe so many people of her acquaintance.

"Tell me about the knife."

"He gave it to me. I asked why not a gun. He said there wasn't much danger. I should just have it for insurance."

Pilakin stood and walked over to the knife, keeping an eye on him the whole time. She picked it up and went back. Turning his head to look at her, his crying turned into a wail. His eyes widened as he formed the word, "Nooooooo…"

She knelt down and sliced through his cuffs. As soon as his hands were free he scrabbled away from her, falling and rolling a few metres away. He lay looking at her, breathing hard.

"I'm sorry," she said.

"What? What did you say?"

"I'm sorry. Not for this," she indicated the roof with a sweep of her hand, "you had this coming for jumping me. I'm sorry for what I did at Pandora's."

"Oh…well great help that is to me now."

"Did the guy pay you up front for this job?"

"Half. Half on delivery of information."

Pilakin shook her head.

"He didn't want information. He wanted you to kill me. I think he knew how you'd react when you saw me. Where were you supposed to meet him?"

"I wasn't. He just gave me a number to call."

"Tell me."

She tapped it into her slab as he recited. The call went through to a dead service line. "You see? You were an expendable tool."

"Story of my fucking life."

She looked at this beautiful boy all bruised and bloodied. She half expected he'd jump off the building once she left. Hell, she needed him out of circulation if only to buy a few hours' uncertainty in her stalker. She approached him again, writing on a card she took from her pocket. He cringed as she held it out with a folded-up ten-credit note.

"Here. Go and see this friend of mine; Clem Starlight. He runs a clean, safe house with a little sideline in cross-dressers. Be nicer work than you've been doing. Tell him Jaq Pilakin sent you."

He reached for it with a shaking hand. She held on for a moment more to demand his attention.

"Stay away from me from now on okay? And be careful who you work for."

He nodded and she let go, turning to walk back to the

stairwell. As she reached the entrance he finally found his voice again.

"Takani."

"What?"

"My name: it's Takani."

I didn't want to know that, she thought as she shouldered through the door.

Chapter 21

W*HERE WAS HE? They usually came out for their mate in the first couple of hours but the body is still sitting there; the rats, mere brown blobs through her rifle sight, swarming over the carcass. The HUD over her other eye tells her it's just coming up on five and her muscles are aching like hell. Soon she'll be losing what they laughingly refer to as light in the Meadow. Another hour and she'll call it quits – heading back, disappointed, for some yeast and grit.*

She cocks her head. A different sound from the burning, moaning and distant stuttering guns. The squidge of boot into mud. The hovering sound of a breathless person trying to exhale silently. Carefully she draws her panic pistol from its neckholster. There's a murmur.

"You don't need that, Jaq."

Frustration.

"Why the erith do you do that, Itzie?

He lies down next to her, so close their sides touch all

the way down and he leans close to kiss her on the cheek. She doesn't move or take her eye away from the sight.

"You spend too long out here Jaq. You don't have to rot one every god-damned day, you know?"

She adjusts the sight to compensate for the deteriorating light.

"I've already done one. I want to get two a day."

"Why for fuck's sake? Tomasz says you're the best he's seen. They already call you the Lion Hunter right round the shell. What are you trying to prove?"

"If I leave this one maybe he'll bite you tomorrow and Tomasz the day after."

"All about protecting your loved ones is it?"

"Why are you here, Itzie?"

"I saw the firerain and was worried about you."

"It's okay; I had my breath and shiny."

"They'll catch you off-guard one of these days, kid."

"Don't you kid me."

"Ooo, yeah. Nearly seventeen – all grown up now."

"Still got a year on you, boy."

She smiles at last and turns her head to face him. He leans in to kiss her properly and she lets him. After a couple of seconds the bullets thump into the mud in front of them and both their faces get splattered.

"Shit!"

Itzie sprays the land around the body with machine gun fire and they both slither backwards. Crawling, then crouching, then running, they get back to the shell.

Dropping into a slit trench they feel each other all over for injuries and then she punches him in the stomach.

"They were waiting for me the whole time and you went and distracted me, you bastard."

He gasps and holds out his hand before getting the words out.

"I bet... I got him... instead."

She grabs his ears and stares into his eyes. After a moment, both smile and embrace. Kissing, they fall to the bottom of the trench.

PILAKIN BLINKED AND took a moment to recall her whereabouts. She was returning on a tube to the inner city and, with an effort, turned her thoughts back to considering the case. It was like a big knotted up ball of fibres. Half a dozen ends were sticking out and she had no idea which one to pull to solve it. There was the added danger that each strand was attached to an organisation with the power to hurt her – everyone seemed to be involved. The Kristanis, the Imps, the Feds; and others she hadn't got a clue about. Water activists? The mysterious assailant who seemed bent on getting her killed? Who was he working for? And she hadn't made any effort to find the mysterious Rimsky since the shootout in the bar. She reached for her heroettes but, finding an empty pocket and remembering what she had done with them, she shuddered. She tapped the shoulder of a guy puffing on an ordinary ciggy.

"Buy a smoke?"

"Point five."

Price gouging her but she was desperate and handed over the coin. After three drags she decided to head to the Federation to see if she could get to the bottom of who was ordering the artillery strikes. Even if the Feds *were* ordering hits for propaganda, it was beyond the bounds of credulity to believe it was coincidence a strike had been ordered at the exact time and place where a bomb went off. But why go to all the subterfuge of ordering the strike? Inside the city it would be assumed it was a shell from outside but if someone had investigated, like her, it wouldn't take much effort to uncover the lie. Maybe the cover up was for someone else…

TWO CHANGES LATER she emerged from Liberty Square Station. Blinking in the unusually bright light, she stood still for a moment, fighting the vertigo most city dwellers felt when entering this place. They projected a startling real blue sky with clouds on to the high vaulted ceiling. It was bad enough for her, who had spent a lot of time in the Meadow. For normal denizens it was horrifying and native city dwellers could be identified as those assiduously looking at the floor or walking around with hands above their eyes as a visor, blocking out the nightmare overhead. Having dealt with the Feds before, she was fairly sure they used it as an anti-riot control device.

The headquarters of the Free Federation of Anti-

Imperial Organisations – the FFAIO, or Feds to the lay-person – towered over one side of the square like a giant bunker. A great, multi-storey blank wall with turrets at each end and windows made to look like firing slits along the top. Again, she had no doubt that they would be used as such, should push ever come to shove. A piece of music she liked started up and caught her attention. She looked up and saw one of her favourite Federation propaganda pieces projected on the wall. The song was sung by a woman bemoaning the end of her money, job and relationship. The images were of her arguing and eventually fighting with a man before running off into the city. Everywhere she sees prostitutes and women being harassed and sex being used to sell everything. The music ups its tempo and the lyrics speak about another way of viewing the world. The character on the screen walks in an apparent daze into a dark alley where steam is billowing out of vents and as she moves through it she is in a wood with dappled sunlight passing over her face. She walks toward a group of soldiers and, as they turn to greet her with smiles, you see they are all women. The caption appears. *72% of FFAIO volunteers are female*. It's time to see the world differently. (*or the xeno-biological equivalent)*

Pilakin smiled and took a quick nip from her hip-flask. She'd seen the same percentage used on adverts in sex joints trying to get men to join. The Feds made themselves out to be saints but she suspected it was all just good marketing. She put away the flask and advanced toward a small queue of people, in both Federation and CDA uniforms and City garb, waiting to pass through the checkpoint in the middle of a long line of soldiers who were permanently stationed in the square. They formed a human barrier 20 metres or so in front of the building. She noted, by accident or design, it looked like they had made sure 72% of them were female. Each person in the queue had their federation badge scanned before being waved through. When Pilakin reached the front, an officer with two bars on her collar, denoting a lieutenant, held up her hand.

"Excuse me, ma'am. I'm sorry, but public access is via the recruitment building."

She indicated a low part of the main building that jutted out into the square and intersected with the line of defence.

"No, I'm not here to join. I'm an FPA and I'd like to confer with Officer Locatore in your Agency."

"Do you have an appointment?"

"No. I could call him and make one if you like?"

The lieutenant chewed her cheek for a moment. "Who do you work for?"

"I'm independent."

A nod.

"Show the sergeant your badge, please."

She held it out to be scanned with the same machine they had been using on the Feds.

"Checks out, boss."

The lieutenant activated her head set. "What's your name?"

"Pilakin."

She spoke into her mic.

A moment passed and although Pilakin couldn't hear the reply it must have been favourable, as the lieutenant turned back to her.

"What weapons you carrying?"

"Pistol in my shoulder holster and a fighting knife at the bottom of my right leg."

"Okay. Please unload your gun."

As she did so, the lieutenant kept talking. "Once we let you through do not reload and do not unsheathe your knife. If you do either it will be regarded as a Tenth Right threat to life and you will be killed or detained pending prosecution. When I wave you through, walk directly to the reception doors in front of you. Go in a straight line and do not run. Understand?"

She spoke into her headset again.

"Okay, I'm sending her in now."

What were they so scared of? Pilakin thought as she advanced through the empty space behind the soldiers. It felt like hundreds of pairs of eyes were on her the whole way and it was a relief to get through the doors and into a strangely normal reception area. Behind a long desk a glass wall gave a good view of a huge open-plan office space with hundreds of people working in it. One of the receptionists smiled and beckoned her over.

"Freedom Protection Agent Pilakin, wasn't it? How are you spelling that? You're an independent, is that right?"

"Yes I am. Is that significant?"

The receptionist was printing off a plastic card and attached fabric hooks to the back.

"ECC and syndicate agents are not allowed in without an appointment approved by the City Liaison Committee. I've informed Agent Officer Locatore that you're here. He'll be right up. Please take a seat."

Pilakin leafed through a copy of *Federation Life*. So many articles and features about the joys and benefits of joining the FFAIO. Nothing in there about Hell's Meadow though. Nothing about fire-rain and nukes and murdering people for a living. Nothing about the likelihood of getting killed either.

"Are you thinking of joining up?"

The receptionist was still smiling.

"No. I spent a couple of years in the CDA. I think I've done my bit."

"Yes, I'm sure you have."

Max Locatore appeared through a door in the glass screen.

"Hi, Jaq. Lovely to see you again. Did you declare your weapons? All of them? Because when you go through this door the scanners will check and if there's something you haven't declared, they'll jump on you. Okay? Good then, follow me."

As she passed through, a wall of noise hit her from so many people working in the same place. The place felt frenetic but fortunately Max quickly led them to a door in the corner and through into a warren of corridors, down a set of stairs and into a part of the building that was immediately recognisable as an FPA centre. They sat down at his desk in the detectives' bull-pen and Pilakin felt suddenly sad and alone, homesick for her desk in the ECC-FPA. She quickly pulled her thoughts back and focussed on Max's words.

"… want some tea, Jaq? It's a—"

"I know what it is. No, I'm good thanks."

"Okay then. What can I do for you?"

"You going to charge me for this consult?"

"No, of course not. This is the Federation – we don't work like that."

"'We', Max? You didn't sound so certain this morning that you were really part of this."

His eyes flitted side to side at the other agents but it was clear none were paying him any attention. He smiled. "Everyone here is a true believer, Jaq. That's why we refuse to take a salary. Well, apart from—"

He stopped short and blushed. That was the great reason for talking to Max. He tried to be discreet. He really did.

"I need some information about how the Federation works. Is that okay?"

"Of course. We have nothing to hide from anyone, apparently."

She smiled back at him.

"So, you have twelve 'commands', right? Things like intelligence, the navy, the army and so on?"

"Yes. That's what the pictures on our badges are about. There's also non-military aspects like propaganda, logistics and commerce."

"Commerce?"

"Fundraising, I suppose. But most of our money doesn't come from appeals. We own businesses like…" he managed to stop himself this time. She waited to see if silence would induce him to continue, but this time it didn't.

"Okay, I get it. So, which command is responsible for defending the city and fighting in the Meadow?"

"None of them."

"What?"

"Each command is headed up by a senior officer who has been elected to the Command Council. There's a lot of politics involved and I don't think they really get on with each other. You remember when old Jones took over Central Two back in the ECC and started trying to take over our territory?"

Pilakin nodded.

"It ended up with that punch up in the Frog Lane Bar. I get you."

"Well, there's too much to be gained out of dealing

with the city. So, partly for efficiency, partly for Federation unity but mostly out of politics they formed a committee called City Liaison. All the commands that have a stake in dealing with the City send a representative. On the other side of the table are reps from the City Corporation, the big syndicates, the Institute, the CDA, major media and so on. All interaction with the city goes through them."

"So that would mean you—"

"That's right. I don't belong to a specific command. We report to City Liaison."

"Do all the commands have equal weight on the committee?"

"I always envied you your detective's nose, Jaq. Of course not. Commerce and Army are the big noises."

"Intelligence?"

"Intelligence seem to be everywhere. I sometimes wonder if they're actually running the whole show but you can never pin them down."

As if on cue, the phone on Max's desk rang. He nonchalantly hit the answer button. "Locatore."

"Hello, this is Major Neuberg."

"Major! What an honour to speak to you."

He looked like he regretted answering it on speakerphone.

"Nonsense, Maximillian. Now, a little bird tells me that you have a certain Agent Pilakin with you. Is that correct?"

"Yes, Major."

"Would you please do me a favour and bring her up here? Thank you."

Neuberg disconnected the call and Max got out of his chair.

"Where are you going?"

"You heard the lady."

"We were having a conversation."

"I know it didn't sound like it but that was a direct order from my boss's boss's boss. She's also intelligence and, given the questions you're asking, I'd rather the answers came from someone up there. Come on, we shouldn't keep her waiting."

Chapter 22

THE INTELLIGENCE STAFF were high up in one of the building's turrets. The hallways were clean and tastefully decorated but the office Max led her into was bizarre. Pilakin had never seen so much real paper in her life. The walls were covered in shelving heaving with folder after folder, each stuffed with papers held together with string or elastic. Several dozen more were stacked up on a large desk. A short figure with her back to them was standing by another table in the back corner of the office on the opposite side to the desk, dealing with a kettle and cups. A large, unruly ponytail sprayed out from the top of her head and down over her shoulders. She turned to look over her shoulder at them. Major Neuberg's warm, brown eyes were framed by mascara, which had run like she'd been crying. An instinctive swell of compassion died away as she took in Neuberg's face as a whole, seeing a warm, calm expression with a serene smile.

"Thank you so much for coming, Agent Pilakin. There's no need for you to stay, Max. Good work on the Pandora's case by the way."

"Oh… er… thank you major. But I was hoping I could stay to…"

Neuberg said nothing but tilted her head and turned her smile upon him. He swallowed, his eyes darting to anywhere in the room except Neuberg. He then nodded his head before leaving the room in a manner that could be described as fleeing. Neuberg turned her gaze back to Pilakin.

"I think he's taken enough credit from you for now."

"He paid for it, he bought that praise."

"Such a strange moral code in this city. The almighty Credit. Can I get you some tea?"

Pilakin's hand fluttered to her money and she felt indecision.

"Oh no, Agent, you are the Federation's guest. I wouldn't dream of asking you to pay. I insist you have some, in fact."

Nice psychology, thought Pilakin. *Saved me from the discomfiture of deciding whether to pay and then saved me from the further shame of accepting or not on the grounds of it being free.* Mind games? She'd heard that about Fed intelligence.

"You Feds really do like your tea, don't you?"

Neuberg handed her a steaming cup and invited her to sit in a chair at the side of her desk. It had to be at the side;

if it had been opposite, Pilakin would have been unable to see the diminutive Neuberg over her paper ramparts.

"Please forgive me, major, but are you okay?"

Pilakin's fingers fluttered to toward her own cheeks before she realised and drew them away. Neuberg's expression did not change and showed no sign of distress or embarrassment. She raised beautifully manicured fingers to the run mascara.

"Oh this; I've made it permanent to show my sorrow at humanity's plight."

"A tattoo?"

"If you like." She pushed some papers aside to give her space to lay down her cup. "You're probably wondering why I invited you up to see me."

"About as much as you're wondering why I came to see Max, I should imagine."

"*You're* here to find out who has been ordering artillery strikes on the City."

Was that a slap down? A smug I-know-more-than-you? The warmth had not left the face but it had been joined by a mischievous twinkle at which Pilakin could not help but smile.

"Okay, I'll bite. How did you know that?"

The smile on Neuberg's face got wider and she did that head tilt thing again. Pilakin could swear she heard her say *go on; show me what kind of detective you are.*

Think...

"Crustetin!"

Neuberg threw back her head and laughed – a light-hearted, tinkling sound. The kind of laugh one almost never heard in the City.

"Yes, Agent Pilakin. She's one of mine. Have you ever considered coming to work for us?"

"No, I like to get paid for a living."

"That's our perennial problem, being based *here*. It means we end up with people like dear Maximillian. However, from time to time it's important to get things done. We have a budget available for handing out contracted commissions."

"Is this why you invited me here? To offer me a job? Is that so you can stop my investigation? A nice little cover-up now that I've started figuring out what the Federation is up to?"

"So many questions, agent. Which would you like me to answer first? Or maybe I can answer with a question of my own that I'm sure you've already considered. Why bother sending ineffectual orders out to Imperial artillery? Who is it to fool? If you're setting off bombs in the City to look like artillery strikes, who on Home are you trying to divert the attention of?"

Pilakin stared at her. Neuberg leaned forward.

"Me, Agent Pilakin. I suspect they don't want Federation intelligence looking too closely into which artillery batteries have started making a nuisance of themselves only to find out that none of them are."

"Why?"

"In any large organisation people can sometimes have the tendency to go... rogue. I suspect one or more of my colleagues on City Liaison may be up to something."

"Are you investigating it yourself then?"

"I've been sniffing around but they're alive to the danger I pose. Even if I caught them out it would be, as you suggest, a cover-up job. Believe it or not, I think there should be at least a modicum of justice in this world. I would very much like you to get to the bottom of this – the fact that someone is trying to kill you would suggest that you're on the right track."

Pilakin took out her slab.

"How much?"

"Ah, I'm afraid I can't offer you any money now. Releasing funds would leave a paper trail and I have no idea who to trust. I offer you any knowledge I might have and you can call on my assistance if you ever find yourself in a jam."

Neuberg reached out her hand, in which was a business card, and tapped it on Pilakin's slab. All her information appeared in the contacts.

"As for your recompense, I'll make sure that if we *are* responsible for this thing there will be an adequate pay out. What are you on? Fifteen percent?"

"Twenty." Pilakin nodded. Compensation was bigger when the rights litigants didn't get their sticky fingers all over it. It could be handy to have a bit of back-up to call on too.

"I want to run some names past you, major. Jeremiah Flow, Youal Fesh, Zeb Lander, Sarah Flow, Oswin, Wade. Have you heard of any of those?"

"None before my review of your case notes."

"How about Artyom Rimsky?"

"No."

Damn. That was the one she really wanted information on. Hang on…

"How have you seen my case notes?"

"You really need better encryption on that thing."

"But when did you even get access to… oh never mind. Do you have anyone other than Crustetin spying on me?"

"No comment."

Pilakin took stock and stared at the calm, amused face of this irritatingly evasive woman, trying to figure out why she wasn't as annoyed as hell. She sighed.

"Anything you need to know, major?"

"Is there anything you haven't put in your notes?"

"No."

"Then you can consider me fully briefed. What do you plan to do next?"

"I'm going to try and find Rimsky."

"Good. How?"

"You have your secrets. I'll keep mine."

"Fair enough."

"Tell me, major, do you have dealings with the Kristani syndicate?"

"Me or the Federation?"

"Either."

"They're in the consortium that sits across the table from us in City Liaison meetings, along with other syndicates, the City Corporation, the CDA, major companies, the Institute and so on."

Neuberg finished her tea while Pilakin sat chewing her lip and thinking.

"Why do you let them exist?"

"Who?"

"The artillery batteries that are left."

"Mercy."

"Really?"

"Well, they don't shoot at us any more, do they?"

"And there's no other reason?"

"Of course not."

Pilakin stared hard at her but she could not see deceit in her face.

"I'd best be getting on."

Neuberg stood and held out her hand. Pilakin shook it but their hands only touched for a brief second because Neuberg yanked it away as if she had touched something burning hot. She leapt backward, staring at Pilakin in wide-eyed shock. The smile was finally gone. She was breathing hard and eventually gasped, "Anjelik danté insa mirs…!"

"Angels what?"

"They walk amongst us, Jaquelinya Denestra Pilyarkin."

Chapter 23

"HOW DO YOU know that name?"

Neuberg's face had gone pallid and her hands were shaking like Pilakin's did during a monumental hangover. She drew her hands together and clasped them. Pilakin reached out to steady her.

"No! You mustn't touch me. Please step back so I can sit down."

Pilakin hesitated with her hands outstretched. She half withdrew them before finally sinking back into her chair.

"Forgive me, Agent Pilakin. Please don't be concerned. It's just shock – I've not been injured."

"You need to tell me what just happened."

Neuberg looked up at her with what might be tears in her eyes. Difficult to tell with the tattoos.

"You're half Anjelican. Your… mother. She's pureblood."

"What?"

"You're not aware. Why?"

"You need to start making sense."

Pilakin pulled the chair back and sat down. Neuberg took a deep breath and a moment later the look of serenity returned to her features.

"When Anjelicans touch we can tell each other for what we are."

"Aren't we all Anjelican?"

"It's true that inhabitants of this world, Athréa, call themselves Anjelican but the purebloods; we are... different."

"I've heard the stories. The ancient race – they have special powers and live for hundreds of years. Are you seriously telling me that you're one of them?"

"Yes. And your mother is too."

"Stop saying that."

"What?"

"That my mother is one."

"She is."

"Was!"

"Oh, my dear girl. I'm so sorry. What on Home happened?"

She saw Neuberg half reach out her hand, apparently automatically, before stopping and pulling it back.

"I was still a baby. Imperial soldiers killed her."

"No."

"Excuse me?"

"I don't want to cause you pain but it's extraordinarily

unlikely that an Anjelican would die by a human hand unless they allowed it."

"You mean suicide. My father said she gave up her life for me. And him. Or are you suggesting she isn't even dead?"

"Do you know your mother's name?"

"No. My father refused to tell me. Said it would be dangerous for me to know before I was old enough."

"Do you think I can speak to him?"

"No."

"He's dead too?"

"Yes. He died working for the Federation, believe it or not."

Neuberg looked deep into her eyes. "Would you want to know more?"

"Of course. You can look him up?"

"Well, yes I can and will do so. But I meant about your mother."

Pilakin frowned. "You got Imperial records or something?"

Neuberg shook her head. "Those powers that we openly mock; it's easier to ridicule than reveal the truth. When I touched you I could feel the residue of your mother. I broke the connection so quickly because it's taboo to access information about other Anjelicans without their permission. We're not supposed to delve into humans either without dire need."

"You keep talking about humans as separate from you.

Are you alien?"

"We, Agent Pilakin. You're part of this too. What I'm saying is that if you let me touch you for longer I may be able to find out more. Your Anjelican elements will retain residual memories of your mother and I will be able to access parts of your consciousness that you were too young to remember. At the very least I will be able to give you her name."

Pilakin stopped breathing. The silence in the office was sudden and complete. She fancied she could hear whispering in her mind. All she could see were Neuberg's eyes. To know her mother? Of course she wanted that. Neuberg reached out her hand and Pilakin was sure the tingling between their fingers was real.

Pilakin saw her mother's face. She had no real memory of it but she was sure. It was a huge face towering above her. She realised it was her perception. She was being clasped to her mother's breast. Her mother's eyes were wet – Pilakin had no conception of how or why that would be. After feeling the warmth and smelling the mother smell she was taken by other arms. Oh yes, the loud one. The one who hugged even tighter than mother. She saw others – loud. They all looked the same. Apart from their faces. Other than their faces they were the same. They held things in their hands. Long things that pointed at her and her mother and the tight hugger. They looked like giant, black fingers. They looked angry. They were making noise. She looked again at her mother and two of the same-lookers were hugging her. More noise. The tight hugger quivered now and turned with her in his arms so she could see nothing.

"Denestra Illanya."

Pilakin wiped her eyes on her sleeve. "Her name?"

"Yes. I didn't know she or her mother existed. Your grandmother was Tuuca Illanya's sister – *she* never told me she had siblings. To protect them I would guess."

"I recognise that name."

"Tuuca married the king of Simplaerosia. I would guess that's why the Imps wanted her relatives. To get some much needed leverage over the king. That, and they fear Anjelicans. They want us all dead. It's why they hate the Cult of Angels too. The Imps think they're our disciples although we try to have as little to do with them as possible."

"So the Imps *did* kill her?"

"It certainly seems that way."

Rage bubbled up inside her chest and burst. A number rode on top – 639. Quite suddenly 639 did not seem nearly enough. She'd had that thought before though and filled her mind with the faces of the men she had killed.

"You said that would be nearly impossible."

"Unless she let them. You remembered your parting from her?"

"Yes."

"But you wouldn't have understood the speech as your brain at the time couldn't process it. Your Anjelican nature let me hear it though."

"Oh god."

"She bought your life."

PILAKIN REALISED THAT neither of them had spoken for a long while. Maybe a second. Maybe a day. The boom and rumble of an explosion came in through the window. It didn't sound so far away. She rubbed her face and sighed.

"Your name's Leda, isn't it?"

"Yes. Part of me leaked into you. I'm sorry. That was unavoidable."

"What do you mean by *aware.*"

"The offspring of an Anjelican is a potential Anjelican only. It would be dangerous for you to have the full consciousness without maturity and training."

"What is it inside that makes… you didn't answer my question. Are we alien?"

"I'm sorry. I really can't tell you."

"Well, fuck you then. I was happy being who I was. Now you bring me this? I don't want this. Fuck you."

"You certainly were not happy."

"Fuck you!"

Pilakin stood up to leave.

"Jaq."

"What?"

"She's back with you now. If you need her, be still. Look inward. You will find her strength and love inside you."

Pilakin could have screamed but she didn't. For all this witch had just screwed with her mind, maybe she'd just given her a precious gift. Or returned something lost. Why this sudden trickle of compassion? Leda just sat there, looking forlorn. There was more to this.

"I'm sorry."

"I'm sorry too."

"We'll work together?"

"Yes."

The intercom on Neuberg's desk buzzed.

"Major? Lieutenant Metoria is here to see you."

Neuberg's face lit up into the most joyous Pilakin had seen it. She felt a pang of jealousy.

"I'll go."

"Thank you so much, Agent Pilakin."

As she walked out of the office she saw a young woman with a fair face and unusually blonde hair; a pair of wings on her Federation tunic. She glanced up at Pilakin from the magazine she was reading and smiled shyly before glancing to the right and standing up. Neuberg was in the doorway, beaming sunshine.

"Lucy! I'm so glad you're here."

Outside, Pilakin wanted to make a call but figured that reaching into her jacket pocket might activate one of the soldiers' security instincts. Once beyond their cordon, she moved off some distance before jabbing the contact for Sam Lyttle at the ECC-FPA. When he answered there was a lot of noise and sirens in the background.

"Hey, Jaq. Whassup?"

"Sam, I need to have a quick root around in the ECC database."

"I'd love to get away but some shit's kicked off."

"I can come to you."

"Where are you? Somewhere central?"

"Liberty Square."

"Oh, walking distance then. I'm down on Sghntana Street. You'll need your badge to get through the cordon."

"Cool, Sam. I'll see you in ten."

AS SHE APPROACHED Sghntana Street in one of the financial zones, several FPA aircars and a couple of ambulances wailed past. A large crowd parted reluctantly for her badge, and the agents who held horizontal stun poles in a line across the street only let her through after she'd convinced them she had an appointment with Sam. Blue flashing lights on a cluster of vehicles and a tang of dust and smoke in the air indicated this was the site of the explosion she'd heard in Neuberg's office. Winding through the vehicles she came across people walking away from the scene with a variety of vessels and containers, carried as if heavy with liquid. At last she stood next to the site. A large hole had been rent in a wall and water cascaded several metres onto the pavement. A huge wet area indicated that when the explosion had happened a vast torrent must have spread over the whole street. It would be the in-house water stash of one of the big banks leaning over the pavement. People held out containers under the supply while Sam Lyttle repeated the same message periodically through a megaphone mounted on one of the FPA vehicles.

"This water is private property. Any person taking it will be detained on a Sixth Right violation."

She sidled up to him and kissed his cheek. He turned to her, grinning.

"Hey, Jaq."

"They don't seem to be paying much attention to you."

"Well, it's bloody ridiculous anyway. The bank staff have no way of catching the stuff and it's just pouring down the street. Rights Enforcement department say we have to make the effort to stop them, though, or the bank'll sue us for failing to carry out our contracted rights protection duties."

"Who did it? Water Activists?"

"Yes, they called it in five minutes before it went off, so there were no casualties. I don't get it. How does blowing this shit up make water cheaper?"

"They don't want it to be cheaper. They want the ECC to collect it all in and then distribute it equally to everyone as part of the standard service package."

Sam made a face of disgust and threw his hand unit into the car through the open window.

"Get in and we'll fire up the old database connection."

They settled themselves and Sam closed the windows. "What do I get for this?"

"You can strike out another favour from our balance."

"Two."

"One!"

"Come on, Jaq."

"No. By my reckoning we're into the times I saved your life now. Stop your whinging anyway. There's only two left after this one. Then I'll have to start fucking you if I want something."

Sam laughed and logged into the ECC grid.

"I'd rather take the money. What you after, then?"

"I've got a name. I want to know if he's real. Artyom Rimsky."

"Fourteen people by that name on the City records. What else can you give me?"

"Might be a hit-man. Might be into hydroponics. Possible connection to the Kristanis. Does business in a bar called Cubilicious…"

"Okay stop. Only three of the hits have been tagged for investigation. One domestic, one petty stealing. The third has a lot of intel but only one arrest. He's been implicated in protection rackets and Tenth Right violations galore but someone always seems to have been watching out for his interests."

"You say he got arrested once?"

"Yeah, for sure. But some older guy with a fake name turned up with a stack of cash and a shit hot rights-litigant."

Pilakin sighed and used her fingernail to burrow into a scratch in the dashboard and work loose a scrap of plastic.

"So, if I wanted him found, what are the chances?"

"I can give you a list of known associates and locations. According to this he's turned up in so many cases, the crimint guys have built up quite a network around him but unless you have manpower or contacts it'd take a long time to track him down."

She didn't have a long time. She didn't have manpower. Her resources were dwindling significantly. And even if the ECC found him they were never going to crack him open. No. If Artyom Rimsky was going to be a lead there was only one way to play it.

"Give me the data, Sam."

"Two favours?"

"Alright, damn you. Two favours."

Chapter 24

PILAKIN KISSED LARS on the cheek before sitting down opposite, self conscious because of her shabby clothes.

"Have you eaten today?"

"Is that why you suggested the Commanders' Club?"

"I need my evening vittles, Jaq. Since you absolutely had to see me right away and you're barred from Kristani owned establishments, decent eateries became somewhat more limited. Although it was nice to use *your* name to get into a place for a change."

"I'm glad I could return the favour. Don't you think it's ironic that most members can't afford to eat here though?"

Her membership had been granted to her for life along with the honorary rank of Commander that had accompanied one of her CDA medals. She'd even heard a rumour once that it would get her into any Commanders'

Club in the galaxy – even Cambouria.

"Most find themselves a patron, Jaq."

"And you've all but shoehorned yourself into that job anyway. Look, can we talk about why I wanted—?"

Lars raised his hand. "Let us please have a civilised moment. *Have* you eaten today?"

Pilakin felt a certain grim satisfaction in being able to answer in the affirmative. "I had a cooked breakfast and rats for lunch, actually."

"My goodness. This case must be treating you well."

"No, not really. Just the right places at the right times."

Sod it. If Lars wanted to pay for dinner, why the hell was she arguing? Picking up the menu she saw tank-lobsters and tried her best not to blush when ordering them. Lars was speaking to the sommelier.

"We actually got a shipment in last week, sir. I know it is not normal to drink Shupillier with the tank-lobsters but if we ask chef to use it in a butter and spinach sauce, you could make use of the opportunity."

"Yes. Bring the rest of the open bottle…" he glanced at Pilakin across the table, "…and another to drink immediately."

"Certainly, Mr Löring-Kristani."

Lars refused to turn to business until the LaMarquois Shupillier had been poured into appropriate flutes and the bottle deposited into at least a dozen credits' worth of ice in a bucket beside the table. God only knew what the drink itself was costing.

"Don't gulp it."

For once she could feel the weight of distance and difficulty between where the cork had been placed in the bottle and where it had been removed. It was a very long time since she had treated a drink with respect.

"Now. What do you want?"

"Actually I have a business contract for you."

"Really, Jaq? You don't have to—"

"I'm serious. Why won't you ever take me seriously? You always say I come to you for hand outs and I never ask for anything."

"Okay. I'm sorry. I just won't have you on the streets."

Always so tempting to tell him she was already an itee just to prick his bubble but she held back, knowing she would regret it the moment it was out of her mouth. Even though he'd set her up somewhere, like a fucking mistress. No. Like his daughter.

"I need you to pick someone up and find out what he knows."

"You run out of favours at the ECC-FPA?"

"No. But this guy will be hard to get, harder to prove a violation and hardest of all to crack. Even if the ECC did a good job I don't have time for a... rights-compliant interrogation."

Lars leaned back and sighed, allowing the conversation to pause as a waiter refilled their glasses. He leaned forward, placing one fist inside the other and rested his chin upon them.

"It would certainly *have* to be a business arrangement. Given the guy doing the questioning takes on full responsibility for the Rights violation, he has to be paid a commensurate fee. And I can't sub it – don't look at me like that – I mean, I can give you a good rate but this isn't something I can massage the books on. It's a very closely monitored aspect of our business."

"I'm flagged."

"We'll use your client's name."

"How much?"

"Tell me more about the subject."

Pilakin hoped he would know who Artyom Rimsky was but he didn't. She told him everything she knew about the man; description, haunts, known accomplices. She came to an end as the lobsters arrived.

"You have all that in a case file?"

"Of course." She had spent half an hour in a bar before her arrival collating it. Lars looked thoughtful as he set about breaking up his dinner. His silence grew irritating.

"So?"

"Five hundred and twenty."

It was Pilakin's turn to attack her dinner without saying anything.

"Can you make that, Jaq?"

"Can you lend me twenty?"

"Seriously? Your hand is so good that you'll bet everything you have left on it?"

"You have to when you don't have enough to buy into

the next game."

Lars chewed for a while longer, the reflection from the ceiling lights flashing on his glasses as he moved his head to take another sip of Shupillier. He picked up the lobster hammer.

"Are you sure this is really you? The way you really want to operate."

He emphasized his point by setting about the lobster's claw with the hammer; smashing the exoskeleton before cracking open the joint.

"Just do the minimum necessary, will you? Don't kill him; I don't want the number on my conscience going up again…"

"You're paying us so that you don't have any responsibility."

"And having got into the business yesterday in the back of a yeast van, I obviously didn't realise that."

She chugged the full glass in front of her to piss him off further. He just refilled it, inverted the bottle and placed it back in the ice bucket while speaking.

"I don't think I've seen you like this before."

She sighed deeply.

"I guess I just know this is it. If I don't get this one sorted, and soon, then I'm out of the agency game. There'll be no way for me to clear my conscience."

"Don't hate me for saying this, Jaq, but you could do something that actually *saves* lives rather than just investigating murdered ones."

"It's not about the lives. It's about the justice."

"You were born in the wrong city."

"I wasn't."

"What?"

"Oh, never mind."

He reached across the table and held her hand. "Where are you staying tonight?"

"What? This again?"

"You talk about justice. I understand; I feel responsible for you getting fired from the ECC."

"It was my sense of justice that made me give him to you. Justice for her."

"But—"

She pulled her hand away. "I knew what you would do when I handed him over. I'm not a naive inny. I did it anyway because justice demanded it. The path to atonement should not be an easy one, Lars."

"You know I'll always be here for you."

They sat in silence for a moment. She grew uncomfortable.

"Listen, can you order a bottle of something cheaper now? I want to be able to relax while I'm drinking."

OF COURSE, THE answer to where she was going to sleep was simple enough. She'd had enough booze to get her stupid fears about the robot under control but Lars had prevented her getting as rat-arsed as she usually was by this time. Eschewing use of the doorbell, she kicked at the grating until the intercom buzzed to life.

"Hello. Is that you, Freedom Protection Agent Pilakin?"

"Yes it is, Plumber's Receptionist Robot. Is the boss in?"

"My apologies, Freedom Protection Agent Pilakin, but Zeb Lander is currently out on an emergency plumbing project."

"Well, I will come in and wait. Let me in. And just call me Agent Pilakin."

"Yes, Agent Pilakin."

By the time the door began to retract she had her gun out and pointed at where Jess's head would be. It was probably wrong to assume that what passed for its intelligence would be contained within but it would still be the most vulnerable point and the ocular sensors were there.

"Agent Pilakin, please stop pointing that weapon at me. I am programmed to protect my structural integrity."

"I feel my life is under threat and you scare me to the point of mental imbalance."

"In that case I withdraw my objection, Agent Pilakin. May I remove myself from your presence?"

So far, so good. She scanned the garage. The van was gone and she was delighted to find revealed what she had assumed would be there.

"Is that Zeb's tool locker?"

"Yes, Agent Pilakin."

"I assume it's empty."

"Yes, Agent Pilakin. Zeb Lander will have taken the tools on the job."

The sturdy, safe-like construction was large enough to contain two or three people.

"Can the door be operated from the inside?"

"No, Agent Pilakin."

"Do you have a key? Unlock it please."

The robot walked to it, taking a key from a small hatch in its side.

"Hand me the key and step inside."

The robot did so and she locked the door behind it.

"Information. Agent Pilakin, how long do you intend to keep me in here?"

"Until Zeb gets back."

And the rest, she thought with a smile.

UPSTAIRS, PILAKIN SET to work searching the living room. She had hoped to get the opportunity to do so and it was a good break in her luck that she could do it now. Finding little of interest, she quickly turned her attention to the section of wall that had sounded hollow when the robot had walked into it the previous evening. Tapping it with the butt of her gun confirmed her suspicion and she set about searching for signs of a door. Ten minutes later and her frustration was rising. Thinking some tea might have the calming effect she'd heard about, it occurred to her to move the base unit of the kettle. Underneath was a small hatch in the surface of the table with a thumbprint lock.

She pulled out her forensic kit and it was the work of a couple of minutes to dust and find one of Zeb's prints on an unwashed mug. She lifted it and photographed it with her slab, then printed a copy on the receipt-printer. Holding this down on the scanner with her own thumb behind, the lock clicked open. Reaching around the small space inside she found a roll of credit notes, some gold coins, a couple of circuit boards, leasehold documents and finally, reaching far inside, a button. She pressed it and, despite half expecting something of the sort, a click and whirr behind her made her jump and spin round. The wall in the corner had retracted, revealing a darkened room within.

Her gun was back in her hand as she advanced towards it and stood on the threshold for a few moments to allow her eyes to get used to the gloom. She'd heard rumours about plumbers and this sort of thing. Inside was a sink, a toilet and a shower head, although the latter was suspended over some kind of low, oblong box rather than in a shower stall. *Looks like a coffin* she thought and smiled grimly. She holstered her gun and walked inside the room with the intention of filling her water bottle from what was clearly Zeb's secret, stolen supply – there was certainly no way he could afford to pay for this kind of set-up.

Passing the "coffin" she glanced in curiously and promptly dropped her bottle. She leapt back to the doorway, scrabbling to illuminate the torch on her slab.

Switching it on, she advanced just far enough to look in once more. She didn't expect her mental description of the box to be true. Inside lay the body of a young woman. She was clean and looked as if she could be sleeping. Pilakin reached forward.

"Hello?"

She touched the woman's cheek. There was no movement and the skin was cold. She straightened up and looked at the shower head. Was this like one of those morgue slabs? What the hell was Zeb up to? The body was in a good state. No smell even. Was it freshly dead or was he preserving it in some way? Why would he want to? Hell, was he one of those perverted…?

A hand landed over her mouth and roughly dragged her backwards.

Chapter 25

S HE TRIED TO bite the hand over her mouth and made to stamp on her assailant's feet. As a reward for her efforts someone kicked the back of her legs and forced her to her knees. She felt cold steel on her temple.

"You need to stop fighting us now and don't make a noise, okay?"

The gun pressed harder against her head and she nodded. The hand left her mouth and she decided to keep schtum. Someone reached for her holster and pulled out her gun. Oddly, he threw it across the room. Guns were expensive. Why wouldn't he want to keep hold of it? She thought about reaching for the knife at her ankle but didn't know how many of them there were. She felt her slab vibrating for a call and wriggled in the hope of tripping the answer button and letting the caller hear what was happening. Another man, wearing a balaclava, walked in front of her and looked into the hidden room.

"It's a bathroom all right. Actual bath, too. Fucking plumbers."

As he turned back Pilakin saw a blue armband with H2O written on it. Water activists. He clearly hadn't been in far enough to see the body in the gloom. She was conflicted about saying anything to them and had just opened her mouth to do so when a ball gag was roughly pressed in as someone else whacked a set of heavy metal scrapes on her wrists. The first man spoke as he tightened a buckle uncomfortably behind her head.

"We're going to have to make an example of you, plumber bitch. Okay guys, we'll take her down to the car and then come back up and melt this joint to shit."

He yanked her to her feet and now she saw that there were three of them. All with balaclavas and arm-bands. They dragged her through the office and down the stairs. As they reached the bottom all stopped dead and stared at the open garage door. Zeb's van was outside and the man himself stood, mouth agape. A good couple of seconds passed before anyone spoke, but then Zeb called out.

"Jess! Agent Pilakin is in mortal danger."

Pilakin's eyes darted to the tool locker and a fraction of a second later the door buckled and flew away from its hinges, clattering to the floor a couple of metres away. By that time the robot had leapt through the air straight at them. Its arm reached out and as it landed, its fingers closed around the gun in the activist's hand and crushed it. Pieces fell to the floor.

"Would you like me to remove the cuffs, Agent Pilakin?"

The robot's voice was calm; it hadn't become breathless because of its exertion. Pilakin nodded and the sound of the locking mechanism accompanied the loosening of her bonds. Meanwhile, Zeb had drawn his own gun and was covering the activists who had their hands up. She fiddled with the buckle of her gag before tearing at it in frustration. Surprisingly it came apart in her hands but the rage that had given the strength to do that then drove her to the leader of the gang and she punched him hard in the face. He screamed but as she raised her fist for the second blow the robot's hand clamped gently but firmly around it and she was pulled away.

"Let go of me, for fuck's sake."

The robot did so but then stood between her and the activists. All eyes were on her and she looked around defiantly. *Damn it.* This was all too much for her to handle alone so she grabbed at her slab and put in a call. It was answered quickly.

"ECC-FPA, reciprocal services."

"Pilakin 814159. I've caught three water activists who were trying to kill me. I need back up. Prosecution share."

"Usual terms, Agent?"

"Yes"

"Help is on its way."

The last part of the conversation had been difficult due

to shouting from the activists. Pilakin told Jess to take their hoods off. Unremarkable looking guys really. What were they shouting about?

"We weren't going to kill you. Sure, do us for a Second Right but we weren't going to kill you."

"A Second? A Second? You fuckwits. Kicking me was a Second, putting the gag in was a Third, preventing me speaking was a Fourth, tying me was a Fifth, taking my gun was a Sixth and we cap it all off with your Tenth against the First. That's almost a full house, buddy boy. You're going to get your arse handed to you for this one."

"No! We don't kill. We never kill."

"'Make an example of me?'"

"Yeah, by melting your bathroom, trashing your van, putting you in a video…"

"Bathroom?" Zeb interrupted loudly. "What the hell is going on, Jaq?"

Damn. She hadn't wanted to confront him about this until the back-up had arrived. She didn't even have her gun.

"Watch them, Zeb. I need to get my gun."

"Jaq, wait. Jaq!"

She dashed upstairs and grabbed her pistol. As she turned she couldn't help looking into the bathroom once more. The bath was empty. *What the…?* She looked all round the room. Had she imagined the whole thing? The sound of sirens grew nearer so she took a deep breath and went back to the stairs. As she reached the bottom, an

ECC-FPA meat wagon screeched to a halt next to Zeb's van. Half a dozen fully kitted agents leapt out. She hastily yanked out her badge as they advanced, grabbing Zeb and the others. The lead activist looked at her aghast.

"You're an agent?"

"Yes, I'm a fucking agent."

"We thought you were a plumber."

"I'd gathered that, dumbag."

The agent holding Zeb addressed her. "The call said three activists. Who's this guy?"

"The plumber who owns this place."

"You want me to let him go?"

"No, not yet."

"Jaq… what the hell? What's going on for God's sake?"

"He's not covered under the terms of reciprocal services…"

"Just fucking hold on to him for a minute, will you?"

She needed time to think, but another siren announced the arrival of an ECC squad car. She felt a certain measure of relief as Sam Lyttle and his partner emerged from it.

"Twice in one day, Jaq. And you're doing my job for me now, too. Some days it's a delight to know you. What have you got them for?"

She listed the violations and once again the activists objected as she recounted their intention to kill her.

"We were never going to kill you. Look there. The

magazine on the floor." He gestured at the broken parts of his gun. "Take a look. They're drill rounds. Not even blanks. Blanks can hurt people. That gun's just for show. Why do you think I threw your gun away?"

That would explain it…

"You're terrorists."

"Water activists have never killed anyone."

Pilakin looked at Sam, startled.

"Is that true?"

He shrugged.

"I spend some of my time on the water activism task force and haven't had to investigate a related death. I've never seen any threats to kill either."

"The threat was still implied when they put a gun to my head."

"You know as well as I do that rights arbiters argue about that one a lot. So this guy." He indicated Zeb. "What's he done?"

She thought about the dead body that wasn't there. They'd laugh at her or worse. Zeb was clearly stealing water from someone. But he'd probably claim that Jer had put it in and he knew nothing about it. Could this really be what the murder was all about? Water?

"Oh, let him go, for fuck's sake. I need to get out of here."

Zeb tried to stop her although with nine agents present he clearly didn't dare touch her. "Jaq. You can't leave. We need to talk."

She barged past him. As she stepped into the street she heard Sam shouting after her that he needed a full case report for the prosecution. Oh, he could wait for that. She had more pressing concerns right now. Like where she was going to sleep tonight. She took out her slab and looked at the pushes, frowning at the missed call from Sarah. And one from Clem. She read an instant message from Lars as she opened voicemail.

We have our subject.

Her satisfaction was short lived as Clem's agitated voice blurted at her, "Jaq, where on Home are you? The shit has kicked off here, big time. Your guest and her boy are gone. Get down here as quick as you can."

Chapter 26

THE SCENE THAT greeted her in Starlight Sophisticates, to an inexperienced glance, looked fine. But Jaq could see chairs slightly out of alignment, more staff on the door, fewer punters inside and a lack of smiling. Clem appeared in a doorway and beckoned her over.

"Bloody hell, Jaq. What have you got me into this time?"

He led her into the observation room, where she could see every client at their play. Not her first time in such a place, but the first in Clem's. It was such a respectable, quiet joint she could almost have believed there wasn't one.

"Well, what the hell happened, Clem?"

He pushed a chair at her and they sat down in front of the large bank of screens, the staff moving aside to a discreet distance. He tapped away at the screen in front of them and brought up some files on the main display.

"We were having our usual quiet night when these guys rocked up."

He opened a file and the security camera for reception popped up. After a few moments the main doors crashed open and several large men were in, overwhelming the security guards and pushing them to the ground. Once the guards were subdued, another man walked in and led them towards the private rooms.

"You know who these people are, Jaq?"

"That man there," she pointed at one of the first men, "is muscle-for-hire. I've used him for back-up a couple of times. The other big guys must be too. The one leading them now though, I'm not sure…"

Clem tapped a few buttons and the screen split – one showing the outside of Sarah's door and the other inside their room. The thug leader walked up the corridor, checking the numbers, and stopped outside Sarah's. Pilakin realised there was a sound feed as he indicated the door.

"This one."

He knocked on it and Pilakin saw Sarah get up and check the monitors. She clearly seemed shocked and leapt back to hit the room's panic button on the table between the beds. At the sound of the alarm the leader stepped back and the thugs started throwing themselves against the door. Paul started shouting.

"What's going on, mum.?"

"I don't know. Where the Hell's the security? Pile

some stuff against the door, I'm going to call Pilakin."

Paul dragged the beds over as she tapped away at her slab.

"There's no answer."

Pilakin grimaced as she remembered her slab ringing in Zeb's flat. As Paul dragged over the second chair, the door crashed open and a couple more thrusts by the heavies outside scraped the barricades aside.

"Which one do you want, boss?"

"Both of them."

Sarah started screaming but within another couple of seconds the corridor outside was filled with more men. These looked well-dressed, wore dark glasses and carried guns. The thugs outside quickly surrendered and a guy from the new group slapped one of them in the face. "You know who we are?"

The big guy nodded.

"Syndicate."

"At the moment I don't care who you are. Tell me which one's Artyom Rimsky and it'll stay that way."

The thug indicated the small man who had re-appeared from the room and was trying to make a break for it. He shrieked as the suits grabbed him, threatening retribution to his erstwhile posse. The new group's boss went through his pockets and checked Rimsky's face against one on his slab.

"Who do you think these new guys are Jaq?" asked Clem.

"Kristanis."

"How do you know?"

Pilakin tore her eyes away from the screen and realised she couldn't answer that question truthfully.

"Oh… I've done some work with them…"

"You move in some interes—"

"Shush!"

The suits had dragged away the protesting Rimsky and the leader beckoned one of his men. "Go in there and make sure that lady's okay."

He stayed outside to release the thugs, who left in a hell of a hurry, but his man was back at his side very quickly.

"Boss! That's Maggie Poulter."

"You're kidding me."

The leader marched in, scrolling pictures on his slab and held one up next to her face.

"Ms Poulter, will you please come with me?"

Sarah's voice rose. She looked even more frightened than when Rimsky had made his entrance.

"I'm not her. My name's Sarah Flow."

The man moved over to Paul and placed his hand on the boy's shoulder.

"I would very much appreciate it if you came with us, Ms Poulter. I sincerely hope there won't be any trouble."

Sarah's shoulders sagged. "All right."

Pilakin watched as the two of them were handed large Starlight Sophisticate branded dressing gowns from the wardrobe and escorted out of the doors.

Clem looked at her. "The Prozzie Poulters?"

"Fuck. FUCK."

"Whassup, Jaq?"

"I failed investigation one-oh-one. Find out who the hell everyone is. The way she reacted to being here; I assumed she used to be a whore herself. It never occurred to me she might have been a pimp."

Damn, this made so much sense. The fact she had a gun and was confident to use it. The bag she packed so quickly when they'd left her flat. She must have had it permanently ready. It clearly wasn't the first time she'd gone into hiding in a hurry. Clem broke into Pilakin's thoughts.

"So you really think she's one of those Poulters? Didn't the Kristanis stage a hostile takeover?"

"Mhm. About fifteen years ago the Kristanis were diversifying and had almost nothing going on in prostitution. The Poulters had made the mistake of specialising too much."

"So they killed them all off?"

"No. They wanted to take over a functioning operation. Most of the middle and junior guys went over without much fuss. Only the core family, senior management and foot soldiers got massacred. Given Sarah's... well, Maggie's, age I would guess at the time she was the teenage daughter of someone senior. I mean, if the Kristanis are still looking for her."

"Why would they still be bothered after fifteen years?"

"Oh, I don't know, Clem! Give me a bloody minute to think, will you?"

He reached out and stroked her arm. "This isn't good for you, Jaq. You should drop it. Come and work for me."

"I'm not going to whore for you."

"I don't mean that. Come and head up my security team. After what happened tonight, it's clear the guy I have is no good. I'll give you a suite, full board, decent pay. You know the kind of place I run. You can do some good here."

Damn, that sounded so tempting right now. Walk away from it all. Do something simple and good.

"No. Thank you but I've got to see this through."

He sighed. "Okay. But you've got to stop sending me your charity cases."

"Sarah's gone."

"Yes, and I still expect payment for that…"

"Soon, Clem."

"All right, all right, I know. Anyway, I mean this Takani character. What am I supposed to do with him? Maybe he'll look all right eventually but he's pretty beat up. I can't put him in front of the punters like that. He doesn't have experience being a tv-chick either. What possessed you to send him here?"

"Show him the security vid will you? See if he recognises anyone. Especially Rimsky – the one who turned up first. Look. This case will either break or it won't. If it does I'll pay everything I owe and get him set up somewhere else. If it doesn't I'll come and work off my debt to you. Okay?"

"Shit. Are things really that bad?"

"Make or break."

"I wouldn't be sorry to see you out of it."

She managed to smile at him but inside she felt sick. If she couldn't do this maybe her guilt would overwhelm her. In which case, who knew what would happen next. Maybe she'd go move in with Choker.

Get a grip.

It was late and she still had nowhere to sleep that night.

Come on, think.

She reached automatically for her heroettes but instead she found Melissa's micro-eye. She could return it and then plead the late hour for a stay on her sofa or something. She found the address and set off.

IT WASN'T A bad apartment block. A bit shabby and spare but in a decent enough neighbourhood fairly high up over the central district. Its location next to an air filtration plant probably meant rents were lower than they might be on account of the noise. Although, once inside, the sound proofing in the place made that point moot. She took the functioning lift up the 19th floor where Melissa lived. She approached the door and, seeing the broken lock and the door ajar, drew her gun. She crouched and quietly pushed the door open. A strange smell wafted out – a kind of sharp, tart odour that made her nose pucker. She stood and checked the rooms leading off the hallway, gun first. A bedroom, bed made, and a small kitchenette. Then she opened the door facing the entrance, which led into a living room. A woman sat tied to a chair in the middle of the floor. Pilakin couldn't tell who though, because her face was missing.

Chapter 27

PILAKIN SHIVERED AS she finished vomiting into kitchen bin. The thought of going back into the other room repulsed her, but she'd have to. She sat on a stool next to the counter and called Dr Vrijbuiter at LRT Forensics.

"Ah, Agent Pilakin. What can I do for you now?"

"I've got another body. Do you do case-interrelated discounts?"

"Sure. You wanting the full works?"

"No. I can see how this one died. Just need to positively ID the body and sweep the room for evidence."

"You'll have to pay up front again."

"I know but can you take the body as part payment? Deduct the release fee for any relatives who show up?"

"Hmm… okay. That'll take the fee to about four-fifty."

Damn. She'd have to use the money she'd promised to Lars.

"Fine."

"Give me the address, then."

She steeled herself to go back into the room to see if she could find anything before LRT showed up and charged her for finding it. The sound proofing would mean that anything happening in here probably wouldn't be heard in other apartments. She studiously ignored the body as she went round the room, although the tart, vinegary smell with the sweet smell of the start of putrifaction was all-pervading. A few pieces of furniture looked like they'd been knocked out of place and one or two items, like a framed photograph of a small girl, lay on the floor. The only object of real interest lay in front of the body. It was Melissa's engineering kit, scattered and smashed to pieces, like every piece had been removed one by one and broken deliberately. Finally she could put it off no longer and turned her attention to the body. The feet were a bloody mess and it appeared as if something had eaten away the flesh. White bone peeked out of the ruins. Further up the legs, huge holes had eaten into the tops of her thighs and the mess that used to be her genitals had Pilakin fighting down the urge to heave again. The breasts were absent entirely, ribs showing in the place where they had been. Finally the face looked as though it had both burned and melted. The mouth was wide open, the teeth fully on show as there were no longer any lips to cover them. The nose was flat and it was difficult to tell whether the eyes were still there.

The killer had started with the tools of her trade – destroying her kit could put her out of work. The victim clearly could not or would not answer the questions, so the killer had moved on to hurting her. Pilakin sat heavily on the sofa and put her head in her hands. She kept thinking of the body as 'this woman' but she could not see how it would be anyone other than Melissa. And it was equally clear that this had happened because she had been drawn into the case. Maybe this was a warning to clear off. The perpetrator was pure evil, but then her thoughts turned to what might be happening to Rimsky right now. Things she had put in motion. For a moment she considered calling Lars and telling him to lay off but lost the urge as she remembered Rimsky was at least involved with the people who had done this. A large sob caught her unawares but acted as a flood gate and she started to cry and couldn't stop. She bent over double and fell off the sofa and onto the floor, curling up into a ball and crying like she hadn't since Itzie had died in front of her. He'd melted too but on that occasion, at least fate had spared his beautiful face.

She couldn't remember having fallen asleep or passing out. Either way she was awakened by Dr Vrijbuiter prodding her with his foot and demanding payment.

"You okay?" he asked as he counted out her credit notes.

"Yeah. It's just… you know… that body is…"

He nodded. "Yes. That's one of the nastier ones I've

seen. I wonder if he cut her vocal cords before he started."

"I don't think so. He wanted information. You reckon the killer was a guy then?"

"The pattern of the injuries would suggest a certain sadistic sexual pleasure."

"You thinking acid?"

"That, Agent Pilakin, is an opinion you have not paid for."

"Oh come on. Look at her. Throw me a bone will you?"

He sighed and turned to his assistant.

"Go and dust for fingerprints in the other rooms?"

The assistant eyed them both and then departed. Vrijbuiter closed the door behind him and gestured for Pilakin to stand by it.

"If he reported seeing me do something that hadn't been paid for I'd probably get fired." He walked over to the body and took an instrument out of his bag. Using a small pair of scissors he cut some flesh away from the burned face and dropped it into a chamber in the top of the instrument. A moment later he read the results.

"Given the bizarrely high levels of fluorine compounds, I'd say the agent used was Hydrofluoric Acid."

"Acid?"

"Yes. It's used as a precursor for various things and it even burns through glass. Very nasty stuff – even if you survive the initial burns it's a slow-acting poison. There was never any intention of letting this woman survive. Okay, you can step away from the door now and I'll get on with the bit you paid for."

Ten minutes later he confirmed that it was Melissa Walden's body and another twenty minutes after that he and his assistant concluded the killer had left no fingerprints or DNA evidence behind. Neither surprised Pilakin in the least.

It was after 3am when they finally left with the body. Pilakin barricaded the front door with furniture from the living room and then gratefully crawled into Melissa's made bed.

She's out there to find some officers that have been reported in the area. Itzie is with her because it's a really hot zone – lots of Imp activity – and she needs someone to watch her back while she focuses on her sights. A forward CDA patrol is engaging the Imps while she lies on some higher ground behind, waiting to pick off anyone who looks like they're giving orders. She listens in to the CDA comms and it sounds like the engagement is not going well. She can see the Imps trying to turn their flank but she can't say anything for fear of giving away her position. An Imp waves at his comrades in an attempt to move advance; to get behind the CDA troops. His soldiers appear reluctant and he points his pistol at one of them. They move on. Officer or NCO? Doesn't matter. He's the one. Rot him and the rest will run. The chatter in her headphones tells her the CDA troops are finally alive to the danger. She ignores them and finds the lion badge.

"Itzie. You see the guy at oh-niner-four with a pistol in his hand?"

"Sure."

"Confirm range and conditions."

Her rifle sight and HUD between them tell her what she needs to know but it's always best to confirm with manual measurements from your partner.

"Range to target one five two metres. Elevation minus one six giving you a downward angle of six degrees on the nose. Wind speed seven kilometres per hour with a cross component left to right of four and headwind of five and three quarters. What will this be, Jaq? Six-three-eight?"

"Hush."

She makes the final adjustments to her sights and brings the cross hairs back onto her target, who's mustering his men for the final push. The lion on the badge flashes into her crosshair and she squeezes the trigger. Split seconds later the man throws his hands up, his pistol flying into the air. Having lost her target she sets her scope back to wide view. The men around him dive to the ground before casting around panicky looks for the source of their leader's death. She resists the urge to shoot another to maintain her cover and grunts with satisfaction as the first jumps to his feet and runs pel mel back to his lines. Another follows a couple of seconds later and, with the dam burst, the rest follow in short order. Itzie nudges her.

"What do you recon, Jaq? Six-three-nine now? Six-forty for your birthday? Stay out for two more?"

Having checked for no more movement on the flank, she turns away from her sights and lets Itzie kiss her.

"Shut up."

They both smile for a moment but then she frowns as she listens to the chatter from the CDA unit. The boss hasn't seen what's happened and is starting to panic.

"Hey, I don't like the sound of..."

She breaks off as she hears the commander call in a firerain strike for 300 metres around his position. A Simplaerosian jet responds almost immediately. In 20 seconds it will fly over and fill the air with flammable vapour before turning and setting it alight. They don't have time to run out of the zone. The look on Itzie's face shows he heard and is having the same thoughts.

Be calm!

Firerain is used to kill Imps on top of you while you survive in your breath and shiny. Don't panic. She throws off her helmet and grabs the gasmask from her belt, pulling it over her head. She watches Itzie do the same. They pull their thermally insulated, highly reflective blankets out of pouches. She puts her feet into one end and pulls it up and over her back, crouching down in one fluid motion so she's like a tortoise in her protective shell. As she bends down she has her eyes on Itzie and the last thing she sees is a rip about five centimetres long across his back. She can hear the screaming engines of the jet approaching. She panics. She almost gets up but that might kill her. She screams herself.

"Itzie, get on your back!"

"What? Why?"

"You have a tear on your back."

The engines are so loud.

"What? I can't hear you."

Liquid pours over her blanket, making even more noise, as if she's been thrust under a shower."

"Itzieeeeee…"

She hears the jet turning and a second later there's a rumble as loud as a battery firing. The temperature in her cocoon rises immediately and keeps on rising. Every time she's used the shiny it's felt like she's being cooked. But this time she ignores it because, above the rumble of the fire surrounding her, she hears her lover screaming. She imagines the burning liquid pouring in through the crack, filling the space inside. She imagines the torment he must feel wondering if it would be better to throw off the blanket. It's supposed to be a humane weapon, the burning vapour in the air devouring the available oxygen and plunging the victims into unconsciousness before they burn to death. Finally, the temperature stops rising and the noise fades. Her HUD flashes the all clear and she throws off her blanket. She stumbles across to Itzie's curled up form. Smoke rises from the hole in his shiny and she smells the reek of burning, all the more sickly for being from the one she cares most about in the world.

His screaming has become hoarse and she sobs as she

rolls him over and pulls away the blanket. Most of his clothing comes with it and what must be skin too. His raw and bleeding body is exposed and she summons the courage to lift off his mask. It has protected his face. He stops screaming and takes a deep breath as she grabs a curette of morphine and bangs it into his arm.

"My angel. My own personal angel."

Pilakin yanks off her own mask. "Hush Itzie. It's not as bad as it feels."

"It feels like hell."

He groans again and tears fill his eyes. His face projects despair for a moment and he squeezes his eyes shut. Then his expression clears and he opens them again.

"I need the second curette. And a third one too."

"No, Itzie. You can't ask me to…"

"Marry me."

"What?"

"Marry me Jaquelinya."

She is crying full flow now. She nods and speaks with as steady and clear a voice as she can muster.

"I, Jaquelinya Denestra Pilyarkin, declare that Itzick Zilberman is… is my husband. I promise that this state will exist between us for the rest of our lives."

"Me too, Jaq. Me too."

She looks down at his destroyed body and accepts he's never going to survive. She looks back at his face and sees the unbearable pain under the happiness of what they have just done.

"I love you."

"I love you."

She stabs two more curettes into his arm and then kisses him deeply. She inhales his final breath and takes part of him inside her forever.

639.

Chapter 28

THE SOUND OF furniture scraping across the floor in the hall awoke her. Someone had opened the door very slowly, probably trying to be quiet. She reached under the pillow for her gun and adopted a sleeping position where she could see the bedroom door and cover it with her pistol below the sheet. She heard the intruder, treading lightly, walk down the hall to the living room. After a few seconds she heard the steps returning and the bedroom door slowly opened. A man with a gun in his hand advanced into the room and froze when she spoke.

"I've got you covered. That's quite far enough my friend."

"Pilakin?"

"What the…?"

She sat up and switched on the bedside light. Agent Manstein stood facing her, shielding his eyes from the sudden glare. She threw the lamp at him and shouted.

"Goddammit. Manstein, you creepy bastard. What on Home do you want?"

"I came looking for you. We need to talk."

"How did you find me?"

"Look. There's a bar called the Potter's Wheel about fifty metres down the road. I don't like talking with a gun in my face, so why don't I go there to wait while you get dressed? I'll stand you a breakfast."

"What time is it?"

"Seven thirty."

"Oh, for crap's sake, Manstein. Why're you getting girls out of bed at this time?"

"I'll see you soon."

He turned and left.

TEN MINUTES LATER Pilakin walked into the bar. She felt rough despite having found some water in Melissa's kitchen and some aspirin, too. Manstein waved at her from a booth near the back and, when she arrived at the table, she found upon it a full cooked breakfast, coffee, a half-bottle of vodka and two packets of heroettes. She eyed Manstein suspiciously as she sat, noticing that he had what she now knew to be a pot of tea in front of him.

"What are you after?"

"Nothing."

"Vatshit."

He pulled the stopper out of the bottle and poured generous measures into two of the earthenware cups that were clearly the theme of the place. It was rare to find any vessels in the city that weren't plastic or metal. He raised his cup in salute.

"Hair of the dog."

She watched him down it before taking her own. It was good quality and sat in her stomach like a hot stone. She fished a heroette out of its packet and lit up.

"So?"

"I'm here to apologise."

"Ah. For what?"

She felt she'd shown an adequate period of disdain for the breakfast and now attacked it with hunger.

"I've been using you."

"You're still working my case?"

"No. I've been doing one of my own. I got hired by an outfit the ECC put together to track down Water Activists. I knew Flow was on their hit list but you found him first. So, I gave you Fesh and then sat on top of your case, waiting for the moment when the activists got involved again. Unfortunately, when you got them you handed them straight over to the ECC."

"You've been keeping tabs on me? How? I can't believe you've managed to follow me around."

"When I gave you my case notes I put a spyware programme in there too."

"You crafty sod. Why are you telling me now?"

"The ECC have frozen me right out of the enforcement case. Say you've done a prosecution share with them."

"Aha. So you *do* want something."

"Let me in will you, Pilakin? I'm not asking for your full stake but just enough to get some leverage. You know what reputation means in our game. If you do, my outfit will chuck a lot of work your way from now on."

Pilakin downed another vodka and poured herself some coffee. Were the activists responsible for Flow's death? From what Sam said and the incident at Zeb's place, it didn't appear to be their normal line of business. She couldn't see the ones she'd met doing those hideous things to Melissa either. Her gut was saying they weren't involved in her main investigation, in which case Manstein's offer would be a good one. On the other hand she had nothing to lose in waiting to see how things played out before making a decision. If it fell apart, maybe she could get a job with his organisation.

"Give me a few days to decide, will you? I'll make sure nothing happens in the meantime."

He smiled at her. "You don't think they did it? The evidence seems very strong to me."

"Stop reading my notes, you bastard."

She pulled her slab out and slid it across the table. "Now get that spyware out of there. I assume there's a tracker too."

He nodded and tapped away for a moment or two before handing it back. He'd set a security scan running so she could see it was clean.

"Okay then, Pilakin, I'll wait to hear from you. If you need any help just give me a shout."

"I'll be fine."

"Oh, one other thing. I hired some muscle to help me out. A guy called Artyom Rimsky. He's dropped out of circulation and I can't get hold of him. Have you any idea what's happened? I know you were looking into him."

She felt cold inside but managed to keep her face neutral. "No idea. I've not been able to find him either. So he's your man? I thought he was the guy who's been trying to kill me."

"I'll admit he's a shady character but he was ideal for trying to get Flow to sign up to something dodgy and thus smoke the Water Activists out. Listen, I sent him to go get Sarah and her son."

"The hell you did. Why? You had no right."

"I heard chatter that the Activists had found out where they were. I thought they were in immediate danger. I was going to contact you as soon as Rimsky told me he'd got them but that was the last I heard from him."

"You should have contacted me first. I mean, shit Manstein, you've been using me and my case as bait."

"I know. And I've said I'm sorry but I think if you interrogate the activists you caught, you'll have it all tied up. And I won't try to muscle in on that action. I want them for other things. I gave you Fesh, remember, and I'll stick to that."

"Oh, very munificent of you."

"We're all just trying to make it, Pilakin. I think you and me could make a great team. Ah well – if you find Rimsky, will you tell him I'm looking for him?"

"Okay, sure. But now I have things to do."

"Thank you."

Standing, she downed the last of her coffee and picked up the heroettes and vodka before briskly walking to the door. Once outside she hurried round the corner and into an alley. She called Lars and fought down her frustration at getting his answer phone.

"Hey, Lars, it's Jaq. Listen. Whatever you're doing to Rimsky can you pause it? Please? It's important. Keep asking questions but dial back on the other stuff okay? Call me."

Shit.

None of this was making sense. Just when she thought she was finally getting somewhere, Manstein turns up and drops his little bombshell. She needed somewhere to sit down and review the case. Checking a map, she saw that Gursky Park was not far away and ten minutes later was queuing to pay a credit to get in. She glanced enviously at the large apartments surrounding it, with views of actual living vegetation; desirable despite the hoards of people. The entry fee, as well as paying for the park's upkeep, was supposed to keep out the dregs. She found an empty chess table under a tree and placed the vodka bottle on it alongside her slab. She took a couple of swigs and opened the case file, perusing the tangled web of links and suppositions.

Zeb, of course, was at the heart of it all. Jer had pretty much ruined their business but with him gone, Zeb had been divested of all his personal debt and had inherited the van, premises and tools. Barring any personal debts he had, at a stroke, put the business back on to a sound footing with only a silent partner taking a share of the profits. There was also the matter of the body in the bath. Where had it gone? Was it there in the first place or was she going mad? Unfortunately, although this was all good reason to point to Zeb for the initial murder, achieving it seemed like the work of an organisation, as did the subsequent attacks on Sarah. Or Maggie, as Pilakin was now going to have to get used to thinking of her.

So was this the syndicates? They'd taken Paul and Maggie and she, Pilakin, had been red-flagged on their records since the very start of the investigation. On the other hand, it was their bloody hit-list to start with. If they'd wanted Jer dead, they could have just green-lit him and sat back. The motive though? She wasn't sure, but it would presumably have something to do with Sarah. Maggie.

Could *she* be the culprit? Like Zeb, Jer's financial mis-gambles had directly impacted upon her life and, more importantly Pilakin suspected, that of her son. The woman was certainly of more sturdy construction that she appeared when the surface was scratched. No surprise really, given that it turned out she'd been raised a Poulter.

So there was certainly some sort of syndicate politics going on. It also hadn't surprised Rimsky as to who she really was. Who'd had access to her case files? Neuberg over at the Federation, certainly. But she'd been the one who asked for help and was suspicious of others in her organisation. It would seem to be an unfeasible double-bluff to throw suspicion away from her and on to others in the Federation when Pilakin's attention had not been on her anyway. She closed her eyes and drank more vodka to blank out the memory of what had happened in Neuberg's office as best she was able.

But it turned out Manstein knew as well. But *he'd* claimed it was all about the Water Activists. There was a lot of evidence stacked against them. Their bungled kidnapping at Zeb's place. The use of acid on Melissa – and presumably on the wailer that failed to sound when Jer was originally killed. That certainly connected the two incidents in a city where acid was hard to come by and the Activists had somehow a ready supply for their use in their attacks on metallic pipes and tank infrastructure. They had their grudge against plumbers, especially ones who went into private practice, as Jer had. There had been an attack on her at the same moment someone was trying to attack Sarah. A hell of a coincidence, again smacking of organisation.

A thought occurred that maybe Zeb and the Activists had something in common there. Zeb wanted to get back to City contracts and the Activists would certainly see that as the lesser of two evils. Zeb had also been conveniently out when they had grabbed her in the flat but, on the other hand, he'd returned in the nick of time to get her out of the situation. Coincidence? Unlikely. Could RK4Jess have alerted him? She was locked in the tool cupboard and Pilakin had already seen she needed to use the phone for calls.

It was a mess of too many possibilities. She had to focus on her one truly solid lead. Rimsky. Although now she blanched as she thought what he might be going through after Manstein's revelation. She picked up her slab and called Lars' office again. This time it was answered almost immediately.

"Lars Löring-Kristani's Office. Rehabilitation and liaison. How may I help you?"

"Hello. This is a personal call. Can I get straight through to him?"

"I'm sorry, Mr Löring-Kristani is not available at the moment. Is that you, Agent Pilakin?"

She felt her heart shrink. "Yes. Has he left a message?"

"No, Agent. Mr Löring-Kristani is currently under a minor investigation. Nothing to worry about. However, some of his evidence could really do with a spot of corroboration."

The woman on the phone lowered her voice and spoke in more conspiratorial tone.

"Listen. I'm sure it would really help if you came in. Jaq, isn't it? He said, if you called, he really needed your help. You should come straight to our office. You know where it is, right? Between you and me he's in real trouble this time. I'm so worried. Please will you—?"

Pilakin cut off the connection. *Shit.* Was this to do with the red flag? The case? Sarah or Maggie? Or something else entirely? But they knew her name. The very last thing she should do right now was head down to their headquarters. On the other hand, he'd probably kept Rimsky away from the books for now and she needed some answers. She laid her head down on the table, the cool erith like a burn-poultice on her brow.

"AGENT PILAKIN, AS I live and breathe."

She looked up blinking, her head not in pain but in that kind of dizzy precursor.

"Neuberg?"

She sat down on the other side of the table and eyed the vodka bottle. Fuck her judgement.

"You want some?"

"No thank you agent. I have other vices."

Neuberg pulled a packet of cigarettes out of her inside pocket and offered one to Pilakin. She took it and lit up with her own lighter. Surprisingly it was just tobacco, but with a taste she had barely thought could be so rich and lacking in lung abrasion. She looked at the packet and saw the broken seal of the royal tariff. Neuberg waved away the smoke and smiled.

"Simplaerosian. If I'm going to smoke something, it

helps to have friends in high places."

"You following me around now?"

"It might be helpful to do so to stop you falling over… but, no. I happen to have a house next to the park."

"A house?"

"Yes. I know – how could I possibly? It was… ah… in the family before the siege."

"Vatshit."

She smiled. "It doesn't actually matter whether you believe me or not. Although do ask yourself whether I'd follow you around or send a minion to do it."

Pilakin dragged on the smooth cigarette and regarded Neuberg's calm eyes for a moment or two.

"Hey, listen. Let's say I have a meeting I need to go to but can't possibly attend in the other person's house. Could you help me out with that?"

"To do with the case?"

"Pretty much."

"Who's involved?"

"A syndicate."

She took a couple of drags, slowly, and looked up at where a real bird with a yellow face and blue wings had started singing some kind of discordant tune in the branches of the tree above their heads.

"Sure. I can arrange that. How soon?"

"Today. Ideally in the next couple of hours."

Neuberg stubbed out her cigarette, only three-quarters smoked, on the table, before flicking the remainder away.

"Is it that important?"

"Yes."

"Okay. Give me the details. Someone will call you in the next half hour."

Chapter 29

IT DIDN'T LOOK like much from the outside. It was one of those streets filled with the usual rough-looking apartments, although an unusual number had hangings in the windows. Elsewhere in the city this would be a cause for comment and anger, but this many clearly signalled that everyone was expected to mind their own business. As Pilakin approached the address, she noticed that, where the other doors had multiple buttons for the various apartments within, this one had a single doorbell. About to press it, she stopped as someone cleared his throat right by her ear. The door was in a small porch and she hadn't seen the shadowed alcove beside her where a large man was standing, wearing shades and a visible gun holster.

"Can I help you?"

"My name's Pilakin. I'm here for the meeting."

He checked a small list in his hand.

"Very good ma'am."

He reached out and pressed the bell for her and a male Federation soldier in full gear opened the door. Inside, another soldier, female this time, stood to the other side of the door. Between the two soldiers stood a striking officer; tall and athletic, and wearing a black uniform tunic with the collar of a crisp, white shirt emerging at her neck, to which the three bars of a captain were pinned. The badge on the tunic was the same as she had seen on Major Neuberg, denoting she was in the Intelligence command. Her highly tattooed face, with several piercings, was framed by black, glossy hair that looked as though it had been ironed flat and her wide piercing blue eyes bore an expression of suspicion and contempt in equal measure. She licked her lips and looked Pilakin up and down before speaking.

"You're the Agent then, I guess."

"Pilakin 814159."

She held out her badge and the officer checked it with an instrument.

"Please hand over your weapons."

She removed her gun and knife from their holsters and put them on a table where several firearms already lay.

"Now, Agent Pilakin, I'm sorry to say I am going to have to ask you to waive your Third and Fifth Rights for a moment and agree to a body search." She didn't sound sorry about it at all. "Which of our lovely volunteers would you like to submit to?"

She smiled as she checked out the guy, who stood

implacably, but when she caught the officer smirking at her, stepped to the female soldier. After a thorough groping, the officer escorted her up the stairs and into some kind of dining room where several figures were seated around a long table. In the middle, facing her, was Major Neuberg, who smiled and indicated she should sit down in the chair in opposite. To the left end sat Lars with a syndicate goon uncomfortably close beside him, although she was relieved to see he looked smart and unharmed. He was not prevented from speaking.

"Thanks for coming Jaq, but I'm sure we could straighten this out without your involvement."

"You and I have unfinished business that can't get done unless you're out and walking around."

"How are you, Jaq? How is it going? Have more—?"

"Stop talking, now."

That was the man at the other end of the table. He was bald and the shape of a bullet, although he wore a suit at least as expensive as Lars'. He had a goon of his own and Pilakin reflected for a moment that taking away everyone's guns hadn't made the meeting safe so much as tipping it entirely in favour of the heavies. Well, to hell with them.

"I don't know who you are but in this city we have something called the Fourth Right."

Bullet-head gave her an unpleasant, sneering smile.

"And I have made no threat against it, Agent Pilakin. But this is a syndicate meeting and we do not acknowledge such rights or your authority to protect them. It just so happens that it is not taking place in a Syndicate facility. So, let's just forget the niceties and get down to fucking business."

Neuberg, who continued to wear her serene smile, interjected. "Mr Kristani, while you are in my house I would ask that you keep things civil. Captain Hashan, please will you step inside?"

The door behind Pilakin opened again and the officer from downstairs marched around the table to stand behind Neuberg.

"Gentlemen. Agent. The good captain has certain non-lethal enforcement tools about her person. I do hope I will not have to call upon her services. Good. Now, Mr Kristani. I believe this is some form of disciplinary hearing?"

"Who the hell do you think…?" retorted the Bullet but his response died on his lips as he met Neuberg's gaze. He shifted uncomfortably in his seat before turning his attention back to Lars. "I have been asked by the Executive Committee…"

Lars snorted.

"What?" said Bullet in a voice that made Pilakin's neck hairs bristle.

"You mean you badgered them for years until a bare majority…"

"I have been asked by the executive committee to look into your relationship with this woman." He indicated Pilakin. "Payments made, courtesies extended, information given and all for very little apparent return on investment. The reason I have been… the committee has tasked me with looking closely into your affairs now is that you have continued to meet with her after a red flag was placed on her file. Put simply, Löring, what the hell is going on?"

Pilakin banged the table. "What on Home have you asked me here for if you're just going to talk *about* me rather than *to* me?"

Lars laid both hands in front of him.

"Jaq, please let me answer Edward's somewhat bizarre allegations. Jaq Pilakin is a friendly and honest Freedom Protection Agent with a strong sense of discretion. She is investigating a murder with a connection to our organisation. Rather than embarrass anyone or make things awkward, she came to see me quietly."

"And you gave her all the information she wanted. What kind of syndicatist are you? Our business is our business. Certainly not an agent's."

"Even when our policies are being breached?"

"Internal matters. We know how to deal with our own as you well understand. Or you will do soon, anyway."

"Surely we should take every step we can when our members' money is walking out of the door."

"Oh, for fuck's sake, Löring. You banging on about those uncleared bounty payments again?"

Pilakin half jumped out of her chair but no further as Captain Hashan's hand moved to the top of a stunstick at her belt. She looked accusingly at Lars instead.

"Why didn't you tell me?"

"Tell you what?"

"Don't get cute. That there'd been other bounty payments."

"Despite what Edward says, I stay firmly within the spirit of our policies. I gave you only enough information for your case to progress. Hopefully you'll also find out enough for me to clear up our own problem."

"Löring!"

It was Bullet's turn to almost get out of his chair. Lars finally raised his voice.

"Edward. This isn't really about Jaq. I know all about your fuck-buddy in the ECC contracts directorate and that teenager from Fed Intelligence you think you've got wrapped around your little finger."

"I'm not the one under investigation. Tell me what binds you to this woman and tell me now."

Lars sat with his jaws clenching.

Oh for gods' sake, thought Pilakin. *I need him out of this. I need Rimsky's information, if nothing else.* Bullet rose out of his seat with an air of finality, so she blurted out.

"The Society Slasher."

"Jaq, no."

"I'm telling him, Lars. I don't know what the beef is between you two but we can't chuck everything away. Mr Kristani, do you have children?"

He'd sat down again. She saw on his face the expression of someone about to crack open a secret sought by many. It was the first time he looked straight at her.

"Two sons and a daughter."

"Then maybe you'll understand. You do remember the Society Slasher?"

"Of course. He raped and tortured his way through the debutants of Engalise."

"I was the deputy lead detective on the ECC investigation team."

"Well, doesn't that just make you a fucking great detective then? Best financed and highest profile case in the last decade and you never got him. What's that got to do with us?"

"The twelfth victim was a seventeen-year old called Nicola Shelbourne."

"What about her?"

Pilakin looked at Lars and he sighed before speaking quietly.

"She took her mother's name."

Bullet finally calmed a little.

"And this Pilakin's been looking ever since?"

Pilakin looked back at him.

"No. Although Lars gave me a lot of support in pursuing the case and we became... friends."

"Then...?"

"I found the perp after the nineteenth victim. His name was Jonathan Westfry."

This time it was Neuberg who interjected. "Son of ECC Finance Director, Gordon Westfry?"

Pilakin nodded.

Neuberg leaned back in her chair and sighed. "Yes. We guessed it was him too. Of course you were working for the ECC, so I suppose that wasn't a fortunate conclusion to reach."

"You could say. I admired my boss's balls though. He detained the bastard, put together the perfect case file and sent it up the chain. Thirty-six hours later he was transferred. I got made lead and told to hand Westfry over to over to a Finance Directorate team that would be with me in a couple of hours. I got hold of some contacts at HQ and found out there was a plan to get him out of the city."

"And you gave him to Lars instead." That was Bullet. He turned his attention back to Lars. "How long did he last?"

"I booked the room for ten days but he only made three. I should have let him sleep."

Despite taking 19 off her 639 in one go, Pilakin shivered as she always did when she thought about that. Bullet grinned at her unpleasantly. "I bet you were popular."

Lars responded for her.

"I pulled every string I had. I went to all the other victims' parents – a lot of rich and powerful people. One was even an ECC board member. Talk about shitting where you eat. In fact that one was the first. Anyway, Jaq was fired but managed to stay credentialed. The father, Gordon, was forced to quietly resign. And a video of his bastard son's punishment was made available to anyone who felt it would help bring them closure."

They all sat in silence a moment before Bullet stirred in his seat.

"Not good enough."

"Now hang on…"

Neuberg leaned forward in her seat.

"Mr Kristani. You don't think this is sufficient reason for a debt to exist here?"

Bullet glowered at her but said nothing.

"Well, then maybe you could help me with something. You and Mr Löring-Kristani are both junior executives; am I right?"

He grunted an affirmative.

"And yet he keeps Löring in his name whereas you, like only the most senior and most junior, are simply Mr Kristani. Are you by any chance a member of the core family?"

"No."

"No indeed. I think there is another reason for this animosity between you."

"What business is it of yours?"

Neuberg turned her back on him and spoke to Lars.

"What happened to your career after the… Westfry incident?"

It was Lars' turn to look uncomfortable. Pilakin

wondered why they were answering this woman's question like lambs. Not a woman, of course.

"I was promoted."

"Why had you not been before?"

"There were questions as to my reliability."

Bullet snorted but Neuberg ignored him.

"How did these questions arise?"

"Because of my performance in running a take-over."

Bullet really did jump out of his seat this time and Pilakin noted that Neuberg held out her hand to restrain Hashan's response.

"Hah. You fucker. I'm glad they screwed you over for that. A lot of my associates died. My friends and family too."

Lars looked him in the eye, defiantly.

"You fought, you bloody idiots."

Neuberg quietly interjected once more.

"Which take over were you in charge of, Lars?"

"The Poulters."

Chapter 30

BULLET BANGED HIS fist on the table.

"I knew it. I knew you were the one. Now, you're going to pay, you fucker."

Pilakin began to figure out what was going on and spoke aloud her theory to Bullet.

"So, you were a middle ranker and, because your syndicate fought back, despite being kept on in the new structure, you were stripped of your name and identity."

"Yes. I don't know how you missed me, Löring, you bastard. But I'm still here. I'm a real Poulter as well. Junior cousin but a real one."

After sitting dumb for so long, Pilakin's mind was finally working again.

"You're missing the crucial point here. Lars? Why were you promoted after killing Westfry?"

"Because I proved I had the aggressive attitude needed for senior management."

"And why was there doubt about that?"

"Because the board felt that, despite excellent business handling, I showed weakness in not going after the senior Poulters' wives and children. After some of my juniors took matters into their own hands and started rounding them up, it was leaked from my office what was happening and the remainder were able to go into hiding."

Bullet laughed in a sneering way.

"Yeah, right. And that just hasn't come up before. What makes you think that I'm going to cut any slack now?"

"Because yesterday evening my department picked up Maggie Poulter."

It was the first time Pilakin had seen Bullet on the back foot. His jaw slackened a little and a certain pallor became evident in his features.

"Maggie…?"

"Yes, Edward. Your cousin's daughter."

"She's alive. How did you find her?"

Lars glanced at Pilakin and she realised it would not be a good moment for the truth. "Never mind that. Just part of my rehabilitation programme. Project loose-ends I suppose."

"You're lying."

"No. Look at the F: drive under missing persons and you'll see a video of her in processing."

Bullet examined his slab for a moment or two and Pilakin could tell the moment he saw the video by the extraordinary expression of joy and anger that crossed his face.

"Where is she?"

"Under protection."

"You bastard. This is beyond—"

"Edward, listen to me. I am serious about my rehabilitation scheme. I have paperwork and litigants ready to take everything to the leadership. I think it's time for the name Poulter to come back. Let's get everyone out of hiding. I think we could be stronger for it. You're angry, I know, so I couldn't suggest it before. But if you bring me down now, then my staff will have to follow the normal clean-up procedures that I *should* have followed the first time round. Come on. Isn't it time for a new, moderate faction? You and I have more in common than most of the other senior executive candidates and more experience in scrapping our way up. Two seats next time – can't we fight to fill them together, Mr Poulter-Kristani?"

The conflict in his mind was clear to see but Pilakin guessed that every moment he did not speak, it was more likely he would acquiesce. Clearly holding a gun to a relative's head was more "business as usual" than an outsider would assume, given Edward's eventual decision.

"Okay, Löring. We're not going to be friends but I think we can work together. I'm assuming you're not handing her over until we succeed but I want your word that she'll be looked after."

"Of course, Edward. And I'll make it clear to her that

she isn't in any danger. She isn't, is she?"

"No."

He stood up to leave.

"I'll have my PA draft a memorandum of understanding. Then we can plan our strategy."

With a nod, he walked out and his goons followed. Pilakin looked at Lars, expecting to see relief, but instead he was smiling. Neuberg lit a cigarette and blew smoke across the table.

"Nicely played."

"Thank you, Leda. It was certainly fortunate that Maggie landed in my lap when she did, although it was only a matter of time before I found someone."

Pilakin looked from one to the other and suspicion formed in her mind.

"You bloody bastard."

Lars raised his eyebrows. "What?"

"You must have realised who she was. When I asked you to pick up Rimsky, you got to kill two birds with one stone. You got Neuberg to find her in my case notes and pass it on to him. All so you can push forward your career. And what does the Federation get out of this? You're obviously as thick as thieves."

She was working herself up into a rage and only the menacing presence of Captain Hashan, who looked as angry as Pilakin felt, prevented her from jumping out of her chair and committing violence. Neuberg passed her cigarette packet and lighter across the table.

"No, Agent Pilakin. I've had no part in this and didn't even know Lars was involved in your case until he got here today."

"Why are you so chummy?"

"We know each other from the City Liaison Committee – he's the Kristani representative. Well, he attends on behalf of his boss – as we all do…"

Pilakin lit one of the cigarettes and dragged on it hard before examining the glowing tip. Everyone in this case seemed to be related to everyone else. She was beginning to wonder who the hell she could trust. Her emotions must have been on show because Lars looked at her with concern.

"I told you Jaq. I'm here to look after you. You needn't concern yourself with my troubles."

Patronising arse, she thought but, before she could give voice to her opinion, Captain Hashan experienced what could only be described as an eruption.

"You misogynistic *fucks*!"

Lars blinked in surprise. "Who?"

"You and that wanker who was just here for starters. You bartered over the ownership of a woman. He wanted to use this female agent to bring you down. She is bonded to you because someone else killed your daughter – who you *also* saw as a possession that someone stole from you. Now you're setting yourself up as some kind of benevolent saviour riding in to bring all those Poulter women out of hiding. Why not just set them free? Oh no you can't do that because then you'd lose control of them. This City is supposed to be about freedom but it's the same old story. How dare you treat us like this? How fucking *dare* you?"

Leda had risen from her seat and put a hand on Hashan's arm. Hashan was trembling but she took a deep breath and nodded at Neuberg. She walked to the door but as she opened it turned once more to Pilakin.

"You need to succeed without them. Otherwise it isn't worth shit."

NEUBERG QUIETLY LEFT after Hashan. Pilakin and Lars looked at each other in silence for a few minutes. It was he who eventually spoke.

"What do you need me to do now?"

"Get back to the office and tone it down with Rimsky. I have information that he was trying to protect Maggie and Paul."

"You want me to let him go?"

"No. I'm not convinced but—

"I understand. I'll get back and call you with what we've got out of him so far. Listen, Jaq. About the politics—"

"Not now. I need to focus on this case."

Something had struck her after Hashan's tirade. About men getting women to do things for them; it had triggered a memory. A tenuous link in her mind. She pulled out her slab and pulled up the retinal scan image from the last thing Jer had seen. She zoomed in on one of the running figures in the background. She picked that one out because, unlike all the others, it was running straight at Jer. Fuzzy and uncertain though it was, Pilakin could not help but believe it was her. She jumped out of her seat.

"Seriously, get to Rimsky and stop what's happening. I have to go."

Chapter 31

S O SHE HERE she was again, pressing the buzzer outside Zeb's garage door. His intercom fizzed.

"What the hell do you want now, Jaq?"

"We need to talk."

"Talking with you seems to lead to all kinds of unpleasantness. Why should I let you in after you ran off and left me with all that Water Activist shit to deal with?"

"Because I've figured it out Zeb. I know who killed Jer and I need your help to catch them."

"Oh hell…"

The door retracted once more.

Zeb met her in the outer office and she asked to step inside.

"I'd like RK4-Jess to come in with us please."

"Why, for heaven's sake?"

"It makes me nervous and I like to have it where I can see it."

She allowed them both to precede her and indicated that Zeb should sit at the table. The robot stood behind him and Pilakin took the seat opposite. She took her slab out and laid it on the table then followed with her gun, which she placed adjacent, her hand still resting on it. Zeb sighed.

"Jess saved your life, you know?"

"Yes. But I think only because you asked it to."

"Why would that be the reason?"

"Let's ask it shall we?" Pilakin looked at the robot's blank optical receptors. "Come out Jess."

The robot didn't move. Zeb took a breath as if to speak but before he could, there was whirring sound in the corner behind her. She knew it was the hidden door opening but the hairs on her neck prickled just the same. She heard soft, padding, footsteps approaching from behind but she hoped the fact that the gun was pointing at Zeb would be deterrence enough to prevent any problem. The robot Jess moved away into a corner and the "dead" woman from the bath took its place, resting a hand on Zeb's shoulder. Pilakin looked at her now animate features and considered the fact that she was willing to use the word "her" to describe it for the first time. The thing stared back.

"You don't blink," said Pilakin.

A smile twitched around the edges of its mouth and its eyes slowly closed and opened.

"I keep forgetting. Doctor Reigel didn't have time to

fully describe my semi-autonomic protocol simulations."

"You're the real Jess?"

She nodded.

"And you control that… thing… remotely."

"Yes I do, fleshbag."

Zeb jumped in his seat and turned to look at her.

"You really did do that? You told me you didn't. Why?"

"She's trouble Zeb. She's dangerous. Look at all the things that have happened since she turned up in your life."

Pilakin cleared her throat and they both looked back at her. "Why the plastiform?"

"So I can be around Zeb when he's with other people. To protect him."

"But you're damn near human. You could get away with it."

"I have a job to go to."

"A job?" Pilakin's hand tensed on the gun at this stunning revelation and she saw the eyes of both robots drop and focus upon it. Jess returned to looking at her while Robot-Jess's eyes stayed on the table. Useful feature, that.

"Yes, Agent Pilakin. I'm a journalist. A very good way to learn about humanity."

"I think there's another reason you warned me off. Jealousy. I think you've imprinted onto Zeb. You want to be with him and protect him."

It was Zeb who answered.

"You mean love."

"Talk about robo-perving."

Zeb looked at her with anger in his eyes.

"Look at her, Jaq. She's beautiful and intelligent and innocent."

"Oh no, Zeb. Not innocent. She wants to protect you – it's clear from the way she treated me. But I think she's been protecting you a long time. And because she has an uninhibited nanomatronic mind, she has no moral compass or sense of proportion. And we're not living in the best of societies to teach her compassion, are we? I think you're a good man, Zeb, despite your perversion. I don't think you're a killer, no matter what Jer had done to almost ruin your lives. But she's looking out for you. She's the one who saw that he had to be taken out of the picture. She's the one who knew about your business enough to set up a fake meeting and plan an elaborate murder. She's the one with a steel skeleton to break a man's legs and get out from under a rock fall."

"I'm that strong, am I?"

"I know you are. You jumped out of the window when I was being kidnapped by the Water Activists. You must have dropped four or five metres with no ill-effects. You're also the one with absolutely no soul who could do things like try to kill Jer's family and burn Melissa's face off."

"Jaq! Enough." Zeb's face was white and he was shaking.

"No. You have to know the danger you're in. I know that Water Activists use acid in their attacks. Jess must have been outside ransacking their van while you came in. She met you outside, didn't she?"

"Well, yes. But she wouldn't come in to expose herself."

"Sure, tell yourself that."

"But what reason would she have to try to kill Sarah?"

"For you, Zeb. So you could finally be unshackled from the financial burdens you were labouring under."

"That makes no sense. Who in their right mind...?"

"She has no morals. She has no right mind. She's a danger to the whole City."

"Jaq!"

Zeb jumped to his feet, so Pilakin followed suit, finally bringing up her gun and pointing it between Jess' eyes. She didn't have to worry about the robotic one. It was under orders. And the humaniform, she knew, had her brain where it should be.

"Jaq, where the hell have you got all this? Where's the bloody evidence?"

"Look down at my slab, Zeb."

"Some fuzzy picture. What am I looking at?"

"The very last thing Jeremiah Flow saw."

"A street with people running in it."

"Find the one running toward him. You see her? Zoom in."

There was a silence that, to Pilakin, seemed more

eloquent than any words could be at this point. Finally he said in a quiet voice, "It's you Jess."

"Of course it's me." Her voice switched to a sarcastic tone and was accompanied by slow clapping. "Oh well done, Agent Pilakin. Very good."

Zeb turned to her. "What were you doing there?"

"You sent me to keep an eye on him."

"You told me you couldn't find him."

She turned her head and gazed at him with a tender expression and touched his face.

"I was ashamed. I let you down. I let him down, too."

Pilakin sneered.

"Very touching but complete—"

Her slab rang with an incoming call. It was Lars. She tapped it to speaker to keep her hands free.

"Hey, Lars. Has Rimsky been singing?"

"Yes I got to him but they'd been working on him a while. I'm afraid he's not in a good way Jaq, but I don't think it matters."

It was Jess' turn to sneer.

"I'm the one without a soul…?"

Pilakin waved her to silence.

"Let me guess. He was pretending to work for Manstein but was actually in the pay of a tall woman who doesn't blink."

"What the hell, Jaq? No. He was working for Manstein alright. Did a whole load of stuff with him, including burning a woman's face off…"

Pilakin swayed before sitting down heavily in the chair.

LARS' VOICE BROKE through the rushing in her ears.

"Jaq? You there?"

"I… I don't know, Lars. Did he say who Manstein was working for?"

"It was the main theme in the second part of his interview. My guys really think he doesn't know. Just a thug for hire, they recon."

"Don't let him die."

"Why not? It sounds like he's done some pretty nasty things."

"Just don't, okay?"

She hung up the call. Jess was looking at her with contempt on her face. A simulation of contempt though, surely?

"Manstein was the one who gave you the Fesh case?" she asked.

"Yes," replied Pilakin. "How did you know about that?"

"You really need better encryption on that thing."

"Shit. You're the second one who—"

"I bet I'm not just the second."

"When did you…?"

"I'm in it right now. Look."

Pilakin gazed at her screen and saw her files moving around as if possessed. Jess frowned.

"Why did you never put Manstein's name in your case files?"

"I must have. Although maybe? Well, isn't it in the files he transferred to me?"

Jess shook her head. "Looks like someone's been through and expunged all reference to him. No here – a virus that automatically deletes his name. Sophisticated too. Was that him who came into Cubilicious when you were in the shoot out with Zeb?"

"Yes."

Pilakin felt cold as she began to realise the correlation between her brushes with death and the proximity of Gregor Manstein. Maybe it wasn't Sarah who'd been the target after all.

"That bloody skunk. What's he been up to? Who the hell is he working for?"

The robot ignored the question and instead said, "You got my face out of Jeremiah's eyes. Clever you, but you often walk around with far better recording devices strapped to your own eyes."

"What has that got to do with it? I was there. I remember what happened."

"None so blind... What's the quote? *Foolish person, without understanding, who has eyes and will not see.*"

Pilakin looked daggers at her but Zeb cut in.

"Using the actual Book of Jeremiah? That's in pretty poor taste, Jess."

"I'm sorry, my love. Agent Pilakin, is this Manstein?"

She indicated the slab where an image taken from her shades showed Manstein standing in front of her after the shoot out.

"Yes, that's him."

Through some invisible means, Jess manipulated the image and zoomed in upon Manstein's collar. And Pilakin could finally see what had been in front of her multiple times.

Two small holes where a collar badge had been removed.

Chapter 32

PILAKIN IMPATIENTLY TAPPED her gun on the table as she waited for Neuberg to answer her call. Zeb looked nervous.

"Can you stop doing that?"

"Mmm?"

Jess' hand darted across the table and held the gun still. Pilakin tried to pull it away but, apparently without effort, the robot held it down tight. She glared and was about to shout when Neuberg answered.

"Agent Pilakin. Is it urgent?"

"Yes it is actually."

Jess released its grip on the gun but indicated with its other hand that she should put it back in her holster. After a moment's hesitation, Pilakin complied.

"Do you have an agent working for you called Gregor Manstein?"

"No, I don't know anyone called that."

Damn.

"I'm going to send you a picture."

She lifted the one from the shades and zipped it over.

"Okay, I've got it. Let me…"

Neuberg went quiet.

"Major?"

"That's Martin Boyd. He's a contract agent for us."

"Don't you people do any kind of background checks?"

"Yes, of course. That's what's concerning me. He was hired by the Commerce Command to do revenue protection work."

"Well, he's my prime suspect for at least three murders."

Jess looked at her angrily.

"You're giving her all this intel? The Feds are pretty good at cover ups."

"Who's that?" asked Neuberg.

"A witness. Listen, you meant what you said about helping me catch the suspect, whoever they were, and getting justice, even if it means getting to grips with elements inside the Federation?"

"Yes, of course. And now you've given me something to go on I can make some inquiries."

"Perfect," replied Pilakin, "and if you could dig around for a motive as well, I'm not very clear on that yet."

"Oh, if he's on contract to Commerce command, it'll be financial in nature, I'm sure. Tell me, do you trust Max

Locatore?"

"Yes but he's a moron."

"I think loyalty and trust are more important right now. And I'm not licensed to make arrests in Engalise. I need an agent."

"Hell no. It's my case – I make the arrest."

"Yes, of course. You have the contract. But if he tries to escape I'll need to hold him until you get here, won't I?"

"Okay."

"Meet me in half an hour at twelve forty three Plankbridge Walk."

Zeb looked at her as she cut the call. "You're not going by yourself, surely?"

"Why not?"

"Jess may be right about a cover up. Plankbridge Walk is an easy place to off people. Literally."

"You coming too then?"

"Yes.

"Both of us," added Jess with a look at Zeb which seemed to dare him to challenge it.

"Why?" Pilakin asked.

Zeb shrugged. "Because despite the way you have treated me I can see the only thing you've actually wanted to do is find my uncle's killer. It might be fun to get into another shoot out, too."

"Zeb!" That was Jess, with a scandalised tone. Pilakin cut in.

"You shouldn't get a taste for it. That's a bad road. But

come along. And bring your gun."

Maybe that dangerous bitch of a robot could be useful after all.

PLANKBRIDGE WALK WAS a narrow boardwalk hanging over the East Central Chasm – a large void hundreds of metres deep that helped to circulate air around the inner parts of the city. Despite the City Corporation's efforts to keep the chasm free of obstruction, the absence of laws and regulations meant that enforcement was difficult. Every time a new dwelling appeared, the owner of the property it was attached to had to be tracked down and bribed into taking a Sixth Right action against the squatters. Pilakin looked down off the Walk at the perilous slums and shacks attached to the walls like...like what? Again nature programmes were her salvation as she thought of molluscs. It was a perilous life alright, she mused, as she regarded the small wind turbines covering the outside of them, whizzing in the perpetual convection induced air-currents. The eye-watering cost of energy in the city along with the lack of housing meant that the wind farmers could make a profit in the five to six weeks before they were moved on.

Rope ladders or swinging bridges connected the shacks to the Walk and numbers were painted on placards, although there seemed to be little rhyme or reason to the order, likely due to the regular evictions. Eventually Pilakin's group found a sign saying 1243 and one of the more substantial cable bridges connected to what appeared to be a small metal porch five metres or so above their heads. They marched up it one by one but when they reached the top Pilakin was confronted by a heavy steel door with no external controls or even any kind of buzzer. She pulled out her pistol and was about to use the butt to bang on it when there was a clunk and it opened outward, so that she had to step backwards. Neuberg emerged into the porch.

"Good, you made it. Who are these people?"

"Zeb is the victim's brother and Jess is his…friend."

Neuberg nodded to Zeb and, on turning her attention to Jess, froze.

"*What* are *you*?"

"Well, that's quite rude. I could ask the same of you."

Neuberg looked at Pilakin.

"You know, right?"

"Yes."

"Well, then why on Home are you—?"

Zeb stepped in.

"Listen, Major Neuberg. We're here to help. Jess protects me and she's very interested in finding Jer's killer."

Neuberg shook her head. "It can't come in. It's too much of an infiltration and security risk."

Jess replied with apparent anger.

"If the place is full of people like *you*, then I'd say it is already fully infiltrated."

"I'm not going to stand here and exchange insults with a—"

The riposte died on her lips as both she and Jess snapped their head round to look along the Plankbridge Walk. A group of men were running along the gantry; heavy set, in body armour, shades and with automatic rifles at the ready. Pilakin looked the other way and saw the same coming from the other direction before turning back to Neuberg.

"They look like they mean business. Please just let me vouch for Jess and we can get inside?"

Neuberg nodded and they all tumbled through the door before she yanked it shut. The clang of its closing was entirely drowned out a moment later by the sound of bullets striking, as Jess helped Neuberg turn the heavy duty locks.

"Are we safe?" asked Pilakin.

"Yes. That door could take a nuclear strike."

"Where the hell are we?"

"You're inside Federation Headquarters."

"Really? Why the back door?"

"It's handy to have an unobserved way in and out. Manstein seems to have riddled our computer system with observation worms so I didn't want him to see you coming in the front."

"Have you got him yet?"

"No."

The sound of a running man came from the corridor

behind them and Max Locatore appeared, breathing hard. He nodded to Pilakin.

"I'm sorry, Major. I can't find him. No-one in the bullpen's seen him but he hasn't signed out. I authorised a security scan but his badge and collar stud are nowhere in the building."

Pilakin kicked the wall.

"Now what do we—?"

She broke off at the sound of sirens. After a few seconds, Neuberg walked over to a comms unit hanging on the wall next to the door and lifted the receiver, dialling quickly.

"Zdravsta. Et Noyberg. Tamne byl sverla zaplanirov na segdinya. Chto yebesh proiskha?"

Jess leaned closer to Pilakin.

"What language is that?"

"Russik. They speak it in Simplaerosia. I'd've thought making you multi-lingual would be easy."

"I didn't exactly have time for a full education. I'm sure I could pick others up rapidly but this is the first time in my life I have heard anything other than Eglitzé-Anjelican."

Life? Pilakin let it go.

"What about spoken media? Surely you've heard plenty of Common Anjelican."

"No. I don't like television."

Neuberg slammed down the receiver.

"Well, that's done it."

"What's going on?"

"We're actually under attack."

Pilakin felt cold.

"You mean the City?"

"No. Just our headquarters, but things could get seriously out of hand nevertheless."

She opened a cabinet next to the door and took out three small, metal rings.

"Attach these to your collars. Normally I wouldn't bother but as of now we are in lock-down so don't take them off and don't leave my side." She fixed Jess with a hard gaze. "Especially you. You so much as think the wrong way and you'll be taken down. Clear?"

Jess opened her mouth as if to answer but then her face unexpectedly grimaced and her whole body twitched to the side before regaining balance a moment later. She looked at Neuberg with a face that, if human, would have been called afraid.

"That was horrible."

Zeb grabbed Jess protectively.

"What the hell did you do to her? You can't…"

"I'm sure I won't have to do it again."

The sirens dropped a level in noise and intensity and Neuberg was able to speak in a normal voice.

"Stop looking at me like that or I'll push you back out of that door. Okay? Right then. I suppose the attack explains those gentlemen outside. They clearly know enough about the place to surround us. Come on. Let's go and find out what's happening and see if we can figure out where Manstein's gone."

THEY WALKED THROUGH interminable tunnels and passageways and Pilakin took the opportunity to quiz Neuberg.

"It's bloody embarrassing to be honest," replied the latter. "It seems he used his Agent status to get licensed as a bounty hunter without anyone noticing. I went and threw my weight around in the Commerce command and they told me he's been raking in money for them, and himself on commission."

"How?"

"They were cagey about that but I'm in a position to make threats from time to time. It turns out he's got hold of all the syndicate hit-lists and has been claiming kills."

Pilakin stopped and grabbed the other woman's arm for a moment.

"I'm beginning to realise the Federation isn't morally all it's cracked up to be, but surely you wouldn't condone that?"

"Certainly not. The way he explained it to Commerce is that the City is a dangerous place, especially out on the rim. He'd just find unlucky people already dead who happened to be on the hit-lists, get some dodgy post-mortem paperwork done to show murder and then make his claim."

"And your Commerce Command people swallowed

that?"

"They're under a lot of pressure to keep the money flowing and it is staffed by *very* profit-focussed people. Manstein was listing profits against all kinds of cryptic things, like 'water redistribution'. But I knew these 'syndicate claims' would be what you were after."

Pilakin blew out her cheeks and started walking again.

"So that's why he went to so much effort to prevent anyone realising there was murder happening. You were right in your office when you concluded it was the Federation itself he was trying to mis-direct. No one in the City would really care. That's what never really made sense about this case. And now we have motive, too."

THEY EMERGED INTO the large open-plan office area behind the glass wall that Pilakin had seen when visiting Max the day before. There were, however, several significant differences. The wall had developed some kind of mesh covering and through it she could see the huge blast doors had closed over the entrance. The large screens hanging from the ceiling now had images of the square outside, where two lines of armed people faced each other. The biggest differences though were in the desks' inhabitants. They were still sitting and doing their work as normal, but every one of them had on body armour and sidearms. On the desk in front of each lay a combat helmet, gas mask and an assault rifle. At every major intersection between the rows of desks stood a member of the heavy infantry, covered head to toe in a powered, armoured exoskeleton. Pilakin felt uncomfortable as the eyes of each followed their party across the room, no doubt scanning the metal circle on her collar for authenticity. Some people with trolleys were moving slowly through the desks and she saw they were distributing ration packs and water canteens.

Realisation began to dawn on her. The Federation was serious. It was organised. She was looking at hundreds of combat-ready soldiers. Thousands, when including the floors above and below. She couldn't help but wonder if whoever had surrounded the place knew what they were taking on. They took a lift up to the Intelligence section and were met at Neuberg's office by a soldier in full combat gear. She snapped to attention and gave Neuberg a smart salute. Pilakin was astounded. Feds were not famed for observing the niceties of military discipline.

"Major Neuberg?"

"Yes. What is it?"

"We've been told that you may have a Freedom Protection Agent called Pilakin with you. Is that you ma'am?"

Pilakin blinked. *Ma'am?*

"Yes, that's me."

"Fleet General Hopper's compliments and she asks if you could please both join her at the forward command post?"

Neuberg answered. "Certainly. A word please,

volunteer." She drew the soldier aside and spoke quietly to her. They both glanced at Jess and the soldier nodded. Jess folded her arms.

"I did hear that, you know?"

Neuberg looked back at her evenly.

"Yes, I'm sure you did."

"Well, don't worry. I'm really not going to do anything."

Neuberg grunted.

"Can I ask a question, major?" asked Jess in a sarcastic tone.

"Okay."

"Why did they send a messenger to get you rather than calling you?"

"Interesting question to cover for the one you really want to ask, I'll bet."

"Alright then. Why can't I hear anything in the electromagnetic spectrum?"

"As part of our standard defence procedure, we are blanket jamming every frequency in the City. All wireless communication is down everywhere for everyone."

Pilakin grabbed her slab and tried making a call. The device just screamed and whistled. Neuberg nodded.

"If it isn't hardwired or LOS beamed, it isn't working."

And with that, she led them off, the soldier bringing up the rear, with her gun at the ready.

Chapter 33

T HEY WERE INSIDE a wide passage that ran the length of one of the long, horizontal windows Pilakin had seen many times high up in the face of the Federation Headquarters building. As she suspected it might, the glass had retracted so that the multitude of Federation soldiers could point their guns and equipment down into the square below. Every few metres there stood a large cylinder on a tripod with a soldier looking through binoculars next to it and speaking into a microphone. Pilakin walked up next to Neuberg.

"What are they?"

"The voices in your head."

Pilakin actually smiled despite everything when she saw that twinkle of amusement in Neuberg's eyes. The latter explained further.

"They project a tightly focussed beam of ultrasound that turns into audible sound when it hits a solid object.

Say, your cranium. Here, come and listen to one."

They gathered round one of the operators and could hear her quietly speaking into the microphone.

"…yes you… there's no point in looking to the right and left… it's you… with the mole on your chin… that's right, I'm up here… I'm a trained sniper, I have you in my cross hairs and as soon as the shit kicks off I am going to paint the ground behind you with your brains… yes, you're thinking of running now… you should… just pack up and go and I'll pick someone else… stay and you'll last about two seconds…"

"So some guy down there is hearing that voice in their head?"

"Yes. Disconcerting, wouldn't you think?"

Pilakin nodded and looked at a strange gun being aimed by another soldier. The front end was a sort of cylindrical cage. She'd seen one before.

"Isn't that one of those pulse guns? The silent ones?"

"Yes."

"So you can vary the strength and it's completely silent – why bother with that now?"

"If we decide something needs smashing or someone needs killing without setting off a bunch of itchy trigger fingers with the noise. It wouldn't be immediately apparent what happened. The person would just collapse. We're at pretty extreme range here though."

"How so?"

"The beam is circular and spreads out as it travels. It'd

be about the size of a person this far away so the operator would need to aim at the ground in front of the target so that the upper line would cross the body."

"And that line would be curved?"

"Yes."

"Interesting."

"Not really. Now come on, we've been summoned."

"Just one more thing – do your agents have access to those things?"

"Yes, I think there are plenty of them in their armoury."

Well, that was how Manstein broke Flow's legs. She nodded as it made sense. Get Rimsky to spike his drink to slow him down. Then take up a sniper position to make sure that if he *did* start to move away from the rubble landing point you could stop him. No one would hear a shot and there'd be no bullet wound to find once the rubble was taken off him.

Neuberg led them on. They arrived at what was clearly the command post in one of the towers at the side of the building, giving an oblique view across the square. A woman with two crosses on her collar – Pilakin recognised her as someone who frequently stood next to the Federation president at press events – was talking into a phone and raised a finger to acknowledge their presence. Pilakin turned to look at the line of Federation troops in their usual position across the middle of Liberty Square. Unexpectedly, a plasteel barricade had risen out of the ground and they were lined up along it, their guns resting in firing loops. Opposite them, along the edge of the square, sat a line of black armoured vans. Behind and around the vans were men in boiler suits, armour and helmets with a range of heavy weaponry. *Damn.* They looked like syndicate. The fleet general slammed down her phone and glared at Pilakin before transferring her gaze to Neuberg, who saluted.

"Hi, Leda."

"General. Shouldn't you be in the command bunker?"

"I don't think we're quite there yet. Is this her?"

"Yes, general."

She looked back at Pilakin.

"I should have you arrested."

"For what?"

"All this!" She swept her arm around over the square. Neuberg cut in.

"General. We've only just got up here. We have no idea what's going on."

"We've been surrounded and threatened by the Kristani Syndicate."

"Who's leading them?"

"Well, that's just it – it looks like they've had a bit of a re-org over there. I've had some baldy bastard calling himself Poulter shouting at me through the comms. Going on about one of our agents killing syndicate family members and then hiding in HQ behind a cover-up. Of course, in the end, I had to tell him I had *no fucking clue* what he was on about and asked him to put Löring on – he always seemed a reasonable man in liaison committee. And *he* said he was concerned about *your* safety, Agent Pilakin, and that I should call back when I had evidence that you were alive and free. I asked how I could do that and he told me to contact Neuberg. I didn't know you'd have the damned woman in here. And who are these others?"

"They're also involved in the case, General. May I suggest we get Löring back on? How are we communicating with him?"

"They've got a lasercom station with them."

Pilakin saw the base unit that would fire a laser at a similar receiver in the syndicate's line. When pointing at each other the light would flash in the manner of an optical fibre allowing data communication despite the wireless blackout, provided the station stayed in alignment. A sergeant made the call as the general beckoned Pilakin to stand in front of the screen.

"Do not give them any information about the security situation here. If I think you're even hinting at it I'll have you in the cells until the matter is over."

Pilakin nodded as Löring appeared on the screen.

"Jaq. I'm so glad to see you're still about."

"Lars, you're on speaker."

"Who else is there?"

She glanced at the general who frowned.

"I'm sorry, I can't say right now. What's going on?"

"Eddie Poulter's gone off on one. When he and I went to the Executive Committee to propose the rehabilitation of the Poulters, he had a whole spiel prepared on the syndicate going soft and losing its standing and power in the City. Said the Federation in particular needed to be brought down a peg or two. He's basically using this as his coming out party – positioning himself as a no-nonsense, uncompromising advocate of Kristani prestige. Unfortunately, there's still a contingent of old firebrands and enough waverers to carry the vote if he could show evidence of Federation moves against us."

"So he brought up the subversion of your hit-lists for profit and revealed that it was a Federation conspiracy?"

"Yes. How did you know that?"

"Because I've got the case solved – I know who Rimsky's boss was working for. The important question is, how did Eddie Poulter know?"

"He was contacted by someone from City Liaison who told him the guy who had done it was also the one who had killed his niece's husband and now the Federation were trying to cover it up. That's why I was worried about you, Jaq."

"Was that really enough to push your executive board into staging this intervention?"

"Poulter did a whole song and dance about family prestige and the killer of a syndicate family member being kept from us. Said if it was another outfit we'd go to war with them and the Federation was a good deal less impressive than our competitors."

"And that did it?"

"You've seen him in action. Too many think we've become too soft."

Neuberg pushed Pilakin aside.

"Lars, it's Leda. Do you know who it was who told him?"

"Hang on. I'm not sure I should—"

"Was it an Agent called Boyd?"

"Would that be significant?"

Pilakin grabbed the screen back.

"Too bloody right it would. That's the killer. His name's really Gregor Manstein – he's had two identities this whole damned time. That means—"

Neuberg cut in again.

"That means he has manufactured this whole situation to create the ideal circumstances for his escape. He must have known we were about to arrest him."

The Fleet General stepped in.

"Lars, it's General Hopper."

"Oh, hello Alice."

"I think we need a meeting. Twenty minutes. I'm giving orders for all members of City Liaison to be summoned."

"Eddie Poulter is running the show. I'm not sure he—"

"Tell him to come – we'll negotiate with him directly. He'll get to act the big man in front of reps from every significant organisation in the City."

"Hm. That should do it. Where?"

"You see our recruitment building jutting into the square? It's designed to be neutral ground in just such a situation as this. See you in Twenty. And Lars? For goodness' sake make sure nobody gets an itchy trigger finger. This could all get out of hand *very* quickly."

PILAKIN STOOD IN a corner of the conference room next to a row of soldiers and adjutants along the back wall. Federation members of the Liaison Committee, including Hopper and Neuberg, were clustered around one side of an oval table discussing tactics while they waited for the last of the other side to arrive in an anteroom. Pilakin looked out of the window at the lines of potential combatants in the square, and her eyes wandered up to the propaganda projections. It was startling to see their tenor had completely changed. There now played an unremitting stream of Federation troops, weapons and vehicles basically blowing the crap out of enemy forces. One particularly gruesome film revealed bodies in the aftermath of a firerain strike. Pilakin ripped her eyes away as soon as she realised what it was and turned to place her forehead against the wall in an effort to still her breathing.

"You okay?"

Zeb touched her shoulder.

"I… I lost someone in the fighting years ago." She turned her head to face him. "I don't know how the syndicate are keeping their guys in place with all these psyops going on." She lowered her voice, "The Feds are looking a bit less like the good guys at the moment, aren't they?"

There was a knock at the door and the Feds quickly took places behind their seats before a soldier admitted worried looking City representatives, who filed in and took places behind hastily made cards with their organisations' names. Once they were all in, Lars and Edward Poulter entered and stood together. Hopper broke the silence.

"Shall we sit? Thank you all for coming. As you can see a situation has developed between ourselves and the Kristani Syndicate and we felt that to resolve it is a matter of City-wide concern."

"I don't see how, madam chair," interjected the representative from the Engalise City Corporation.

"We will get to that shortly, I promise you. But if you'll indulge us, I think it would be best to hear the Kristani representative's position."

Lars nodded.

"Thank you, madam chair. I would like to request the meeting recognise my colleague, Edward Poulter-Kristani, as speaking for us today."

"Any objections? No? Mr Poulter-Kristani, you have the floor."

And the tirade started. He vehemently outlined his allegations and read out from evidence that had presumably been supplied to him by Manstein. At several points Hopper tried to interrupt his flow but to no avail. She finally succeeded when he got to the point where he accused the Federation of now orchestrating a cover-up and demanded that Manstein be handed over.

"Mr Poulter-Kristani. Believe it or not, we acknowledge that there have been some irregularities and are currently seeking this man who has turned out to be a rogue agent. But we are certainly not going to negotiate with a gun to our heads and—"

She broke off as a lieutenant bent over beside her and whispered in her ear. Poulter seized the opportunity to start speaking again but trailed off as first Hopper and then all of the other Federation representatives stood up.

"Mr Poulter-Kristani. You may not be aware but those of us on this side of the table actually sit here as proxies for the relevant members of the command council. I have just been informed that those currently in residence have decided to attend the meeting themselves."

Pilakin looked on in stunned amazement as several of the infamous 'Triple X's', so called because of the three X shaped rank bars at their collars, walked into the room and took the seats just vacated by their underlings, who bent to whisper into their ears. Neuberg was speaking to a good-looking man, apparently in early middle-age, who looked across at her for a moment, smiled and nodded. Davito Stravinski: Commander of Intelligence and Internal Resistance, Segondo Prince of Simplaerosia and Carraerosia and, it turned out, her grandmother's nephew.

She felt her face flush as his eyes briefly bored into her. Then all attention in the room went back to the door as a tall, brown skinned woman with four X's at her collar limped into the room and sat in front of Fleet General Hopper. Pilakin had never even seen a picture of this woman before but knew her to be the reclusive Dharuna Chandramogen, Chair of the Command Council of the Free Federation of Anti-Imperial Organisations. She was the Empire's most wanted. Pilakin daydreamed for a brief second about the bounty she would get if she turned up at an Imperial base with her.

Poulter looked at her with a sneer.

"Dr Chandramogen, I presume. Am I supposed to be impressed? Is this supposed to intimidate me?"

She stirred in her seat for a moment before speaking in a calm, deep voice.

"I thought it would be useful for me to conduct the last part of this meeting so there is no doubt that we mean what is about to be said. Withdraw from liberty square and stop your offensive action or we shall have to take over the whole City by force."

Chapter 34

PILAKIN THOUGHT THE silence following the statement was stunned but Poulter broke the tension by laughing.

"Take over the City? You lot couldn't take over a coma ward."

"Commander Stravinski."

"Yes, Madam Chair."

"I know we don't have a Propaganda and Media representative here but you task them on City matters. What has been their primary directive?"

"To portray the Federation inside the City as a good-natured bunch of bumbling incompetents."

"Would you say they have been successful?"

Laughter rippled around the Federation ranks in the room. Pilakin glanced at Max, who had gone red. Poulter blustered.

"No. This goes beyond perception. You couldn't do

it."

"It is not a matter of couldn't. Unless you disperse, we will seize the City Corporation Headquarters and multiple key infrastructure points."

The ECC representative paled.

"That would be a coup d'état."

"There is no état to be couped against. It would just be a hostile takeover."

"But you're *against* tyranny and *for* freedom."

"Not at the cost of our own survival."

"The people would rise against you, as would the syndicates, I'm sure."

A murmur of agreement went round with Poulter resuming the role of spokesman. Chandramogen turned her attention back to him.

"Any organisation that rises against us will be occupied. Any insurrection from amongst the population will be suppressed."

"How? A few dumb administrators with weapons."

"We have a trained volunteer militia in the City of twenty thousand. At any given moment we have no less than three infantry and two marine divisions in reserve here. Headquarters staff total around twenty thousand and we have a reciprocal agreement with the CDA that will raise another ten thousand. That's just shy of a hundred thousand trained and equipped personnel that we can deploy in less than half an hour."

"We have plenty of people."

"You lot never work together on anything. And how are you going to carry out command and control? Have you noticed your communications are not working? That is City wide and every wireless spectrum."

"But how are you—"

"…going to control our own? All units returned immediately to their secret barracks all over the City as soon as the attack alarm went off. We are hardwired into all locations naturally."

The Institute representative chipped in.

"The people. Th…th…they wouldn't have it. Sur…suppression would cost t…t…tens of thousands of l…l…lives."

Chandramogen's face did not register any emotion as she replied. "Hundreds of thousands, I would think. And if things do not calm down quickly we will cut off power and food. Blind, starving people fall into line pretty quickly."

"Y…you wouldn't!"

"Damu'us naee."

Pilakin jumped as, in response to Chandramogen's assertion in Old Anjelik she would do what was necessary, every Fed in the room chorused loudly, "Damu'us naee."

Chandramogen stood and clicked her fingers. Several troops who had been standing at the back of the room rushed forward and dumped large bags on the table in front of each of the commanders, now also standing. They opened the zips and took out body armour, which they quickly donned along with helmets. Then each pulled out a large assault rifle, which they loaded and cocked. The faces of all the Feds in the room certainly no longer looked amiable or incompetent. They looked determined and frightening. The people on the other side of the table rose too. The ones who were not syndicate looked like they wanted to run. Even the ones who *were* syndicate looked worried. Except for Poulter. Pilakin had to hand it to him – he either had balls of steel or he was one hell of an actor. She glanced at Neuberg, who had always seemed so reasonable. Now she looked grim. Pilakin couldn't take it anymore.

"This is inhuman! Whatever you really are, the one thing we all know is that you're for freedom and liberation and rights and justice. You won't do these things. You could just sit in your fortress and it'll probably blow over. Worst case scenario, you kill everyone who comes against you here…"

She stopped as every person in the room had turned to look at her. Stravinski, oddly, was smiling. Chandramogen scowled.

"You must be Pilakin. Well, agent, our agenda is Galactic in scope. This City has tremendous symbolic importance but its contents have no strategic value whatsoever. The Emperor wastes his armies against it purely because it exists and it is only successfully defended because *we* are here. Why do we bother? Because it is vital that we are able to say to the rest of the Galaxy that the

Empire cannot dislodge our headquarters from within its very bounds. But think about it. We control all information that leaves this place. All we have to be able to do is to *say* we hold it, even if all that is left inside is Liberty Square and the Sink Field Generators."

Finally she had achieved shocked silence. Neuberg looked downright angry and leaned forward to whisper animatedly in Stravinski's ear. After a moment he waved her away and spoke quietly to Chandramogen. The latter stood like a rock, staring at Poulter even when Stravinski had finished. Poulter stared back and the only sound in the room was people shifting nervously from foot to foot, fingering their weapons. Pilakin heard exhalations of relief when Poulter spoke.

"Is that a declaration, a threat or a bargaining position?"

"You have six hours to withdraw entirely and reduce your street presence to normal levels."

"We're not going until you hand over Manstein."

"We are happy to send out our people to detain him and hand him over for prosecution under the City Corporation as neutral arbiters."

"We're not letting any of you out. We will detain any Federation personnel we find in the streets."

And then Pilakin saw why she was here. What this whole damned charade was about. She looked from Neuberg's face, to Lars', to Stravinski's before fixing on Chandramogen's.

"It's my case and I'm neutral. Let me go and get him."

"Neutral?" Poulter sounded incredulous.

Chandramogen nodded.

"Half an hour ago I was reviewing a proposal for Agent Pilakin's arrest."

Pilakin's anger rose but she kept it in check. "I'm going to need help."

"You will *not* take anyone from the syndicate side. We'll be watching."

Pilakin looked at Zeb and Jess.

"Well, I guess it's just us, guys. You up for it?"

Both nodded.

Poulter leaned forward with his knuckles on the table, looked at Pilakin and then back at Chandramogen.

"So, the deal is when we see evidence that Pilakin has detained Manstein, we will pull back."

Chandramogen looked at her watch.

"And that will happen by precisely six hours from… now… or we will take over the City."

Pilakin looked at her watch and noted the time. As did everyone else in the room.

IN LIBERTY SQUARE, outside the cordon, Pilakin watched a livid Edward Poulter shouting at the other syndicate representatives. Some were displeased at the results of poking the Federation bear but he was making a forceful argument that these threats were precisely why they had to get together and make a stand. Lars touched her shoulder and led her away a little with Jess and Zeb. She raised her eyebrows at him.

"That all seemed rather planned."

"Yes. I had a word with Leda about how we could play it while we were waiting for the other committee members. Apparently Stravinski was on her side with regards to finding a compromise but he had to talk Chandramogen down off the ceiling."

"So, those threats were real then?"

"Certainly – as is the deadline. Unfortunately it's why I'm also not in a position to help you…"

They were interrupted by the arrival of an ECC agent; the Corporation representative himself had high-tailed it away in a convoy of sirens as soon as they had got outside.

"Agent Pilakin? The director ordered me to put my squad car at your disposal. What's going on?"

"What's your name?"

"Pohl."

"Well, Pohl, it's a manhunt on a deadline."

"I'm afraid our comms are down."

"Yes, I know."

"What do you want to do then?"

All of them were looking at her, damn them. A robot, a syndicate manager, a City Agent, a businessman and it was her – the creditless, screwed-up itee, who was going to have to lead them and save the City. *Come on, Jaq, think.* It was the kind of responsibility she had been dreaming of since she got fired. What would that bastard, Manstein, be doing? Getting rid of all remaining accomplices and witnesses and/or leaving the City. Maybe a bit of revenge, too? Given the state of Melissa's body, he was certainly vindictive. She could think of no reason, other than downright sadism, for that particular piece of work. She should warn Takani but did she really have time? She needed more information and the only people who must have had contact with Manstein, and she hadn't interrogated yet, were the Water Activists. Surely he'd been the one to send them to Zeb's. Sam should still have them at Central 1 and Starlight's was on the way.

"Okay, let's go."

PILAKIN HAD ALMOST forgotten how exciting it was to fly through the City at speed, lights flashing and siren pinging. Fortunately the squad car was air-capable so they were able to shoot along a couple of metres above the heads of the pedestrians. In places, around electronics shops or comms stores, the crowds were thickening and the mood looked to be getting darker. Agents and squad cars were everywhere but there didn't look to be nearly enough of them.

"Looks like things will start getting ugly." She turned to look at Jess in the back who was looking out of the window. "I'm surprised you're not taking pictures for a story."

"I am."

Pilakin shivered. No doubt she'd be uploading stories

live to her news feed if it weren't for the signal jamming. They screamed to a sharp landing outside Starlight Sophisticates where Clem's security boys were lined up in front of the man himself outside the entrance.

"Jaq! Looks like you got yourself a posse. Business must be on the up, eh? Does this mean you've come to pay me?"

Pilakin told the others to wait in the car and hustled Clem inside.

"Get Takani, quick."

He looked at her face and nodded, dispatching a receptionist.

"Sorry, the comms are down."

"Yes, it's the whole City. Listen, you need to close. Just for a few hours."

Clem started to laugh but then his face fell. "Seriously, what's—"

Takani walked up the corridor towards them and Pilakin was actually relieved to see he was okay. She held out her slab for him to see.

"Is this the man who set you onto me?"

"Why should I tell you?"

"Because he tortures people to death for fun."

His face whitened, making the fading bruises more prominent.

"Yes that's him."

"Is there anything, anything at all, you haven't told me?"

He shrugged.

"Only that I saw him at Pandora's the night I met you. He was heading down to the dungeon."

Shit, shit, shit. He liked revenge and he liked hurting people. Still, maybe it'd be a good thing if he wasn't just planning to disappear immediately.

"Clem. Takani is in serious danger. Put him in your panic room. Send all your clients out and shut the place down. Lock everything up and don't let anyone in."

"Jaq, no! I'm not going to—"

"Not only is this incredibly serious, Takani is a key witness to prosecuting a case that will make millions. I'll be able to pay you double everything I owe you. This guy turns up," she indicated Manstein's picture, "see if you can nab him but be careful. He's really dangerous. If you get him, sit on him. Call the ECC-FPA – you got a hardwire line?"

"No. Who the hell does?"

"Well, then send someone out to find an agent. Tell them it's related to what's happening in Liberty Square and the fact that no one has comms."

She shouted this last over her shoulder as she ran back out to the squad car.

STATION CENTRAL 1 of the ECC-FPA was in chaos when they arrived. Several agents with drawn weapons were holding back an angry mob but their squad car was able to fly over the unrest and into the courtyard. Pilakin led her crew into the building and made directly for the detectives' room, hoping that Sam Lyttle hadn't been deployed. They tended to keep detectives in reserve and she was relieved to see him when she burst in.

"Jaq!"

"Sam. Listen, you still got those Activists, right?"

"Yeah, sure. What the hell have you got into? We've just been issued city-wide instructions to give Agent J. Pilakin all assistance possible."

Well, that was going to make what she wanted to do next a hell of a lot easier.

"I want the leader scraped to a chair in an interview room, right now."

Chapter 35

WELL, HE CERTAINLY *looked* worried. The activist's eyes followed Pilakin, Sam, Jess and Zeb as they walked into the room. His hands were cuffed behind him to the back of the chair. Pilakin let him sit for a few moments before talking to Sam.

"I want the recording equipment removed, then you and Zeb should leave the room."

Sam pulled the floppy hair out of his eyes.

"You sure, Jaq?"

"Yeah. You shouldn't be here to expose yourself to rights violation action. You too, Zeb."

Sam reached up and ripped the camera off the wall. Zeb leaned close.

"This is wrong, Jaq. If you just explain to him what's going on… And Jess – what about her exposure?"

"You know rights don't apply to her. Now go."

He and Sam left and Pilakin noted with satisfaction

that the Activist's fear seemed to have gone up a notch. Good. She marched forward, threw the table aside and punched him hard in the face. He screamed.

"What the…?"

She walked around behind him so he couldn't see her face. She wasn't enjoying this and only her resentment at the way he had previously humiliated her was carrying her through. She grabbed his hair and spoke close to his ear.

"That hurt my hand."

"Your hand? *Your hand?* What about my *face*?"

"I don't think I really did enough damage to it. You see my friend there?" she held his hair so he was forced to look at Jess. "She's a robot. She has steel fists. Show him will you, Jess?"

The robot righted the table and then punched down into the middle, snapping it clean in two. The man gaped.

"Bu… bu… a robot? They won't hurt humans. They can't. Can they…?"

Jess walked up to him and grabbed at where his left nipple would be and viciously twisted her fingers through nearly 360 degrees. The man squealed and she let him go. Then she pulled back her fist and seized his collar.

"You going to answer the agent's questions?"

"Yes, yes, for the love of God, yes."

Jess nodded and stepped back. Pilakin came back round the front and slapped him once more for good measure. He looked terrified. Perfect. This interview would now proceed at the optimum efficiency.

"Someone set you on me?"

"No."

"Someone sent you to the plumber's where you found me?"

"Yes."

"Who?"

"He never told us his name."

"Him?"

Jess held up a picture of Manstein. Printers in every ECC Agency station in the City were churning them out so they could be handed to agents, since the picture couldn't be broadcast to all their slabs automatically.

The man nodded. Pilakin hit him again but more gently this time.

"I can't hear you."

"Yes. It was him."

"Why?"

"Why what? No don't hit me; I honestly don't understand."

"Was he telling you how to find targets?"

"Yes."

"Was there anything special about this one?"

"He didn't usually give us plumbers. We can find them for ourselves – they have to advertise after all. He also said we could expect trouble unless we went in hard."

"What was he finding for you?"

"Secret stashes, large water tanks, unregistered reservoirs and so on."

"What was in it for him?"

"Money mostly. The odd litre of acid."

"Acid?"

"Yes."

"Why?"

"He never said."

"And you have enough of it to give away?"

"Yes. We…"

He hesitated. Time for some carrot.

"I have no interest in passing on information unrelated to finding my man. That missing camera works both ways."

"Okay. We have our own lab for synthesizing it."

Jess broke in.

"Why do you use it?"

"Easier to get hold of and less likely to kill people. We find a pipe or tank we want breached, we pour it all over and then it gets diluted when the water pours out."

"But you use explosions sometimes."

"Just when we have to get through a wall or want to destroy some equipment. Look we never kill—"

Pilakin waved her hand.

"Yes, we know all that. So how much have you paid to this guy?"

"Thousands in the last year but money is a problem so we were happy when he asked for the last payment entirely in acid."

"How much did you give him?

"Fifteen hundred litres."

"Say that again."

"Fifteen hundred litres."

"That's one and a half tonnes. How on Home did he collect it?"

"He had a van."

"Any markings on it?"

"No. None."

"Is there anything you can tell me, anything at all, that might show where he is? Listen. Some very big shit is going down and if you can help us find him there are going to be a lot of very grateful people. Think."

He flapped his mouth open and shut for a few moments, like a fish in a restaurant that's just been taken out of the tank for the chop.

"No. Honestly. I'd tell you if I could. He always found us. Always in person. No messages. No calls. He'd just appear. And he came to us to pick up the acid."

PILAKIN AND JESS joined the others, who had commandeered the Station Manager's office so they could use the hardwired line. After routing via the ECC's headquarters she got through to the Federation and eventually Neuberg picked up.

"Ah, it's good that you called. I've found out some things that might help you."

"Sure. But quick, tell me, have you got a van missing?"

"Hang on... Yes. Number fourteen isn't in the garage

and… Hell! It was signed out by one of Locatore's murder victims from outside Pandora's two days ago. The one that he said was an itee. I'll need to chew someone out for this screw-up – you reckon Manstein's in it?"

"Yes. He's got over a tonne of acid to cart about. Can you track it?"

"Normally we could, yes, but with the jamming…"

"Why the fuck don't you stop doing that? It benefits him and disadvantages us."

"Listen, Chandramogen doesn't care how this ends as long as the Federation is still standing afterwards. The rest of the command council has put its foot down to give a chance for a peaceful resolution but she's not going to do anything that helps our enemies even slightly. I think she's also seeing this as an opportunity to show dominance and slap down the syndicates."

Pilakin kicked the desk and took a deep breath.

"Okay then. So, what's your news?"

"I've been working through Manstein's server records. He covered his tracks pretty well but I'm pretty certain he's the one who reported himself to the Kristanis. There's a message full of accusations of a cover-up and he goes on about disaffection in the ranks and how most of us are aching for some competent outfit like a syndicate to come in and take over. It explains a lot about that Poulter character's bizarre take on the situation."

"He manufactured the whole crisis to cover his escape."

"Looks that way."

"So we have a totally self-serving psychopath on the run with a vat full of acid."

"There's something else. He seems to have run a search through our whole intelligence net for any mention of you. I fear he's fixated on you as the agent of his downfall."

"Well, surely you don't have that much on me."

"No, but there's significantly more since I started looking for your father. Pilakin, he's seen everything about your relatives on the shell – Tomasz and Vanya and your cousins. I wonder if he might…?"

Pilakin thought about the whole case – about everything she had heard – and suddenly some things that hadn't made sense fell into a horribly feasible pattern.

"Shit!"

"What is it?"

"He's going to attack the tower and then escape into the meadow. We have to stop him."

"How?"

Pilakin outlined her theory and silence fell for a moment. Then Neuberg answered.

"I think you're probably right but there's nothing I can do at this end – all troops inside the City are spoken for and I have no way of communicating with those outside. The CDA won't have anyone spare either – Chandramogen activated the assistance contract. Everyone left out there will be inside their towers."

"What about Crustetin?"

"I can try going through CDA management."

"And while you're at it tell them to get some shinies to exit fourteen. We'll be there in half an hour."

She slammed down the phone and looked at Sam.

"What can you give me in back-up?"

"Nothing. Disorder's breaking out everywhere. The boss has just sent everyone out – even from the detective pool. We're it."

"Well, the squad car had better still be out there."

Chapter 36

T HE SQUAD CAR wailed its way through the City and Pilakin gazed out of the window at the milling crowds. So much of the damned City was wireless, from communications to utility control networks. *But it's deeper than that,* she thought. Everyone was so plugged into information, there was never a question in anyone's mind that was not instantly answered or a thought not instantly expressed. Right now people had no access to any information whatsoever. To have such a safety blanket so completely removed was fundamentally unsettling. She tried to imagine how she'd be feeling if she wasn't actually aware of what was happening. Even the people trying to keep order would have little clue.

If the Federation's objective in jamming was to cause chaos and confusion it was working. Occasional groups of Freedom Protection Agents could be seen but, of course, they had no power to tell anyone to do anything unless they actually started committing rights violations. The first violence she saw was outside the Rottan Rode tube station, where a large crowd being denied access to the trains had turned its anger onto adjacent shops. ECC Agents and security guards were beating people with batons but she was relieved to see no one was resorting to guns yet. She started to realise how close to the edge this City was. Like most people, she'd closed her mind to it for years. Damn, she'd better be right about Manstein or things were going to get a hell of a lot worse.

They arrived outside a small, non-descript building and Pilakin led them through the door. Inside was the large atrium to CDA portal 14 – the same route through the sink field she had taken just the previous day. A group of city defence agents sitting at desks eyed them as they approached.

"You must be Pilakin then."

"Oh good – did the Feds get through to you?"

"That's right. They said the unrest is to do with a murderer who's getting away and you're going to stop him."

Jess held out Manstein's picture. Pilakin hoped to hell they'd recognise him and felt both relief and fear when the agent nodded.

"Yep. He came through about twenty minutes ago. Had credentials as a City Engineer – going to do shell maintenance. What's he done?"

"Torture, murder and pissed off everyone from the

Feds to the ECC and the syndicates."

"Shit. Why didn't you tell us sooner?"

"It's a developing situation. Did he have a van with him?"

"Yes. We put it in the garage."

"Can we see it?"

"Sure. He left the keycard with us but I can tell you there's nothing in there."

"Really? You sure?"

"I guess you're looking for that big tank thing he had with him?"

"Big enough to carry about fifteen hundred litres."

"That's the one."

"How the hell was he carrying it?"

"He had four of those spidery jobs with him – you know, the ones they use to maintain the net. That's why we didn't question him too closely – who controls those things apart from ECC engineers?"

Melissa Walden, thought Pilakin grimly.

"I tell you what though. It didn't look like the spiders were designed for the job. He was having to go very slowly."

"Good. Hopefully that means we won't be too late. Did you get the message about the shinies?"

"Yes. There's a stack of them on the other side of the portal. You going through now?"

THE AGENT LED them through a door to an inner room

and recited the familiar mantra.

"You will be passing through the magnetic field that holds the sink plasma in place. This field is of the order of several teslas so you must remove all magnetically reactive materials. Do any of you have any metallic devices inside your bodies?"

Jess grabbed Pilakin's arm.

"I can't go out there."

"Of course. Agent, my colleague has a number of medical implants so she'll have to use the coffin."

The agent sighed.

"Really? Can't you do without her?"

"I need as much backup as I can get. Any of you lot going to come out with me?"

"No. We have firm orders to guard the portal. Half our people have gone off into the City already."

"Then get it out."

Jess leaned close and spoke with quiet intensity.

"You're not listening. I *can't* go out there."

Pilakin spoke back so the others couldn't hear.

"It's okay, honestly. They have a big metal box constructed with really high permeability materials. It acts like a Faraday Cage does for electricity. The magnetic field finds it about five thousand times less resistive than the air so you'll be safe inside."

"You're... not... listening..."

Zeb came up to them and put his arm around Jess' shoulders.

"It's okay. You can do it. Think about how important it is. We won't be leaving the shell will we, Jaq? I mean we won't go into the meadow."

"You're *scared*?"

Pilakin did not manage to keep the mockery out of her voice.

"Fuck you, fleshbag. No, I'm not scared. I just don't have any parameters… my construction and programming is totally City based. I have no way of conceiving anything beyond the shell. It's like trying to know heaven… or hell."

"Well, you get the advantage of having a return ticket to find out. So *that's* why you won't learn languages or watch TV." Pilakin couldn't help but laugh. Zeb glared at her.

"This isn't funny."

"I was thinking – old Professor Reigel failed, didn't he? Your robotic nature isn't manifested in your blinking problem or your sturdy construction or your wireless capabilities. It's in your lack of curiosity and sense of adventure."

Jess looked like it was about to hit her.

"Alright. Put me in the damned box."

That did the trick.

HAVING PUT THEIR weapons and devices onto trays they all passed through hyper-sensitive metal detection arches. The defence agent's eyebrows raised as the sirens sounded for Jess.

"Given these levels, that must've been one hell of an accident. Anything of you left that's you?"

Jess glowered at him. He led them around a defensive barrier and they stood in front of the sink plasma itself, looking just the same as it did at the location of Manstein's bomb outside the Southwind Building. A large yellow-hatched box on the floor showed where the magnetic field was at significantly high levels. It was cold in this chamber, as the plasma greedily consumed the warmth in the air. A small bridge jutted out to where an ovoid portal, the shape of a teardrop, split the plasma as it flowed down the magnetic field, deep into a crack in the ground. A long tube, made from the same high permeability materials as the "coffin" stretched from outside the magnetic danger area on either side, passing through the portal. Inside was a conveyor belt and an agent placed their guns and equipment on for passage to the other side. Meanwhile, two more agents were manhandling a long, heavy sarcophagus into a groove in the floor with a rail on the bottom to secure it in place. Sam came up to Pilakin.

"I've been to portals before but I've never seen all this shit. I was given the impression that nothing metal goes through. Period."

"This is a secret CDA portal. It's handy to give that impression in the public ones but how do you think we get our gear in and out?"

Sam slapped his hand to his forehead and set out

across the bridge at a signal from the defence agents on the other side. Pilakin followed him and then turned to watch Jess getting into the box. The walls and lid were extremely thick and Pilakin had known real humans who had needed to be sedated to fight some primeval fear-of-burial claustrophobic response. As Jess lay down she reached up an arm and pulled Zeb down for a kiss. Then the lid closed and the heavy box rolled forward, the bridge flexing and creaking as the magnetic field tried to rip it free of its bearings. Pilakin watched anxiously as Jess emerged but any internal conflict was impossible to read in its features. It seemed to be functioning normally as Pilakin invited her crew to gather round. She handed each of them a shiny from the stack she had been given.

"What the hell are these for?" asked Zeb.

"Normally they're for cocooning yourself when exposed to fire weapons but they're also designed so that if you pull those tabs there, they'll ruck up in such a way you can wear them as overalls."

"I still don't get it."

"It's for protection against laser weapons. They're more than ninety-eight percent reflective against incident radiation in the visible spectrum and quite a way either side. So, put on the body armour and then get this over the top."

Sam looked at her quizzically.

"You think he's got lasers? We haven't heard any evidence that he has. Why would he bother with something so—"

"He's got the spiders, you doink. They have heavy cutting lasers and it certainly sounds to me like he has them under full control."

"Ah…"

"So they're our initial target before we try and catch Manstein – alive is much better, remember. The four spiders should have fundamental robotic brains in them, including safety controls to prevent them targeting anything close to a human in shape. So, keep your limbs moving and spread out and hopefully he won't have been able to override that feature. Although we get some protection with our suits, they'll still be able to target and hit weapons and maybe our faces if we don't look human enough."

"Or he's overridden it."

"Thank you, Mr Sunshine."

"But will you please tell us what you think he's doing?"

"I think he wants to take revenge on me by killing members of my family. I think he's going to use that tank of acid to get inside the big metallic tower they live in and kill them all in some way. Then I think he's going to leg it over the ramparts and run off into the meadow."

"Wouldn't that be suicidal?"

"No. People in the City imagine some kind of Imperial ring of steel out there. It's not like that. There are old trenches and shell holes everywhere. There aren't enough soldiers to form coherent lines. And those there are have been so demoralised that they rarely leave their dugouts and bunkers. One man alone, with some decent equipment, will slip through easily. Then he'll get to a starport and we'll have lost him."

Jess cocked her rifle.

"So, let's get out there and stop him."

Chapter 37

T HE SQUAD CAR driver point blank refused to go out. With one look at the sky he turned and fled back through the portal. Argument would consume time they did not have but he agreed to wait inside so that Manstein or footage of his capture or death could be driven back to Liberty Square at the greatest possible speed. Jess was unreadable but both Zeb and Sam quailed a little. She told them to lower their helmet visors and not to look up or over the parapet. They nodded and all four of them advanced up the allure to Tower 17. At this point Pilakin gathered them together.

"This is the last bit of decent cover between here and Tower Eighteen. Sam and I will advance on the parapet side. Zeb, you and Jess walk on the other side, next to the inner wall. Keep low and close in. The light is bad enough that Manstein should have difficulty seeing us. It may be that he has the spiders' ocular sensors on his controller but remember – they're not really autonomous the way Jess…" she glanced at Sam, remembering he was unaware. "…the way Jess feared they might be."

She led them out and as they rounded the tower, a breeze came at them from the meadow. Pilakin was prepared but the stench caused Sam to gag and she looked across to see Zeb with a hand over his mouth. Jess was, of course, unaffected. She'd have to learn to react to things like that if she was going to stay safely anonymous. They advanced in the shadows, the need for stealth testing Pilakin's patience. As it came in sight she signalled for the others to stop and drop even lower. She distractedly noted how her military experience had come back naturally and the others were obviously deferring to it. She raised her rifle and looked through the sights at the path ahead and the tower. It seemed clear at first glance but a large bulky shape loomed on top of the tower itself. It was at the top of the service ramp on the rear side, which gave access to the automatic anti-aircraft battery perched on the roof. Manstein must have guided the spiders up the ramp with that damned tank. Someone or something was moving next to it. She glanced across in time to see Jess turn to her and hold up two fingers before pointing ahead and down, indicating the ramparts.

Pilakin took another look and this time just made out the black legs of two spiders drawn up in the shadow right under the wall. From her angle she couldn't see the bodies so she turned back to Jess. She pointed ahead and then held up her hand and used her fingers to mime pulling the trigger; exaggeratedly doing it twice. Jess nodded and Pilakin held her fist up to the other two, hopefully in warning that when Jess fired things would happen quickly. She watched Jess take aim and noted that the robot did not have to go through the usual sniper rituals of calming breathing or seeking the most restful position to hold the rifle. It crouched there like stone, the barrel of the gun moving almost imperceptibly. Pilakin fought down the urge to hiss at her to get on with it.

When it came the two shots were so rapid that they almost sounded like one. Pilakin's eyes darted back to her sights and she saw a host of black legs flailing and twitching. She moved her sight up to the tower and saw that the figure had disappeared and a moment later two more spiders appeared over the top. She presumed they had been guarding the approach on the other side. Now that their cover had been blown she could give orders.

"You see the other ones coming? Open fire – just keep shooting. Sam, spray the top of the tower – avoid the tank; just make sure he keeps his head down… shit."

The last comment came as a green laser sliced through the smoke and dust. It missed, slicing a line through the back wall. Zeb hadn't noticed and both he and Jess were showering the targets with automatic fire. Next to her, Sam was firing short bursts at the top of the tower. One of the spiders went limp and collapsed to the ground. Jess must have noticed the other's laser protrusion swing round as she stopped firing and lunged to grab Zeb. It was a dumb thing to do. Where the laser had meant to hit the gun, Jess' action had moved his arm into the path. The laser reflected from him and hit Sam, cutting his gun in half and removing the tips of three fingers on his left hand. Pilakin raised her own gun and emptied an entire clip of bullets into the spider which twitched and flew backwards, finally becoming still. Quickly she reloaded before turning to Sam.

"Jess. Zeb. Cover the top of the tower. Make him keep his head down. Don't kill him though and don't hit the damned tank."

Sam had been looking at his fingers in stunned horror but now started screaming. Pilakin grabbed his hand in a firm grip and sprayed the tips with a cauterizing spray she had taken from the tool belt attached to her armour. A foam followed, encasing his hand in an immediate sterile cast combined with a local anaesthetic to numb the area completely. He looked amazed for a moment. Then grateful. Then he pulled out his pistol and nodded at her. She smiled. Good old Sam. She'd have asked him out long ago if he wasn't into guys.

Jess and Zeb had stopped firing but both were still aiming intently at the tower top. She was considering her next move when she heard Manstein's voice shout.

"Pilakin. I think it's time to talk, don't you?"

"Talk? How about you just surrender and let me detain you? Better still, stand up and I'll shoot you."

She heard him laughing.

"I *am* going to stand up, but if you shoot at me everyone under me dies. Do you believe I have that capability?"

She looked at the tank, looming with menace, and kicked the wall.

"Yes, alright."

Manstein rose, holding his hands up level with his shoulder. In his right hand was a small black box.

"Now come closer so we don't have to shout."

She stood, gun still trained upwards.

"Bring your friends too. I want everyone where I can see them."

After hesitating, she nodded to the others. They advanced, line abreast, and she didn't take her eyes off him. He looked calm. The bastard still had an escape plan.

"That's close enough."

"Jaq? Is that you?"

She looked down from where Manstein was standing on the tower roof to the armoured door in front of them to see Tomasz's face at the hatch.

"Yes. Is everyone okay in there?"

She heard Crustetin swearing in the background.

"Yes, we're fine. This maniac on the roof has sealed us in. Welded the doors shut – this one and the escape hatches and the one into the meadow. Did them all at the same time with those damned spider things."

"Where's your metal cutter?"

"CDA sold them all years ago."

Manstein cut in.

"Touching reunion but from this moment on I speak and Pilakin replies. That or no-one comes out of this alive."

"I'm sorry Tomasz, I think he means it."

She saw her uncle nod and hold up an RPG, indicating that he might fire at the roof. She shook her head.

"Wise choice," said Manstein. "Now, Pilakin. You know what I have in this tank?"

"Yes."

"Say it please, so there is no ambiguity."

"Acid."

"Oh, come on. That doesn't sound anywhere near scary enough." He raised his voice. "It's one and a half tonnes of concentrated hydrofluoric acid. Not only will it burn through pretty much anything, including the materials of this tower and the people inside, it also blocks certain mechanisms in the body so even a small burn usually follows up with organ failure. Oh yes – added bonus – the vapours are highly poisonous too. I have set a small explosive charge on the bottom of the tank and have the controls in my hand. So if anyone pulls the trigger, my final act will be to hit the button that sets it off immediately. Are we all clear on the nature of the threat?"

Pilakin controlled herself.

"Yes. Look, why are you threatening these people. What have they done?"

"Your fault, Pilakin. You refused to die. I try shooting you through a window, sending your Pandora's victim after you, setting the Activists on you, setting Poulter on you, starting a war and you *won't fucking die.*"

"But why do you want to kill me?"

"Because you were getting in my way. People don't get to do that. I finally found a nice job killing people for money. I was on commission for the amount I brought in and the Federation commerce rep on liaison didn't give a toss how I was doing it. He had a career to carve out."

"Okay. That's me. That's all those poor sods you've killed for the money. But what about Melissa? What the hell was that all about?"

He laughed again.

"Ah yes, that stupid bitch. She was in it for the money too. I needed spiders for cutting the netting. I found her selling the services of the spiders she'd hacked – made a nice little programme for taking them off grid and controlling them through a slab. She cut the net where I said and when I said. Only had an attack of conscience when you showed up and put faces and names to the victims. Then I found out she was helping you catch me. I paid her a visit but I still wanted the spiders. I think she guessed that once she gave me the access codes and programme I was going to off her anyway so she resisted. She gave up fairly quickly but by then I was pissed off so she took the long way out."

Pilakin shivered and felt sick as she remembered

Melissa's body, and for a moment imagined being in the room during the torture.

"Of course at that point I didn't realise you were going to get close to me or I'd have stood back and killed you at my leisure. Instead you nabbed Rimsky. Got to say I admired you for that move. And maximum respect to you for what you did to him next."

"I'm not like you."

"No, you're not. You're a cretin. I was all over the Federation computer networks. I knew as soon as you contacted Neuberg with your suspicion and I knew about their overkill, armageddon-style plan for dealing with an attack. It's brought me this far. It's made sure that even if you found me, you wouldn't have back up. And it means that no-one's going to chase me."

"How?"

"By making a bet."

"What?"

Manstein laughed.

"I have another setting on this control for five minutes. I'm going to bet that you'll spend five minutes trying to disarm it rather than chasing me. Tata!"

He dropped something he'd been concealing in his other hand and acrid smoke billowed out as it hit the roof. Before Pilakin could react, Jess had jumped in front of her, back towards Manstein. Gunshots rang out and Pilakin felt Jess's body being jolted into hers by bullet impacts until they both fell. It was a moment before Pilakin could gasp for the others to get after him. By the time she'd mounted the ladder to join them, the smoke had begun to clear. A rope hung over the front of the tower and she could see Manstein nearly at the bottom, abseiling down. Zeb aimed his rifle and Sam his pistol.

"Don't kill him. Get after him for fuck's sake. We'll deal with the bomb."

The two men looked at each other and the drop but she didn't have time to deal with them now. She turned her attention to the bomb where Jess had yanked off the cover and had her hands on the detonators.

"Drop them! They're probably barbed. We use them out here for booby traps – a barbed end in the explosive that snaps if you pull them out and sets it off."

Jess stared at the explosive intently for a moment.

"Yes, you're right. I can just make them out. Here, give me your slab."

She grabbed the stylus and started drawing on the screen at manic speed. In a few seconds Pilakin saw emerging a perfectly laid out circuit diagram. She looked at the mess of wires and boards and marvelled at the robot's ability. Then she focussed and dredged up memories of her time studying electronics in the Institute. After a couple of minutes the diagram was complete and both she and Jess stared at it. How much time had already elapsed? *Concentrate, you dumbag.* With a flash she saw the pattern. Could almost see the current flowing. *Damn.* Had she actually beaten the robot to the punch? She pointed at a line. The robot hesitated for a couple of seconds, presumably extrapolating every ramification of cutting that wire to the circuit as a whole.

"I agree."

Pilakin pulled out her ankle knife. There was no theatrical cliché of a digital display timer but within one of the chips, a binary timing circuit would be counting down to 00000000. Well, one thing about the lack of display, Pilakin didn't see any time to sit second guessing herself. She held her breath and yanked the blade through the wire. Nothing happened. Nothing at all. They yanked out a detonator. The barbed end was missing but they were all still there. They'd done it. She patted Jess on the back.

"Well d—"

She pulled her hand away. It was covered in a red, sticky substance. She leaned back and saw multiple patches of gunk soaked into Jess' clothes where they could be seen through the holes in her shiny. Then she noticed the robot had not used its left hand through the whole procedure with the bomb and there was another hole clean through her forearm; a glint of steel tendons visible within.

"Fuck, Jess. How badly damaged are you? Where the hell are you going to get repairs?"

The robot looked her straight in the eyes and shouted, "Manstein!"

Damn!

Pilakin leapt up and ran to the twitching rope. Zeb and Sam had found the courage to head down and the broken foam at her feet showed Sam had removed his hand cast so that he could handle the rope. He deserved a sodding medal for this. Looking out, she could see Manstein running into the Meadow, from shell hole to shell hole. He had a hell of a lead on the other two, even if they could navigate the dangers they'd encounter out there. At least they'd had the sense to take off their shinies. She cast around for her rifle but realised she'd left it on the parapet. She descended the ladder, Jess not far behind.

"Jaq!"

She turned to see Tomasz beckoning to her.

"Well done my girl. Very well done. Here."

He drew back and a rifle butt emerged from the hatch. She grabbed hold and a moment later was holding her old sniper rifle.

"Go get the skunk, Jaq."

She walked to the parapet making adjustments and Jess followed her with the slab.

"Why did you jump in front of me and not Zeb?" Pilakin asked.

"Manstein had no personal reason to shoot him but plenty to go for you."

"Well… thank you. You gonna film this?"

"Yes."

Pilakin watched Jess set the camera, zoom in and start scanning the ground for their quarry. She brought the rifle up to her face and rested it on the parapet, quartering and sweeping the ground over the area she expected Manstein to be in.

And she started to shake. The gun. The stench. The sounds. Searching for someone to kill. A man. She tensed all her muscles and the shaking stopped. *Be in the moment.* A mosquito whined past her ear. She needed a piss. Jess spoke.

"Oh-eight-three. You see the wrecked lander? Up ten. Two left."

Pilakin turned to the heading and scanned up to the wreckage, moving on to find the target. There he was. Disappearing and appearing out of shell holes. The bastard didn't look so dignified in a rapid jog, repeatedly glancing over his shoulder. He looked like a frightened soldier, running. When Pilakin tried to take a breath it was a big, gulping sob. 639. 639. She'd not murdered a man since Itzie. One or two in self-defence or to protect a life. Wouldn't this be that? He'd killed. There was no doubt in her mind he would kill again. The rifle sight was pinging him at 412 metres. 413. 414. Every step a harder shot. He stopped abruptly, looked at his watch and turned. Was that anger on his face? The bomb! It hadn't gone off. He kicked the ground. He was a stable target. The sight said wind seven from the left but a smoking crater next to him indicated a two points, three K shift. She adjusted. Her finger tightened on the trigger. Then she saw it. So vivid it surely couldn't be imagination. A lion badge over his heart. She felt the presence of 639 ghosts behind her and Itzie's breath on her ear. Justice was a hard taskmistress.

"Jess. Will God forgive me?"
"Yes, Jaq. Of course he will."
She pulled the trigger.

Chapter 38

PILAKIN SAT ON a large sofa in the lobby of the Engalise City Corporation's Rights Enforcement building. She pulled at the collar of her old CDA uniform, increasingly tight in places, as she watched with disgust the scurrying of rights litigants between tribunal rooms. She looked at the smoking tip of the cigarette between her fingers. One of Neuberg's good stock – she'd sent over a few cartons as a thank-you gift. During the latter part of the case, Pilakin had been drinking less and drugging hardly at all and the adrenaline had carried her through. She smiled. Good tobacco and drinking mostly after midday was pretty good progress. A bit of psychiatric care after shooting Manstein, funded by Lars as his thank-you, had helped too.

After firing the shot, she'd fallen to the ground. Jess had carried on filming dispassionately.

"What are you waiting for?" she'd asked.

"The boys to get to him."

During the wait Pilakin had curled up in a ball and wept.

"Okay, they have him. I'll get this to Liberty Square immediately."

She'd got back in time and the syndicates had accepted the evidence and pulled back. Wireless was restored and the whole crisis had publicly been put down to the machinations of Imperial agents and a virus they had released into the communications networks. This meant the uniform she was wearing now was quite popular and would make a good impression as well as being the only thing left, other than her last dress, that was still smart.

The case's parties were in pre-trial negotiations – the Feds on one side of the table, the victim's families on the other. She'd watched them all go in. Sarah/Maggie Poulter and Paul. Edward with them. Zeb with Jess holding his arm – it turned out the Feds were able to do something of a patch up job on her but she still moved in a somewhat jerky fashion. Mrs Fesh and her children. Melissa Walden's parents. None of them had come over to say thank you but they probably all assumed she'd done it for the money and her 20% was looking pretty mercenary to them right now. Fees always did on this side of the case. Pilakin had to wait out here until the trial proper started, then there would be days of building the case, calling her witnesses...

The door to the room was flung open unexpectedly

and a cadre of people in Federation uniform poured out. She leapt up and moved to intercept them.

"Ah, here's the bitch who blew out my right kneecap."

Manstein still had the joint in an elaborate harness and was walking with a stick.

"I had to fight muscle memory to avoid your stupid head."

"I'd compliment you on a hell of a shot except it showed how weak you are."

Pilakin lunged at him but several Feds jumped in and pushed her back. Neuberg appeared, so she shook off the people holding her.

"What's going on, major?"

"The Federation has settled."

"What?"

Manstein cackled.

"Hah, you dumb bitch. You think Flow was the first? I was hired to raise revenue. I got a commission on everything. And my contract shows the Federation is liable for all my compensation payments. Cheaper for them to settle now and they can keep the whole thing hushed up."

Pilakin turned a horrified look on Neuberg.

"Is he serious?"

Manstein cut in again.

"And you, Pilakin. Once I'm better, I'm looking forward to searching you out to finish *our* business."

Neuberg signalled to two large Fed security agents.

"Get him out of here."

Pilakin watched as a laughing Manstein was jostled out of the building before turning her fury on Neuberg.

"I need the exposure."

"You can't have it. All parties have signed a confidentiality agreement. The payout is big. I've made sure your share is already in your account."

"It's not about the money."

"I know. It is about the justice and it turned out he's done this forty three times. With collateral damage, you can put another sixty two in your solved column."

"They going to get compensation?"

"Yes but obviously you can't…"

"I know! But it's the confidentiality that's killing me. I don't *want* to be famous. I *need* to be. To get the cases. I'm back to square one. Damn you. *Damn you all.*"

"Jaq! Come back."

She ran from the building.

PILAKIN SAT IN the Calva Club, drinking apple brandy out of a half-litre mug while watching coverage of a hangarball game. New Simplaero were hosting the Engalise Angels and giving them a total womping. Of course part of their home advantage was an empty blue sky and Pilakin concentrated intently to catch glimpses of it. Maybe she would go out and see it for herself someday. After all, she didn't have much to live for here, did she? Despite her success, still no reputation to trade on. She'd also picked up a psychopath intent on revenge. And found a man she'd finally liked, who was shacked up with a robot.

Neuberg appeared at her table.

"Fuck off."

"It's taken me twenty eight hours to track you down so I will not fuck off."

She took the seat opposite and dipped her head to get a better view of Pilakin.

"You look awful." She looked at the tray of drugs paraphernalia on a trolley next to the table. "What on Home have you been taking?"

"DrAlcohol. Keeps you *wasted* for longer." She belched. The way Neuberg winced, her breath must be pretty rancid. Good.

"Your uniform's in a right state."

Pilakin looked down at her dishevelled appearance.

"Ironic really. First time in years when money's been no object and the CDA is so popular no-one lets me put my hand in my pocket. Can't you see? I'm a bloody *hero*."

"You've done a good thing, catching Manstein. And not killing him showed a level of mercy and justice I admire very greatly."

"And what did you do? Hushed it up and let him go."

"No. That contract he hid behind is watertight in another aspect. We pretty much own his ass for the next eight years, so I've arranged a posting for him."

"Oh?"

"He's going to be a resident investigator at one of our more unpleasant prison colonies. Tiny, cold place it is.

Dark too."

"An eight year sentence for what he did? That's not much."

"We control all access to the place. At the end of his contract he's going to find it mysteriously impossible to leave. Ever."

Pilakin grunted and smiled for the first time in many hours.

"Good. You want a drink?"

"Not just now, thank you."

Neuberg took out a cigarette packet and lit two before passing one to Pilakin.

"Why do you cover the flame like that when you're lighting them? There's no wind."

"Oh? I didn't realise. Military training I guess – hide the light."

They sat in silence for a few moments before Neuberg spoke again.

"I really am sorry about the confidentiality agreement but it was a case of Damu'us naee. Are you going to stay independent?"

"As opposed to what?"

"Well, I'm sure the ECC must have offered you something by now."

"They have no money for more detectives. After what happened they've decided to create a security service of their own with intelligence and paramilitary arms. They offered me something in that but I'm not going to be able to get justice for people in there. I really have to hand it to you lot – you're pushing this City straight from anarchy to tyranny."

"I know. That's unfortunate but it isn't going to be for much longer. I promise."

"Oh?"

"The revolution is coming, Jaq. And it will start with the end of this siege."

Pilakin looked at her face with its permanent tear marks.

"Are you serious?"

Neuberg raised her eyebrows and tilted her head. "By the way, have you been watching the news?"

"No."

Neuberg switched the channel to one where the president of the Federation was making a speech.

"…led to certain members of the leadership team pursuing a policy of leaving the remaining Imperial batteries and missile stations intact. We recognise that this was the wrong decision and led directly to the deaths of City denizens. We have reversed the policy and as a display of our commitment to the defence of the people, will now make a compensation payment of one hundred thousand credits to the families of anyone killed by Imperial artillery or missile strikes. We will be funding the ECC's efforts to increase the strength of the net and have launched operations against all Imperial heavy ordnance in range of the City. Furthermore, as a gesture of goodwill, we will now make similar compensation payments to the victims of the forty three strikes that have occurred since the mercy policy came into effect."

There was loud applause from an off-camera audience. Pilakin looked at Neuberg.

"Part of the deal?"

"We couldn't keep that many people quiet. Or afford the compensation levels your clients got."

Pilakin looked once more at the screen. The president was moving down a line of people handing out Federation credit notes, handshakes and apologies. Behind him, a large screen played military footage of bunkers being destroyed in airstrikes. A cheer from the off-camera audience accompanied each. Pilakin cried as she thought of Oswin, Wade and the other men she had interviewed. No justice for them. No justice for the millions of miserable souls dying out there for an Empire they didn't believe in. She reached out and switched off the TV.

Neuberg looked at her with shining eyes.

"I'm leaving."

"Oh?"

"I don't like this place at the moment. There's a mission coming up to a world called Ijjalion. Stravinski's leading it and I've asked to go along. I'll need some investigators. Come and work for me, Jaq."

"No. I think, despite it all, you're a good person, Neuberg. How can you bear to work for an organisation that has done all this shit?"

"Humankind needs saving from its fate. A key part of that is to overthrow the Empire, at pretty much any cost. I'm not happy doing what I do at the moment but my soul is less important than the path we must take for the salvation of all."

"Is this an Anjelican thing?"

"Humanity is broken. You must sense it. Engalise is an extreme example but it's the same everywhere. History is missing. No-one looks back. People accept actions by their rulers that a moment's objective thought would see as unacceptable crimes. Slavery, genocide. Human advancement is supposed to be just that but we're sliding backwards. Technology isn't where it should be. A.I. is almost absent and no one questions why…"

"What are you talking about?"

"I'm sorry. It leaks out of me sometimes and I forget you're not…"

Pilakin waited for her to continue but she did not. "So, you're not going to find out what happened to my father?"

"I've handed it to some people I trust and I will check up on progress every time I'm back. I promise."

Pilakin dropped her cigarette butt into the dregs of her drink and put her head in her hands.

"Go please."

"Jaquelinya, I…"

"I said *go*."

She heard Neuberg get up and leave.

She spoke to Itzie.

"I'm alone."

PILAKIN SAT UPRIGHT in the chair next to the desk, swaying slightly as she tried to control her body in an I'm-not-plastered way. The man returned and sat down with a friendly look on his face.

"Well, that all checks out. If you sign here, you'll get instant upgrade to platinum membership."

She picked up the pen and smiled. She could fight that loneliness here.

"That's excellent, Francis, thank you."

"We're always delighted to see our long term members back and clear of… inconvenience."

Pilakin finished the tumbler of water on his desk. Someone walked in behind her and they both stood up.

"Eric will show you up to the exclusive modules."

She turned to face him.

"Would you step this way please, Dr Pilakin?"

Author's Note

I have written this book partly in the hope that, as well as inside, people outside the City of Engalise may also read it. As such, I have included passages to explain what life in our City is like. To my fellow inhabitants, I apologise for telling you things you already know and hope you agree with my depiction of our home.

The story is largely based on the truth of a case as I understand it and, in spite of its fictional style, the characters portrayed do live in the Free City. This has been done without their knowledge or consent. Inaccuracies will be many but I invoke my Fourth Right.

Finally, I would like to thank my translators for their assistance in changing the story from my native Eglitzé-Anjelican into Galactic Standard and other languages, so that it may be read across the sentient galaxy.

Wilsha McKatie

Originally published as *Falling Rubble: An Agent Pilakin Mystery* by Angel Media, Speaker's Plaza, Engalise.

THE END

Acknowledgements

They say your second novel is the toughest one to write and I'd like to thank Sara-Jayne Slack of Inspired Quill for patiently waiting and then deciding to publish what I produced. Also at Inspired Quill, Rebecca Hall gave the manuscript a thorough going-over and Venetia Jackson produced another excellent cover, finally giving her wonderful lion the top billing it deserves.

For the best part of two years I read excerpts of this work at the Leicester Writers' Club and received professional and valuable feedback. A more insightful and supportive group of people would be hard to find.

I would like to thank my cold-readers, Jo Baldry, Michelle Foxon and Clive and Denise Wilkinson. Their initial feedback led to some plot refinements, which I think has made the finished work better. I must again thank my wife, Helen Child, for pushing me to pursue my writing and her unwavering support in everything.

Finally, thanks to Charlie and Toby for inspiring *Bookdog and the Worm*.

About the Author

David lives in Ashby de la Zouch, land of Jaffa Cakes, Ivanhoe, the National Forest and Adrian Mole's Cappuccino Years. He is a physicist and, after years of being a research scientist for the Government, now works for the Institute of Physics. Married, his wife eventually got fed up with him talking about all the books he was going to write and told him to get on with it or shut up.

Writing science fiction in a universe he has been perfecting for decades, his stories are devoted to plot and characters. Influences range from Asimov, Niven-Pournelle and childhood science fiction through to the new style Battle Star Galactica. Having learned his trade with Writing East Midlands, he is now a member of the established Leicester Writers Club.

In 2015, his debut novel *We Bleed the Same* was shortlisted for the East Midlands Book Award – a general award, which shows the cross-genre appeal of his writing.

David fills his time outside of authoring and his full time job with raising two children, being a visiting fellow at Nottingham Trent University and walking two tiny dogs.

Find the author via his website:
anjelican.wordpress.com
Or tweet at him:
@anjelicanspace

More From This Author

We Bleed The Same

When the leak of sensitive information is traced back to his computer console, Government official and minor celebrity Danny Parque's bright future comes crashing down.

Found guilty and sent out as a conscripted criminal to fight for an Empire he once loved but comes to despise, horrifying combat leads to capture by the terrorists he is supposed to fear. Danny joins their ranks; persuaded that they are pursuing the same freedom he craves. But the time soon comes when, entangled in a new web of lies, Danny wonders if the price of freedom is his own conscience.

When asked to betray everything – and everyone – he once held dear, the decision must be made…Whose side is he on?

Paperback ISBN: 978-1-908600-30-1
eBook ISBN: 978-1-908600-31-8

Available from all major online and offline outlets.

www.ingramcontent.com/pod-product-compliance
Lightning Source LLC
Chambersburg PA
CBHW031614180726
48284CB00005B/1543